Arth

Winding Paths of Life
– The Stories of Pilgrims and God Seekers –

Arthur Pahl

Winding Paths of Life

– The Stories of Pilgrims and God Seekers –

FRICK VERLAG GmbH - Postfach 447
D-75104 PFORZHEIM

Bibliographic Information of the German Library:
Die Deutsche Bibliothek verzeichnet diese Publikation in der
Deutschen Nationalbibliografie; detaillierte bibliografische Daten sind im Internet über http://dnb.ddb.de abrufbar

Translated from „Verschlungene Wege", 2009
ISBN: 978-3867440745

Published by:
Frick Verlag
Postfach 447, 75104 Pforzheim, Germany
www.frickverlag.de

1. Edition 2013

Christian C. Tiews, Translation

Helen Ranger, English Editor

Front Cover by Dr. Davorin Wagner, Photography
www.photoimagine.de

Brigitte Jach, Layout

Druck: Books on Demand GmbH, Norderstedt

ISBN 978-3-939862-27-7

To my mother,
who never stopped praying for me.

Table of Contents

A Word from a Friend

Travel is one thing, a pilgrimage is another. Although each involves moving from place to place, a pilgrimage is a journey of faith. Pilgrims in Europe recognize this essential distinction. It helps the pilgrim-traveller to set his/her sights on great persons, places and events of faith and to seek to assimilate more deeply the mysteries and the acts of God that have helped to produce the great culture which we have inherited. I am happy to recommend this book to all who are undertaking such an exciting adventure.

PAX,

✠ Most Reverend John J. Myers
Archbishop of Newark

Author's Foreword

How do you "do" life? Do you just go about it with no particular plan? Or do you do something meaningful? Do you just "check off" your childhood, school, job, family--all the usual stuff? Is your life a success story--or a failure? Are you kidding yourself about your own life, living an illusion, or making up stories, which over time morph into their own reality?

Didn't we all once have a dream, a vision...wishes and hopes that we would one day lead a better life and even make this world a more humane place? Weren't we all once really curious about life, eager to try 1,001 new things? Didn't we all hope to meet interesting people and see far-away places, to meet that one-in-a-million and once-in-a-lifetime soul mate? Didn't we want to show the world what we'd got... fall in love, have kids, find success and happiness? Well, of course we did... At the same time, we know that life is not a quiet and gentle river. Rather, life is one big adventure, up one day, down the next, weaving back and forth. Life is a daring feat, like canoeing down Niagara Falls. And finally--if all goes well--while you might not win, hopefully you can at least quietly moor in a safe harbor when you get old... even with bumps and cuts and bruises all over. No one escapes unscathed. Life is unpredictable, and very few people are able to do something useful in the few short years they are given on this earth. A lot of things depend on coincidences--directed by God--some happy, some not so pleasant... We bump into people, we are attracted to ideas, to the love of money, to the power of grand feelings. Sadly, we are also marked by the foolish things we do.

When I was young, how often did I hear the old folks say, "I just wish I were young again!" Only when we have safely reached the harbor of old age do we have an inkling of the gist of it all: When things work out halfway well, life comes full circle. But yet, we still ask ourselves, "Was that all? Really? Was it worth it? Will any part of me remain? How will the people in my life remember me? Did the good things I did in my life outweigh my thousands of weaknesses, vanities, and missed opportunities? Until not too long ago, thoughts like these swirled around in my mind.

Sixty years of my life left their mark on me. I met thousands of people, came to know countless ideas, feelings, and points of view. I suffered much. And while there were also many moments of happiness, somehow the "hub" was still missing. But finally, I found that "hub." It is love--the master key of my life, the blueprint of happiness. *Eros* (sensual passion), *philos* (friendship with people), and *stoika* (attraction to material things) are the three worldly forms of love that all of us are more or less familiar with. And I had come to know all of them. They are marvelous and you can't do without them. Still, they are not sufficient. Only when I discovered Christian *agape* love, did I finally cross the finish line. *Agape* love is a metaphysical and spiritual form of sacrificial love. No one could describe it better than St. Paul does in his first Epistle to the Corinthians, chapter thirteen:

> *"If I speak in the tongues of men and of angels, but have not love, I am a noisy gong or a clanging cymbal. And if I have prophetic powers, and understand all mysteries and all knowledge, and if I have all faith, so as to remove mountains, but have not love, I am nothing. If I give away all I have, and if I deliver up my body to be burned, but have not love, I gain nothing. Love is patient and kind; love does not envy or boast; it is not arrogant or rude. It does not insist on its own way; it is not irritable or resentful; it does not rejoice at wrongdoing, but rejoices with the truth. Love bears all things, believes all things, hopes all things, endures all things. Love never ends."* (1 Cor 13:1-8, ESV)

Had I not experienced this *agape* love, I would never have dared or been able to write a book. Only the assurance of being safe in the love of God gave me the power and ability to put my experiences on paper.

***

In my folks' home in Würzburg, Germany, we most certainly didn't have any paintings by Picasso or any valuable encyclopedias. My parents, my brother, and I lived in a modest apartment in Würzburg's Old Town. Hard work, duty, austerity, and obedience--those were the virtues I was taught. My father was a skilled craftsman--a machinist, whose skills my brother seemed to have inherited entirely because I have none of these gifts. But the parent who influenced me most was my strong-willed and very devout mother, who always believed in me--all those years.

When it was time to choose a profession, I selected the hotel business. After my apprenticeship as a waiter in a Würzburg hotel, I struck out on my own and moved to Switzerland, where I learned the refined art of the Swiss restaurant business. I was trained as a hotel management assistant in institutions such as the world-famous Baur au Lac Hotel. However, after a while, Germany and Switzerland seemed too small and provincial. I needed to branch out into the big, wide world. So I jumped at the first opportunity that presented itself and signed on as a steward on ocean liners, serving on such famous vessels as MS "Bremen" and MS "Europa." We plied the North Atlantic route and so I regularly visited New York, a city that fascinated me. Sadly, it was also on those visits that I yielded to the Big Apple's seductive lure and its many temptations.

One day, as we were berthed in New York, I left my ship and never looked back, preferring to live in that great city for several years. I found work as a dish washer, waiter, taxi driver, shoe maker, tombstone salesman, and took many other odd jobs. At last I met a young Columbian woman who had worked in New York for a while and who wanted to return to her home country. We fell in love, got married, and--without giving it a second thought--we moved to Bogotá. That was a beautiful time in my life. We were blessed with two daughters. I was hired as the director of gastronomy at a well-known country club and had the opportunity to learn the languages of South America--Spanish and Portuguese.

Years later I returned to the U.S., working as sales manager for a Columbian firm. I separated from my family and lived all over North America until 1991--from Miami to L.A., from Chicago to Vancouver--working as a gemmologist and even as a stock broker.

I remember well--back in the '60s, on the streets of Lower Eastside --when I met Indian guru Srila Prabhupada, a walking legend. You could often run into him--wearing his orange-colored silk robes and being trailed by his disciples--introducing the Hare Krishna Movement to the West. This man triggered a yearning for something spiritual deep inside of me. I became a "seeker"--looking for the meaning to life and even dabbling in Buddhism and Hinduism for a while. Gurus such as Baghavan Raijneesh and Maharishi Mahesh Yogi were important role models during that period.

I finally returned to Germany, disappointed and frustrated. I was forty-five years old and had seen and experienced so many things. But I felt tired and empty, staring into a void. Everything I had ever started seemed to be a failure. What to build on? What to believe in? I had tried a number of things, but couldn't connect to my earlier life. Within a short period of time I tumbled into a deep spiritual crisis. I began to doubt everything, especially myself. I needed time to think about my life and overcome my depression.

Then an astounding opportunity presented itself-- I had a shot at living in a sparse log cabin in Canada for a whole year. Nowadays they call these times of reprieve "sabbaticals" or "Sabbath years." Reduced to the bare minimum, I lived off the land. Once again, I came to learn what really counts in life: dependability, a sip of water, a piece of bread, and the hope that you'll make it the next day. That year changed my life from the ground up. I found my way back to the important things in life and renounced everything flashy, deceitful, crazy, and lustful. Up there in Canada's deep winter solitude I led an ascetic and Spartan life. And I found my way back to God--or rather, I quit rejecting His attempts to reach me. The old Bible I found in the cabin helped me on my way back. I swore that I would start a new life, and so I returned to Germany.

I stayed with my mother for a few weeks--my father had already passed away by that time--and we discussed what I could do with my life. I reflected on my skill set: I was fluent in four languages, was a "people person," and most certainly knew my way around in the hotel and restaurant business. Perhaps most importantly, I was trying to get back to Christianity.

Then one day, an old friend in the U.S. called me up and told me about pilgrimage tours mainly throughout Europe that he was organizing for American tourists. He was looking for a tour guide and offered me the job. We would test the waters with a trial trip. That was back in 1992. Since then, that one trip has led to several hundred other journeys--small ones, big ones, some of them wonderful, some of them less so--but many of them unforgettable. Famous Brazilian author Paulo Coelho writes in one of his books: "Pilgrimages have always been one of the most objective ways to attain enlightenment. To purge your sins, you keep on walking, keep on meeting new challenges. You are rewarded with thousands of blessings, which life generously grants the one who asks for them."

As a tour guide in Assisi, Lourdes, Fatima, and Avila, I can affirm that this statement is true. Every trip changed me a little bit more. On the one hand, I was just a "regular" tour guide, responsible for everything and anything: get two Aspirins here, take someone to the hospital there... and all the while feeling just as responsible for finding the teddy bear of a fifteen-year old girl as helping a priest locate his lost cassock. Yet, on the other hand, I was also one of the pilgrims. I prayed with them, I accompanied them on every procession, and participated in every Mass. I headed up many discussions, talked about the Holy Father, connected believers with the Church--all the while being drawn ever closer to Holy Roman Catholicism. A sense of inner peace started to grow in me and I soon began to radiate it. The people whom I accompanied felt my peace and sincerity and often confided in me. I have no clue how many life stories they shared with me on my many trips. Some of the stories they told me are in this book. And they happened exactly the way I wrote them down.

Years ago I started sharing some of these stories with the people on my tours--sometimes after dinner, or on long bus rides. I was amazed how much the people loved these stories. As soon as I finished one story, they would beg me to tell another. This went on for several years.

And then there was that long trip with Dennis Yosick, an elderly American gentleman dying of cancer. He had traveled to Europe, planning to depart from this life at the holy sites. When I saw how this poor soul entrusted himself to God and to Our Dear Lady--even while suffering extreme pain--something inside of me went "click." I was suddenly standing at a threshold. Behind me I saw my old life. But ahead of me I saw a blooming landscape, which attracted me like magic. Intensive reading, prayers, retreats, and many conversations later, "paradise" finally opened up for me. I had found *agape* love--the humble, dedicated love for God. Or rather, it had found me... I wanted to devote the rest of my life to this love. Over and over, I recalled the life motto of Pope John Paul II and Brother Roger, those two great theologians united in ecumenism: "Love, and express that with your life."

And so, in only one year, I was able to recall and put down on paper many of these stories. They are about individuals who made testimonies on a different kind of life--brimming with decency, responsibility, courtesy, goodness, and love for your neighbor. These are the stories of people who communicate that living a life for God is not a thing unto itself, but rather a way of making our world more humane.

***

Of course, no one can write a book like this alone. So many people have helped me with this project. Unfortunately, I only have enough space to thank a few of them. I would like to mention Father Grigus, whom I met many years ago on a pilgrimage and who appears in several of these stories as a protagonist. I am especially thankful for his friendship and constant support-- especially in spiritual matters.

From the very start, his Excellency the Archbishop of Newark, New Jersey, John Meyers, amazed me with his trust and generous support. I wish to thank this shepherd of the Roman Catholic Church in North America. American author Laurie Manhardt; my American friend, Dennis Gaetan; and my translator, Christian Tiews, from St. Louis, Missouri: all of them continually inspired me to keep on pushing myself. Also, Jim Melornick, professor of literature at the University of Minnesota, Rochester, provided me with useful tips. Most of all I would like to thank Mr. Rainer Gerlach, a specialist in German studies, without whom I wouldn't have been able to write this book. I will never forget his encouraging words, "Write, write, write!"

Frankfurt am Main, Germany, August 2008

The Experience of a Lifetime

Only human beings are capable of receiving the gift of faith. Only humans can believe in the existence of God, the innocent expression in the eyes of a new-born, or in the fact that humans can do good deeds.

But, sadly, this capability to believe, embedded in us from conception, can be crushed, wither, and die under certain circumstances, for instance when people have the misfortune to live under totalitarian governments prohibiting any kind of religious instruction.

Some scientists and intellectuals have great difficulty believing in immaterial things—things that can neither be touched, heard, nor smelled. This tendency is like a steep, icy slope propelling them into the abyss of unbelief.

Sadly, such people lead their lives more or less completely rationally, beholden to a materialistic worldview. As such, they are usually governed by mistrust, skepticism or doubt—not by faith, hope, and love. And, tragically, such people usually wind up emotional paupers.

But that yearning for faith, hope, and love - while often suppressed by the outside world—will at some point in their lifetime attempt to work its way back into their lives, knocking on the door of their impoverished hearts. Tragically, many of them will reject this gift of belief, while others will receive it.

***

One winter's day in Frankfurt I met one of these seekers in a most unlikely place—the fitness center right around the corner from my apartment.

The winter months are a very peculiar time for us tour guides. We finally have time to recuperate from the stressful travels of the previous summer. But the flip side is that we don't make any money during those bleak months between November and February. So during this off time I usually just kick back, sleep, take

17

long walks, and read…Not unlike a bear hibernating—except for the walking and reading, of course. Sometimes I work out and try to shed some of the pounds I had gained the previous summer, when I ate in all those fancy restaurants on pilgrimages.

This story begins in December 2005—a winter's break during which I had decided not to take a ski vacation, but chose to stay home instead.

One Friday afternoon I thought I would go to the fitness center right around the corner from my apartment. I had been a regular there for some time. That particular day, it wasn't good ol' Monika sitting at the reception desk, but a young woman I had never seen before, who greeted me in a very friendly way in an accent I pegged as being Eastern European. Her name was Anastasia, as I later found out. She was probably twenty-one or twenty-two, slim and of medium height, and a brunette. With that deep timbre that sometimes characterizes Eastern European women, she was reviewing with me how to do the new Nautilus exercises the staff had worked out for me on my previous visit. As I was acquainting myself with the new work-out equipment, I occasionally glanced over to Anastasia sitting at the reception desk. Whenever she had nothing to do, she read a paperback.

A few days later I was back and noticed her again. Taking a break from my Nautilus, I sat down at the bar and ordered a power drink. We struck up a conversation and I noticed that she was still reading the same book. I glanced at the title and was surprised. It was Paulo Coelho's famous diary, *The Pilgrimage: A Contemporary Quest for Ancient Wisdom*, one of my favorites. Published in 1987, this book has triggered a plethora of pilgrimages to Santiago de Compostela, Spain, and spawned a wealth of other books on that topic.

In between sips of pineapple juice, we talked about her book. Anastasia was exuberant about it, as young people excited about something are often apt to be. What apparently intrigued her was not necessarily the Camino de Santiago (also known as the Way of St. James) itself or even that gorgeous part of Spain, but rather the mystical experience many pilgrims encounter on that pilgrimage, which Coelho describes in great detail. It seemed very clear that was the kind of experience this young woman was looking for, too.

Over the next few weeks, I worked out at the fitness center more often than I had ever done up to that point. Pumping iron and using all that equipment did work some small wonders on my excess pounds. But, much more importantly, my frequent visits blessed me with a paternal relationship with a young woman whose openness and seeking intrigued me. A few weeks later we were already on a first-name basis (something very special and relatively rare in Germany between people of different generations). I invited her for a cup of coffee at a popular café in our part of town, because I had guessed that Anastasia was searching for a heart-to-heart conversation.

It didn't take us long to get back to our special topic, the Camino de Santiago. I told her about my experiences on the Camino, how often I had been there with my pilgrims and so on.

"Somehow there's something so mysterious and fascinating about the landscape of northwestern Spain," I told her, already lost in thought as I contemplated the region of Galicia in particular.

"I've been thinking about doing the Camino for a long time now," she explained in her distinctly Slavic accent. "But I never figured out how to go about it. Could you help me find the way?"

"Of course I can—and I will. But do you realize what this walk means? Are you sure you want to walk hundreds of kilometers? And besides, for what?"

"I can't really explain it. There's something magical, something mysterious about the Camino. I can feel it drawing me. It's like I'm being sucked into something from which I just can't wriggle free. I can't get it out of my head. I've got to experience this Camino. That's the only way I can kick this obsession."

"Are you a believer?"

"Hardly. Actually I'm an atheist. My family members are atheists, too. We're originally from Kiev in the Ukraine. When I was a child, my mother and I moved to Germany. Back in the Ukraine, religion was suppressed. Besides, everyone in my family is an academic or an intellectual, and you can't be an intellectual and a believer at the same time. It's like oil and water. They don't mix. Practically everyone in my family was a successful academic in the former Soviet Union. I can't remember ever reading the Bible or praying."

The first of those three gifts of the Spirit—faith, hope, and love—came to my mind. "Faith is absolutely lacking in this young woman," I thought.

She told me about her mother, now a teacher of Slavic languages in Frankfurt. Her father had moved back to Kiev, she said. She told me about her grandparents who were chemists and physicists. Anastasia was an architecture major at the Technische Universität Darmstadt.

As we were talking, I discretely observed her and noticed she was having a difficult time keeping still. She kept on fidgeting and bouncing from one topic to another, too. Somehow she seemed driven by something—distracted and lacking inner peace. As she described her day-to-day life, I realized what her problem was.

In order to pay the rent while going to college, Anastasia worked as a waitress in a Russian nightclub by night and occasionally at the fitness center by day. I wondered when and how she ever had time for her studies. What's more, her nightclub employer had been withholding her pay for months and she was living solely on tips—which are not 15% of the bill as in the U.S., but on average only about $1.00 to $2.00 per order. Her relationship with her boyfriend was in a rut as well.

"Achim and I live in two totally different worlds," she described their relationship. "And I no longer have the energy to keep fighting for our relationship. Everything seems so futile. So do these part-time jobs. And even if I ever do graduate, I'll probably never get a job as an architect anyway."

This young woman was sending out conflicting messages. On the one hand, she was high-spirited and joyful about life. On the other hand, she seemed to be looking for something deeper in life—something to hold on to, something with meaning.

I tried to distract her and ordered another piece of cake for each of us. We ate silently, lost in thought. But my attempt at distracting her didn't last long: just a few minutes later we got back onto the Camino topic again.

Anastasia was absolutely convinced that her life would change and that she would find the kind of mystical experience she was searching for, if only she were able to go on that oldest pilgrimage in Europe. I was skeptical about the whole idea and subtly pointed out that I had reservations about her wanting to put all her eggs in the "Camino basket," so to speak, which would just disappoint her if it didn't work out.

But I couldn't convince her. On the contrary, when we were about to leave, she asked me quite bluntly, but with a gleam in her eye:

"Arthur, please walk the Camino with me. You're an experienced tour guide. You can show me all the special things and can explain this myth to me that so many pilgrims are fascinated about."

This caught me off guard. Should I let her drag me into this whole thing? On the other hand, how could I flatly turn down such a charming request? I just didn't have the heart to say "No" and felt somewhat pressured. So I sort of nodded my agreement.

Anastasia beamed. She had gotten what she wanted.

But before she could make this project even more complicated, I quickly added, "OK, we could do this next August... I'll come along, but I've only got two weeks to spare. We'll only be able to walk a few hundred miles (200-300 km)—tops. I don't have time to do more."

When we left the café and said good-bye on the street, she gave me a hug and then vigorously pumped both of my hands. Then we parted ways, both of us absorbed with the Camino.

Over the next few months we saw each other regularly and talked on the phone a lot, coordinating all the gear we had to purchase: clothing, comfortable shoes, light knapsacks, warm sleeping bags, etc. We also stocked up on all the necessary lotions, salves, and pills we would be needing.

I purchased a "Camino Pilgrim Passport" for each of us on the Internet. This is a little booklet for collecting stamps from the various hostels and specially designated locations along the way. It also entitles you to spend the night for free at the various refugios. We would have to present this booklet at the Pilgrim Office at the end of the pilgrimage in Santiago de Compostela, if we wanted to receive the compostela, the prized pilgrimage certificate.

By late August, Anastasia and I were equipped and mentally prepared for our long hike. We flew from Frankfurt to the Spanish coastal city of Santander, where we boarded an overland bus to Leon.

We spent the night at a simple hotel and, the next morning, took another bus to Ponferrada, a town close to the border of Galicia, an autonomous region in northwestern Spain. The first night on our pilgrimage we spent with several hundred men and women in the dormitory of a large hostel. We both slept uneasily that first night, because we were eager to begin the first leg of our trek—from Ponferrada to Villafranca del Bierzo—by 5:00 the next morning.

In the early light of dawn we marveled at the green vineyards, interspersed with elephant-back hills overgrown with strange scrubby bushes. A light summer rain accompanied us on our first twenty miles (30 km). By late afternoon we had almost reached Jato's hostel, situated on a steep mountain. We reached it a short time later—gasping for breath.

Most every Camino pilgrim knows Jato's hostel—a plain but romantic place. Pilgrims spend the night more or less outdoors there, enshrouded in much the same atmosphere pilgrims have been experiencing for centuries. Jato's food is simple, but tasty and plentiful. We sat at long tables with dozens of other pilgrims and enjoyed the engaging conversations with pilgrims and "mystery seekers" from around the world.

Jato, the owner, attended to every single pilgrim personally, making them feel very special. Anastasia and I discussed the next leg of our journey, up to the mountain village of O' Cebreiro, the highest elevation of our hike, 1300 meters above sea level. (About 4300 ft)

Somewhat embarrassingly, the next morning already found me complaining about sore muscles and blisters on my feet, whereas Anastasia had no problems. In contrast to me, she was well rested and full of energy.

The hike from Ponferrada to O' Cebreiro was not very long, but unusually arduous. The route goes up and down, up and down, up and down—and then at the very end of the day—practically straight up. As you hike, the hostel of O' Cebreiro is always in your line of sight—like a mirage that never seems to be getting any closer. Pilgrims really have to dig in their heels to make it up the steep mountain at the very end of the day's trek.

Since the 9th century, the East Galician pilgrimage village of O' Cebreiro—the Gateway to Galicia—has been a famous stopover for pilgrims. Due to the precipitous incline at the very end of this leg, it took us a full four hours to conquer the last three miles (5 km). I'm sure Anastasia would have made it up a lot quicker if she hadn't been burdened with me.

Unfortunately, the higher we climbed, the more the green pastures and gray rock around us disappeared in the cloudy mist. At one particular point we penetrated the cloud line, after which it drizzled non-stop and visibility dropped to maybe fifty feet (15 m). We finally reached our goal of the day soaking wet and bushed, only to find that we still had to line up behind hundreds of pilgrims, all of whom were hoping to find a place to spend the night. But eventually we did find a place to stay.

Exhausted, we dumped our rucksacks and rested a while, looking forward to exploring the ancient Celtiberian village, which has been able to retain much of its timeless charm. The little thatch-roofed houses are made of sandstone and all nestled up to one another, radiating a feeling of peace and safety. We couldn't spot a single villager and presumed they might all be in the local church, the Santa Maria, which we soon located. In the 12th century at this very spot a Eucharistic miracle occurred, which has since been recognized by the Vatican.

Sure enough, most of the villagers were in church.

It took a little bit of persuasion on my part, but Anastasia eventually agreed to step inside the sanctuary with me. We entered just as the priest was preparing the Eucharistic Mass and decided to stay a while. The young priest had provided translations of passages from the Pilgrimage Book in twenty different languages and invited congregants from the various nations present to step up to the chancel and read a passage in his or her native language. I stepped in front of the congregation and read a verse in German. I was pleased when Anastasia decided to do the same, but unfortunately they didn't have a verse in Russian.

By the time we left the church and stepped outside, it had stopped raining and the sky had cleared. Then all of a sudden the evening sun painted the landscape golden, dipping everything in a deep red, which got darker with every passing minute. We both marveled at the breath-taking view and the beautiful colors spread across the sky, highlighted here and there by a few stray clouds.

Anastasia sat next to me. Both of us were enveloped in silence. She had pulled her knees under her chin and her arms were wrapped around her shins. Apparently the combination of the hike, the Eucharistic Mass, and now this beautiful gift from nature had triggered something deep down inside of her. I could tell something was going on by the look in her eyes.

I tried to imagine the Holy Spirit knocking on the door of her heart and envisioned the thoughts, that might be tumbling through her mind. I didn't dare interrupt her reflective mood and the working of the Spirit. So I silently said a prayer and waited for her to speak up.

"How do you think my life will turn out, Arthur? I wish I knew the future. I have so many wishes and hopes for my life, but I'm also scared and have doubts about the future."

I waited a few moments, before answering.

"Well, Anastasia, you need to push all those negative thoughts from your mind and just concentrate on what is beautiful." The second of those three gifts of the Spirit—faith, hope, and love—came to mind, so I replied, "You still have your whole life ahead of you. Fill your heart with hope!"

"I wish it were that easy."

"At your age, hope should be really easy."

We were silent for a long while, intently focusing on the stillness. When the first breath of evening started blowing across the meadows, we finally got up.

The night was pleasant and we slept soundly and deeply. The next morning we were awakened by the first rays of the sun. As it turned out, the weather was sunny and clear from then on out—all the way until we reached Santiago de Compostela several days later.

Over the next few days, Anastasia and I got into a steady rhythm of hiking, eating, sleeping, and contemplating. Our route was at times formidable and we both had to learn that living in close proximity with others requires a lot of patience.

For example, a few times I was careless and forgot some things at the hostel where we had spent the previous night, so I had to trek back to retrieve my belongings. I could tell that backtracking with me without uttering a single complaint was a struggle for my Ukrainian friend.

In moments like these she was upset with me and I could literally feel the atmosphere thicken like the approaching clouds of an afternoon storm in the mountains of Galicia, but not once did she comment on my goofs. She accepted them all with a generous measure of grace.

Mornings were especially tough for Anastasia and me. While I have for years grown accustomed to getting through the first hours of the day without eating or drinking, Anastasia couldn't walk a single step without having a bite to eat. If she didn't have at least a croissant and a cup of coffee, there was simply no communicating with her—something that was hard for me to accept.

On the other hand, when I wanted to stop somewhere and have breakfast, she was so full of vim and vigor that I could hardly contain her. But we pretty much managed to control our tempers about the things that irked, irritated or even drove us insane about the other person.

After about ten days we had almost made it. We now only had one day left on our pilgrimage and woke up that day to a beautiful late summer's morning. We took our time getting ready for the last few miles to Santiago de Compostela. Descending from Monte de Gozo (Mountain of Joy) around noon, with our pilgrimage walking sticks in hand and our traditional scallop shells dangling around our necks, we climbed the last hill, behind which lay Santiago.

Over the centuries, this village has become world-famous—thanks to the millions of pilgrims who have concluded their pilgrimage at this place. Tradition has it that one of the twelve disciples, James the Elder, came to this area very soon after Pentecost to spread the Gospel. Supposedly his missionary work was not successful and so he soon returned to Palestine, only to meet a martyrer's death.

But legend also has it that St. James' disciples Atamasius and Theodorus brought their master's body back to the coast of Spain by boat and buried him at this very place.

Early in the ninth century a hermit named Pelayo is said to have rediscovered the spot where James' body was buried. Christians quickly spread this news and pilgrimages to Santiago began soon afterward. For several centuries, his remains were hidden by monks during the period of Muslim occupation. The gorgeous Cathedral of Santiago de Compostela we know today, was built at that site after the Moors had been driven out and James' body had been returned, now entombed in the sanctuary. In recent centuries, the modern city of Santiago has grown up around the Cathedral of Santiago de Compostela, the town's most famous landmark.

Relieved and somehow also deeply moved, we finally reached our goal and reverently passed through the narrow medieval city gate, which marked our official entry in Santiago de Compostela. From there we headed to a cobblestone square in the Old Town.

We stood around awhile, reflecting on the purpose of our journey, after which I said a silent prayer and crossed myself. I waved to a pilgrim walking by, handed him my digital camera, and asked him to please capture this special moment for us.

Only then did Anastasia and I dive into the crowd of thousands of pilgrims milling about the narrow alleys and squares of Santiago. We drifted along in the throngs of people, listening and looking, taking in the sights and sounds.

After we had come to our senses somewhat, we noticed that we were at the Plaza de Obradoiro—probably the most important square in Galicia, over which soar the moss-covered spires of one of the most beautiful cathedrals in all of Christendom.

Anastasia and I were happy--each of us in our own way. We had come to the end of the road--literally. At least that was what Anastasia thought...

"Somehow I pictured Santiago differently, but I can't believe how exciting it is to be here," exclaimed Anastasia with a laugh. For me too, this was an incredible experience--even though I had already been there so often with my various pilgrimage groups.

Only now that I had actually walked to this town, could I consider myself a real Camino pilgrim. Our next stop was the Pilgrim Office located right next to the cathedral. We got in line behind what must have been hundreds of people, all waiting to receive their compostela. Only people who can actually prove that they have walked at least the last one hundred kilometers are authorized to receive this prized document. It took more than an hour until we were proudly holding our compostelas, written in Latin and probably looking much the same as they would have in the Middle Ages. Anastasia was beaming with joy and waving her certificate through the air. "Guckt mal, ich hab' sie!" ["Look, I got it!"] she shouted in German to the people still standing in line.

Only now did we visit the cathedral. But rather than walk through any of the several main portals, we chose to enter through the famous Portal de Gloria (Glory Door), a masterpiece of Romanesque architecture built in the eleventh century and named for the gloria--glory and honor--that all believers who walk through it are said to receive.

Walking through this portal symbolizes that the pilgrims who have come this far have left their old lives behind them and are now beginning a new life. Like pilgrims for over a thousand years, we too wanted to thank St. James for the Camino, so we got in line to embrace and kiss the bust of the disciple. It took more than an hour until we had reached the saint's tomb, which is located directly behind the high altar. As we were about to leave, the cathedral was being prepared for the Eucharistic mass, so, once again, we decided to stay for Holy Communion. Anastasia, I noted with interest, wanted to see a pilgrims' mass.

During the very ceremonial High Mass, a murmur went through the crowd as several monks started setting the famous Botafumeiro—one of the largest censors in the world—in motion over the throngs of people. Over five feet (1.6 m) tall and hanging from a ninety foot (27 m) rope attached to the ceiling of the cathedral, the huge silver-colored censor swung back and forth majestically over the heads of the congregants, dispensing incense.

When we were finally back on the crowded streets of the Old Town more than two hours later, we noticed how tired we were. So we sat down at the first café we could find, relaxed, and enjoyed a large cappuccino, observing the throng of pilgrims and letting their voices and cries in dozens of languages wash over us. Anastasia and I we sat there for awhile, just chatting, contemplating, and processing all we had seen and experienced the past ten days.

"Anastasia, say, did you know that the Camino does not really end in Santiago?"

"You're kidding... I thought we had reached the end of it."

"Actually, we haven't. The Camino really ends in Cape Finisterre, a French word that means 'edge of the world.' From here in

Santiago the pilgrims used to walk an additional fifty-five miles (90 km) to the Cape. That is truly the end of the road—a little fishing village at the edge of the Spanish mainland, situated on a peninsula of granite. In days gone by, pilgrims used to publicly burn their tarnished and tattered pilgrimage robes at that spot—as a sign of a new beginning."

"Hmm," she replied. "You leave your old life behind you and begin a new life."

"Exactly."

I could tell that she was intrigued by this concept. In fact, it even seemed to electrify her. After a few moments of silence she burst out, "So why don't we push on to Cape Finisterre?"

"I would love to complete the pilgrimage with you," I replied, "but my time is up. I've got to be back in Germany in two days and, besides, my legs hurt. I can't go on. Oh well, I've been there so many times anyway. I know what it looks like, but for you it would be a wonderful experience that would really be worth your while."

"You want me to walk there all by myself?"

"Anastasia, you don't really think I'd suggest something like this without already having a solution at hand, do you?" I asked her with a wink. "You know, earlier when we were in the cathedral, I happened to be standing next to a German couple who couldn't find a vacant seat. You were already sitting up front. They said they'd be driving to Cape Finisterre tomorrow. I asked them whether they might be willing to take along a young woman who desperately wanted to see that place and they said it would be no problem."

"I won't go without you," she pouted.

"Nonsense! They're really nice people. Look. I'll stay here and rest, and will wait for you. You'll be back in a few hours. You can't miss Cape Finisterre."

It took me a while, but I was finally able to persuade her to go along with those German tourists. I was certain that that place, which is supposed to have supernatural powers, would have something special in store for her, but I didn't mention this to her. It only took one cell phone call and we got everything squared away. Next we looked for a place to spend the night and came across an old seminary where they let us stay for free—thanks to the fact that we were now "certified pilgrims."

By the time I woke up the next morning, Anastasia had already left. She had set off about 5:00 a.m. and I expected her back that same evening.

After all those strenuous and exciting days, I enjoyed having a day of rest all to myself. I slept in, had a sumptuous lunch, and just kicked back. That evening, as I was having dinner near our quarters, I saw her coming from afar, walking down the street with a bounce in her step. I waved to her, eagerly awaiting what she had to say.

"Well, how was it? Tell me!"

She plopped down next to me, ordered something to eat, and looked at me with huge sparkling eyes. I knew something special had happened.

"Arthur, it was simply amazing. Cape Finisterre is incredibly beautiful. It'll take me a while to process what I experienced today. The sky... the water... the air... and then that incredible feeling..." That was all she said.

The next day we flew back to Germany and, sadly, it didn't take long at all for us to get back into the rhythm of our lives—she into hers and I into mine. Before long, it was early September and I had to go on several pilgrimages, which took up all of my time. Anastasia called me in mid-December and wished my Merry Christmas and a Happy New Year. We didn't see each other until the following summer.

About that time she called me and we met at that little café around the corner from my apartment, where we had already been several times before. As I walked in the room, she was already waiting, grinning from ear to ear. We hugged and I noticed that something was pulling at her heartstrings. I had barely sat down and it all started bubbling out.

"Arthur, my life has changed."

"Really—and how?"

"Everything has changed... my private life, my career, my attitude towards life—I can't believe all of this."

"Tell me more!"

And then it just started spuming out of her. She told me what she had experienced the past year. Not only had her shaky relationship

29

with her boyfriend greatly improved, now they were even talking about getting married and having children. "We're so happy, Arthur. We've moved in together and are so deeply in love."

This was incredible. And Anastasia's professional life had changed as well. She had quit that horrible job in the nightclub and the stint at the fitness center as well. She was now freelancing in a well-known architectural office in Frankfurt and thought it was quite likely they would hire her full-time before long.

"I would never have thought that so many things could turn for the better in one year."

"What do you think changed everything?" I asked, having a pretty good hunch what was going on.

"I've been thinking about that for a long time, Arthur. And I'm convinced it was the Camino. I want to experience that again. That's right, Arthur, I want to do the Camino again, but this time I want to take the same route that Paulo Coelho took."

"Whoa…slow down, Anastasia… Let's first talk about last year. When you were out there, did you experience anything mystical which could be the reason your life has changed so much?"

"Well, on the Camino and after that I didn't become what you would call a Christian. I still struggle to believe in God. But I do know something was going on. I know I felt something, but I just can't put my finger on it. I don't really know what it was."

"Well, just give it a try…"

"There were a few things that I learned on our pilgrimage, like that I have to be more patient and tolerant, that I shouldn't give up easily and I need to follow through with things. And, even if it seems a long shot, I have to find a way to reach the hearts of people. Before the Camino I had always focused on myself. The three most important people to me had been me, myself, and I. Before the Camino I hadn't been very attentive to my fellow humans… to their needs and sorrows.

But since I've been relating to other people better, they've been relating to me better, too. Since I've been respecting other people more, they've been respecting me more. What a wonderful experience that is."

"Aha," I thought, "The third of those three gifts of the Spirit— faith, hope, and love."

She was beaming so that I didn't want to interrupt her. Finally I did however.

"Tell me," I asked. "Did you have any kind of, how should I say it, religious or spiritual experience out there?"

"I've been thinking about that, too. Now—about a year later--I think I would definitely have to say 'Yes.'

You know, Arthur, when I arrived at Camp Finisterre that morning with the German couple, we agreed to meet again in the evening and then said goodbye for the day. I looked around, and that afternoon I sat down near an old campsite on a cliff on which waves were crashing over and over. I looked out at the ocean and concentrated on the sunbeams reflecting on the water. Wind... waves... the rapidly changing colors... the fascinating kaleidoscope of the clouds flying by. All of a sudden everything was different. I experienced a moment of complete inner peace. This feeling of peace just bubbled up inside of me, erupting in a plume of joy and absolute freedom that I had never experienced before. Have you ever felt anything like that?"

I nodded and bade her to keep on talking.

"So I just sat there and suddenly became blind to the outside world. It was as if I was looking inside of myself. I could see myself sitting there on that cliff; I could see my life and the things I had to do. All of a sudden I was one with the universe--like a small insignificant drop of water in the endless sea. I don't know how long this feeling lasted. But it was so breathtakingly beautiful that I wished I could hold onto it forever"

We were both silent for a while, meditating on this feeling of hers. Finally I said to her:

"Anastasia, in the future if anything should ever happen to you, anything horrible in life, something that might throw you into huge trials and tribulations, then try and remember that moment, remember that feeling that you got to experience at Cape Finisterre and which you can't put your finger on. You know, there was once a very wise man who wrote these words: "Now we see but a poor reflection as in a mirror; then we shall see face to face. Now I know in part; then I shall know fully, even as I am fully known. And now these three remain: faith, hope and love. But the greatest of these is love." That feeling you had didn't actually come from

31

inside of you. It came from an outside source, something we call the Holy Spirit."

She looked at me in surprise, and I could tell she didn't really grasp what I was saying me, so I just let it be.

But I smiled to myself because I knew that one day Anastasia would understand.

The Private Audience of Doña Aurora

Sometimes people ask me, "Arthur, what do you do for a living?" They probably think I'll say, "I'm a teacher" or a physiotherapist or the like. Most of the time I just reply, "I've got the most wonderful job in the world." And I mean it, too. You see, when you like being around people and enjoy speaking foreign languages, when you love getting around and rising to new challenges every day, then my reply isn't really as cryptic as it sounds. I'm still experiencing new things in this profession, even though after fifteen years on the road as a tour guide, you might think there can't possibly be anything new under the sun. Well, I guess there is—as the memorable experience I had with a lady I call Doña Aurora demonstrates.

Our story begins in the beautiful City of Lisbon. the capital of Portugal, which holds a special place in my heart. I always love returning to that town—and to Portugal in general. For years I've been accompanying pilgrims to the various sites in Fátima, the small but world famous village northeast of Lisbon where the Virgin Mother appeared in 1917. Every year more than a million people go on a pilgrimage to Fátima, bringing prayer requests to the Chapel of Apparitions. And for the most part, every pilgrimage to Fátima by travelers from overseas begins at Lisbon Airport.

***

Once again, I was scheduled to accompany a tour group from the United States, slated to land at Lisbon airport at 10:30 a.m. local time that warm October morning. This particular group was on a pilgrimage from Lisbon to Rome. As is my custom, I was there on time, so I'd be able to resolve any issues that might have cropped up with the airline or customs. Holding up a sign declaring "ETS Marian Shrines," I stood there at Arrivals and waited for my guests. After a few minutes I spotted them. Their priest was paving the way through the crowds, his jet-lagged flock dragging along behind him. Our greetings were pretty low-key because even the most exuberant travelers tend to get droopy if they've been deprived of a good night's sleep. I remember that day well. Even trying to hustle these pilgrims into the motorcoach in an expedient fashion so we could reach Fátima that same day was a bit of a struggle. We needed to hurry along because our itinerary called for a visit to the Church of St. Stephen in Santarém that afternoon, where we would celebrate Mass.

The Church of the Holy Miracle in Santarém

Santarém is the capital of the region of Ribatejo, named after the Tejo River that you bump into all the time in that part of the country. Santarém is situated between Lisbon and Fátima, about 60 miles (90 km) north of the capital. After about one and a half hours on the road, we were finally approaching our goal, the Church of St. Stephen. Locals call it the "Church of the Holy Miracle" because of a Eucharistic wonder that occurred in the 12th century, which ever since then has made the sanctuary a magnet for Christians around the world.

Here's what happened: according to legend, there was a woman who sought the advice of a Jewish fortune teller because of the sinful, adulterous life her unbelieving husband was leading. The fortune teller listened to the sorrows of the poor wife and prophesied that her husband would turn his life around if the wife were to bring the soothsayer a consecrated host from the Lord's Table. This was a steep price for the wife to pay because misusing a consecrated host was considered an enormous sacrilege. But the prospective reward—that her husband would repent and turn from his sinful ways—was so great that the wife decided to pay the price. So the wife went to Communion to receive the Body of the Lord. But instead of partaking of it, she hid the wafer in her clothes, quickly making her way to the fortune teller. Shockingly, while the wife was hurrying through the streets of the village, the host began to bleed profusely, causing quite a commotion among passersby who, of course, thought the wife was bleeding. She panicked and ran home.

34

In haste, the wife placed the host in a handkerchief and laid it in a container, which she wrapped in thick linen.

The next night, the wife and her unfaithful husband were awakened by a blinding light radiating from the container with the host. As if this weren't dramatic enough, angels were kneeling around the container, worshipping the host that they had removed from the handkerchief. At this point, the wife confessed to her amazed husband the sin she had committed with the host. According to legend, both husband and wife spent the rest of the night praying on their knees. The next morning they called the priest for help who in a procession returned the host to the Church of St. Stephen, where he sealed it in melted bee's wax. Many years later, a priest opening the tabernacle was astonished to see that the block of wax containing the host had broken open, but that the host was sealed in a crystal pyx. This famous Eucharistic Miracle occurred in 1247.

Today the Church of St. Stephen is in the center of Santarém's Old Town and can only be reached by navigating narrow alleys. So our tour group had to get out of the bus, which we had parked some distance away, and walk the rest of the way. I led my tuckered out travelers over the uneven cobblestones and down the dusky alleys. Glancing up, we marveled at the graceful colonial balconies of Santarém, brimming with bright orchids, gerberas, lilies, carnations, nigellas, snapdragons, and many other sweet smelling flowers, which brightened up the narrow passages. A pleasant summer wind was blowing the exotic floral aromas through the alleyways.

"Tudo bem Senhor Arturo!" the female sacristan exclaimed, greeting me affectionately, as people in this region are wont to do. She gave me a hug and kissed me on the cheek. As had so often occurred before, I accompanied the priest into the sacristy where he robed up, while the sacristan was preparing the altar. After celebrating the Mass, our group was allowed to step up behind the altar into a separate room where the famous 13th century host is displayed. It took a while before everyone had a chance to view it. On their way out, some of our travelers bought religious souvenirs. Then we shuffled back to the bus and continued on our way to Fátima.

Fátima

After a short drive, we arrived at Fátima, where we checked in at the Hotel Santa Maria. Unfortunately, the Hotel Fátima, where I usually stay when traveling with tour groups and which would have been my first choice, was sold out. Apparently, Imelda Marcos—the widow of the former Philippine dictator—had taken up residence there at the same time. As we soon found out, Ms. Marcos—with forty-three suitcases in tow—and her entourage had booked the entire hotel.

Be that as it may, we enjoyed our sumptuous meal at the Santa Maria. Some of our travelers were already working on their second or third glass of Portuguese wine in very short order. Everybody was in the best of spirits and extremely talkative. After all, we wanted to get to know each other better because we would be traveling as a group for quite a while. Nevertheless, before long, most of our travelers were struggling to stay awake. The time change, the long flight, these first exciting experiences in Portugal—and not to mention the Vinho verde—had all conspired to make our pilgrims very sleepy indeed. So it wasn't long before they retired to their rooms, most probably making a bee line for their beds.

But, as on every trip, there always seem to be a few die-hards, determined to shake things up, long after the others have hit the sack. So, a bright-eyed and bushy-tailed remnant of our group crossed the street to the Cova da Iria and headed toward the Chapel of Apparitions, where a Rosary Procession takes place every night in the summer. I joined this group of people, but trailed behind somewhat. At one point I noticed an elderly lady—one of our travelers—walking next to me. I had already noticed her at the airport. She smiled in a strangely peaceful and humble, yet charming way, and made a very pleasant impression on me. Seemingly Latin American in origin, she was slight of build and her black eyes sparkled with energy. She wore her hair, which must have been jet black in her youth but which was now highlighted by a few gray streaks, in a tight bun at the back of her head. The lady spoke so softly that I could barely hear her. Her gestures were minimalist as well. She was demure, yet you could tell there was a lot of pluck bubbling beneath that serene surface. Somehow she reminded me of the *Mestizas* I had met years ago in South America and whose captivating ways had always caught my fancy.

"Tambien habla español, Señor?" ("Do you speak Spanish, too, *Señor*?") she asked me, speaking so softly that at first I couldn't understand a word she said. I asked her to repeat the question, which she did.

"Claro" ("Of course"), I replied in Spanish, triggering a barely perceptible smile.

We continued to converse in Spanish and I noticed that she spoke with a Mexican accent.

"How nice!" she replied. "I heard you speaking Portuguese and I figured that someone who speaks Portuguese might also be able to speak Spanish. And, sure enough, you do. Are you Colombian?"

"No, German."

"Ooh, I was *really* off... Is Germany very far from here?" "No," I replied, "Not too far, only about three hours by air. Europe is not as big as the Americas."

"I see. Señor Pahl, my name is Aurora, Aurora Benitez. Please call me Aurora," she said, extending a dainty hand and, once again, giving her charming smile.

"Doña Aurora..." I said, wanting to address her respectfully, but she cut me off. "No, no, please, Señor...Aurora, just plain Aurora. Please don't call me Doña. I'm not an elegant lady. Please just call me Aurora. May I call you Arthur? I would prefer *Arturo,* but you introduced yourself to our group as Arthur."

"True enough, but all my Latin American friends call me Arturo, as do my friends in Spain and Portugal. Please do me the favor of calling me Arturo, too."

As we were talking, we had reached the Cova da Iria and the Chapel of Apparitions.

The Rosary Procession had just begun and Aurora worked her way up to the front, so she wouldn't miss a thing. The benches were already crowded, but this determined little lady wouldn't be stopped by that minor obstruction. In a dignified yet energetic manner, Aurora managed to find herself a good seat. I couldn't help but grin. It's always amazing what some women—even the petite ones—are capable of accomplishing. As always, Fátima's

Procession of Lights was deeply inspiring. And I was pleased that so many attendees—apparently from around the world, too—were attending, praying intensely and singing hymns from the bottom of their hearts.

As opposed to Aurora, I was not able to find (or create) a vacant spot up front, so I was forced to sit further back. When the procession was over, I started drifting back to the hotel, alone but content with the first day of this pilgrimage. Traipsing along and thinking about turning in for the night, I happened to notice that my new companion Aurora was once again walking beside me.

"Wasn't it beautiful, Arturo?"

"Yes, absolutely, Aurora."

After these two comments our conversation pretty much fizzled out, so we strolled back to the hotel in silence. "This lady is amazing," I thought, ruminating about how rapidly, yet elegantly, she just floated along, silently and smoothly—almost like an angel. Yes, somehow she fascinated me. As we were entering the hotel, she spoke up again.

"Arturo, do you know the story of Fátima by heart?"

"Of course I do. I've been here *so* many times. Besides, Fátima is my all-time favorite place. Sometimes I come here even without tour groups, just for some R & R."

"But you live in Germany, don't you?"

"Well yes, but sometimes I have a yearning for Fátima, so I take a cheap flight down for the weekend and come here.

You know, Aurora, for us believers the apparitions of Fátima contain many messages. I'm not a theologian and I certainly don't come up with any new interpretations about Fátima, but when you take a closer look, one thing seems crystal clear: Something very special happened at this place. Besides, I'm a big fan of Pope John Paul II and *he* has a very high regard for Fátima, too. You probably know that he has visited Fátima several times. In fact, you know the bullet that almost killed him back in 1981 when there was that attempt on his life? He donated it to Fátima. You can still see that bullet today—they've inlaid it in the priceless crown of the Virgin Mary."

"Where can I see that crown?" she exploded. "I've just got to see it!"

"There's a permanent exhibition called *Exhibition for Light and Peace* right across the street from the Cova da Iria. They have a collection of the priceless artifacts given to Our Lady of Fátima over the years. That's where the crown is exhibited. Aurora, you'll be standing right in front of it tomorrow and you'll see the bullet that injured the Holy Father. It's the 9 mm bullet from the pistol of the man who shot the Pope on May 13, 1981.

A few years ago a jeweler placed the deformed bullet into the crown. Just think, when he inserted it into the crown, the bullet fit instantly! All the jeweler had to do was attach it to the crown with a thin strip of gold. It looked like the center of the crown was *made* just for that bullet. Normally you'd have to file and drill for a long time to make a foreign object fit into a work of art like that crown."

"Incredible," she whispered pensively, "Absolutely incredible."

"You know, Aurora," I continued, "the Virgin Mother has several crowns. But the crown we're talking about, the one with the bullet, is the most elaborate one. They only use it once a year, at the procession every May 13th. After the procession they return it in the permanent exhibition until the following year."

After a short while Aurora asked me, "Arturo, would you do me a favor and tell me the story of Fátima?"

Although I was tired and not exactly thrilled about telling the long story of Fátima then and there, I nodded and moved towards a couch and coffee table in the hotel lobby.

I suppose she read the look on my face and guessed that I wasn't too thrilled, so she tried to sweeten her bid. "Arturo, please, you're my guest. I'll order something for us to drink and you tell me the story of Fátima, *de acuerdo* (alright)?"

I grudgingly agreed, but was uncomfortable about her inviting me. I was pretty sure she wasn't a wealthy woman. She was probably a Mexican immigrant. Her English was still pretty rough. Perhaps she had scraped together her nickels and dimes to pay for this trip and here *I* was mooching on her for a drink that she could barely afford. But I gave in and ordered a cup of tea. At least tea wasn't that expensive…

Before launching into the story, I waited for the waiter to bring our refreshments. I took a sip of tea, Aurora nipped at her espresso, and then I commenced with the story.

"On May 13, 1917, three children were shepherding a little flock of sheep in a field called Cova da Iria—at the very spot where we were just a few minutes ago. In the meantime it has, of course, all been built up. Even back then that area belonged to the parish of Fátima.

The children were Lúcia de Jesus dos Santos, age ten; her cousin Francisco Marto, nine; and her other cousin, Jacinta Marto- -Francisco's sister—also age nine. It was around noon and the village was baking in the mid-day heat. As was their habit, the children had just prayed the rosary. Afterwards they started playing, at the very spot were the basilica now stands.

All of a sudden the children saw a brilliant flash of light. At first they thought it was a lightning bolt. Lucia, the oldest child, immediately grabbed the two younger ones by the hand and they frantically looked for cover from what they thought was an approaching storm, but lightning bolts seemed to be following them. Down by a holly oak, which is where the Chapel of the Apparition was built years later, they saw yet another flash of light, but this time it was even brighter than before.

Then a beautiful woman appeared to them, as brilliant as the sun. She was holding a white rosary in her hands. The children looked up at her in amazement and full of curiosity, but without a trace of fear. The woman urged them to keep on praying and to come to that same place at the same time of day, on the 13th of every month, for the next five months.

Of course the children found all of this extremely exciting and actually followed the instructions of the unknown apparition. And that unknown lady did, in fact, reappear on the 13th of June, July, September, and October. Every time she spoke to the children. Needless to say, the children were not able to keep this miracle to themselves. First they told their friends and then, after the news had spread like wildfire, they finally told their parents, too.

Unfortunately, the children were not able to meet with her in August, so the woman appeared six days later, on the 19th, in an area called the Valinhos, about 500 yards (0.5 km) away from the village. You see, on August 13 they had been locked up by the mayor of Vila de Nova de Ourem, their village. At that time, Portugal was governed by atheists who had closed down parochial schools, prohibited church services, and secularized convents. The atheistic government locked the children up because it felt challenged by these three young shepherds and wanted to prevent them from meeting with the Virgin Mother that particular month. So the authorities had the children kidnapped and thrown in prison in the county seat of Ourem. The authorities lied about the children's arrest, telling the parents that the children had been summoned by the local priest.

As you can imagine, all of these miracles had a huge impact on the population. At the Virgin Mother's last appearance on October 17, 1917, some 70,000 people waited—in the pouring rain—to see a miracle.

On that day, once again, the radiant lady appeared and spoke to the children. 'I am the Lady of the Rosary, I have come to warn the faithful to amend their lives and ask for pardon for their sins. They must not offend Our Lord any more, for He is already too grievously offended by the sins of men. To show that you agree with me, I ask you to build a chapel in my honor at this place.'

At that point, the world famous 'Miracle of the Sun' at Fátima began. The rain ceased and the sun took on the appearance of a silver disc. The disc started to turn, first slowly, then faster and faster until it was whirling at a terrific speed. Almost out of their minds with fear, the spectators fell on their knees and began to pray. They later described the Miracle of the Sun like this: This disc shone "like the most magnificent fire wheel that could be imagined, taking on all the colors of the rainbow and sending forth multi-colored flashes of light.' The countryside, people, animals, and vegetation were bathed in violet, green, red, yellow, and blue light. Suddenly the sun seemed to move from its customary place in the sky. At a terrifying speed it started falling to the earth in a zigzag pattern, abruptly stopping and then returning to its customary place in the sky in a zigzag pattern. Although the whole event lasted only about ten minutes, it had a shocking and long-lasting effect on all the spectators. The bizarre movements of the sun were visible even twenty-five miles (40 km) away from Fátima.

A few journalists had come from Lisbon just for this event, claiming they wanted to report on the miracle that had been prophesied. But atheists all, the *real* reason they had come was to

41

uncover what they thought was a swindle concocted by the Roman Catholic Church. Even though the journalists had witnessed seventy-thousand spectators screaming for their lives as the sun appeared to be crashing into the crowd, they did everything in their power to discredit the miracles. And so, the flaccid articles that appeared the next day in Lisbon's newspapers belittled and ridiculed the entire event.

But their shoddy journalism wasn't able to smear the 'Miracle of the Sun' at Fátima. Big news spreads—even without journalists. This is why every year millions of pilgrims come to Fátima to worship the Mother of God. And every year there are more."

Aurora remained silent for a while, as if she were waiting to see whether my story was over or not. Then she asked, "What ever happened to the children?"

"Jacinta and Francisco died just a few years later, while they were still children. Amazingly, Lucia is still alive. She has been living in a convent in Coimbra, Portugal, for years. She must be well over ninety years old by now. You know what? In a few days we'll actually be driving by her convent on our way to Spain."

"You're such a wonderful story teller, Arturo. I could just sit here and listen to you for hours on end." Then she paused and yawned, softly uttering, "But now I really am very tired. I need to go to bed. '*Buenas noches*,' she said, getting up and slowly making her way to the elevator. The elevator door opened, closed, and she was gone.

A few days later, our motorcoach drove us northeast from Fátima towards Spain. We stopped at Coimbra, where Sister Lucia was at the time still living in the convent with her fellow Carmelite nuns. We got out and our priest held Mass in the convent chapel. Unfortunately, we did not see Sister Lucia.

Next, we moved on to the Chapel of Santa Clara, where St. Elisabeth, the patron saint of Portugal, is interred. She was queen of Portugal and also the great-niece of St. Elisabeth of Thuringia. After her husband died in 1227, the queen joined the Third Order of St. Francis. She died four years later in Estremoz, Portugal, and was canonized after four years after her death, in 1235.

We then journeyed on to Spain. Our first stop was the Castilian town of Salamanca, the oldest university in the country—founded in 1218—and one of the oldest universities in all of Europe. Today, one in four residents of Salamanca is a student. We spent the first night on Spanish soil in Valladolid. The next day we visited Burgos, where we celebrated Mass in a beautiful chapel by the ocean. From there we pushed on to France, finally reaching Lourdes, the next highlight of our pilgrimage.

Lourdes

For the past few days, Aurora had been seeking my company. She seemed to enjoy the fact that we had become closer. And I enjoyed it too, I must admit. One evening, when I had a bit of downtime, I went up to my room, lay down, and thought of Aurora before falling asleep. Yes sir, she was something special, no doubt about it. Somehow she reminded me of my grandmother—and my mother as well. Aurora was like an amalgamation of the two, I thought. Even though I am a typical Central European and my ancestors were Anglo-Saxons, I somehow felt that there was something familiar about Aurora, as if she were a member of my family. To be sure, she came from different continent and spoke only Spanish. But her disposition reminded me of the old nuns from my boyhood home of Franconia (Franken) in Germany. She had something motherly about her, too, a characteristic in women I have appreciated ever since a child. Women like Aurora are able to communicate feelings and ambiance without words. All they need are gestures. Even from a distance you can tell what they are thinking.

Not to mention, I've always been intrigued by older people, in fact, even fascinated by them, provided they are not grumpy, know-it-alls, or mean-spirited—which is often the case.

Aurora radiated such kindness, wisdom, and piety that she touched me to the core. I'll never forget the few questions she asked me in that soft voice. They were to the point, but full of compassion, warmth, and feeling. They never irritated me. On the contrary, I found them amusing. At any rate, I answered all her questions as pleasantly and in as much detail as I could.

Aurora was especially transfixed by Lourdes. I observed her deep in prayer at the grotto of Massabielle, where the Virgin of the Immaculate Conception appeared to Saint Bernadette in 1858. "Go and drink at the fountain and wash yourself there," the Blessed Virgin had told Bernadette Soubirous the ninth time Our Lady of Lourdes appeared on February 25, 1858. Massabielle spring—the "Water of Lourdes"—wells up to this day, renowned across the globe for its healing properties. For the past century and a half, there have been reports of all kinds of miraculous healings resulting from this water. The Roman Catholic Church has officially recognized sixty-seven of them, of which forty-eight are directly connected to this spring water. Aurora was captivated by the healing water of Lourdes and filled up several bottles to take home, but didn't buy very many souvenirs—once again probably due to the fact that she didn't have as much spending money as the others.

A Disappointment

After an in-depth tour of Lourdes, we continued our journey through France, heading toward Carcassonne, a fascinating medieval town some forty miles (70 km) northwest of Perpignan. Founded in ancient times, Carcassonne was designated a UNECSO World Heritage site in 1997. Its city walls go back to the time of the Migration Period of the 5th and 6th centuries A.D. Positioned on a hill above the Aude valley, Carcassonne for centuries benefited from the fact that it was on a heavily trafficked and strategic trade route between the Mediterranean and the Atlantic. Because this ancient town was basically untouched by World War II, Carcassonne has largely been able to retain its medieval character. Tourists are thrilled by it, as was Aurora who had never before seen a medieval castle. As usual, she didn't say much, but the expression on her beaming face spoke volumes.

That evening after the official sightseeing program, the two of us took a walk through the festively illuminated town. Aurora and I sat down on a bench near the Château Comtal, the Castle of the Viscounts, enjoying the balmy air. I had already gotten used to the fact that Aurora didn't say much. In fact, I actually appreciated that particular attribute of hers. Silence can be quite enjoyable. Both of us realized that we had become friends. She seemed to feel well taken care of, understood, and safe around me. And I just plain liked her. So it came as no surprise that she started to tell me stories from her past.

"Arturo, may I share some things about my life with you?"

"Yes, I'd love to hear about your life. Please go ahead."

"You know, my children gave me this trip for my birthday. I turned seventy last year. I have five children—two sons and three daughters. Yes, I'm very proud of them. They're good children and they are repaying me richly. They gave me this trip because I would like to see the Holy Father so much. Do you treasure our Holy Father too, Arturo?"

"Absolutely, Aurora, I honor him greatly. In fact, in many ways John Paul II is one of my heroes."

"Well, at my age, you've got to be really careful with the heroes you pick. But John Paul II really *is* a hero. I revere him. Will we be able to see the pope on our trip? That would be my greatest dream."

"You certainly will be able to *see* him, Aurora, I promise you that. In fact, next Wednesday we will have a Papal Audience."

"We will? That is so wonderful. Then I'll be able to see him face to face. Now that my life is slowly coming to an end, that would be a dream come true." She was silent for a moment, but before I could say anything, she continued.

"Arturo, I just want you to know that my children didn't give me this trip to Europe for no particular reason at all. They did this because they wanted to make that dream of mine come true, so I could just once in my life step before the throne of the pope and see him up close."

She hadn't finished her sentence yet, but I felt I just *had* to interrupt her.

"Now wait a minute, Aurora, I think there's a misunderstanding here. I can't *promise* that you'll see the pope face to face. We'll be attending the Papal Audience along with hundreds of other believers and we *will* see him from a distance. But it's highly unlikely you'll get to see him up close."

A cloud of disappointment passed over her face.

"But my children *promised* me that I would be able to see the pope up close," she gasped, placing her right hand in front of her mouth, her features stiffening.

Now I could see that her eyes were welling up with tears and I thought to myself, "Please, dear God, don't let her cry, not at this beautiful place, not right here, on this wonderful evening. Please, Lord, help me. What can I tell her to calm her down?"

My only option was to distract her.

"Look, Aurora, look at what I've got here..."

I reached into the travel bag that I always carry around and took out two caramel candies. I had bought a bag of them at Frankfurt Airport, at one of those ridiculously expensive gift shops. Although I'm always trying to kick my candy habit, these particular caramels let my good intentions crash and burn. Whenever I fail, I am always reminded of Oscar Wilde who supposedly said, "I can resist anything—except temptation."

Anyway, I wondered whether she too would succumb to that strange weakness that almost every female seems to have for bonbons or pralines. Aurora reached for the caramel, peeled off the wrapper, and popped the candy in her mouth. As she was sucking on it, she looked at me mischievously and said, "You're very clever, Arturo. You're trying to console me and cheer me up. But you still haven't answered my question."

I had to grin. She had caught me red-handed.

"Aurora, we *will* see the pope. I promise you that—on my honor. But it's simply not in my power to guarantee that you'll be able to get all the way up to the front and see him face to face. Please understand and don't make my life so difficult!"

"I won't make your life difficult, Arturo. I like you and that's why we'll change the subject."

I had actually been able to dissuade her from that topic! We exchanged a few more platitudes, and then walked back to the hotel. That evening in Carcassonne I was convinced I had succeeded in talking Aurora out of her greatest dream. Little did I know how wrong I was.

The next few days Aurora avoided me. Had our little conversation cooled our relationship? It certainly seemed so.

From Carcassonne we drove down to Nice and then to Monaco, moving further east along the Cote d'Azur and then down the Italian Riviera. We passed Ventemiglia and San Remo and spent the night in La Spezia, a quaint little beach town on the

Ligurian Sea. Everything went like clockwork, nothing out of the ordinary happened.

On the way to Rome we drove through Tuscany. My American tour group was impressed by the gorgeous and ancient northern Italian cultural landscape, where the legendary Etruscans and the ancient Romans had made their mark on history. We visited exquisite landmarked churches and buildings in Siena, in the university town of Pisa, and in Florence, the capital of Tuscany with its countless art collections. As we worked our way south, we also spent two days in Assisi, where St. Francis once lived. But the closer we got to Rome, the less we were able to focus on our sightseeing. Everybody seemed to be concentrating on the highlight of the trip—Rome and the Papal Audience, trying to envision how the Audience would go. Without a doubt, our trip was rapidly approaching its conclusion and culmination.

During the next two or three days Aurora began to seek my company once again, like at the beginning of our trip. Here and there she asked me little things—the names of persons she had not heard of yet and so on—but she didn't bring up the whole pope situation. Once again she was smiling, which really made me feel good. I figured she had resigned to the fact that having a Private Audience with the pope was a dead issue.

On Monday evening we arrived in Rome late, had dinner, and went straight to bed because we had a busy day of touring ahead of us. On Tuesday morning—one day before the Papal Audience—Giovanni arrived at our hotel. I've known him for many years and regard him as a highly competent *cicerone* for the multitude of sights in Rome. Giovanni had at one time been an attorney and had a law practice together with his brother. He has always been interested in the history of the city of Rome, having read reams of books on the topic. He knows all the famous and even the less well-known tourist attractions in the Eternal City up and down, right and left. Sadly, at about the age of forty he lost his faith in his profession and no longer wanted to deal with other people's "dirty laundry," as he called it. So for him, the next logical step was to turn his hobby into a profession. When the opportunity arose to do just that, he hung up his attorney career. Giovanni is a practicing Catholic and for us travelers he was often the "go-to guy" whenever we had a religious question. Over the years I've gotten to know him better and better, and today he and I are good friends. We spent a busy, but also strenuous, day in Rome with him, taking the "classic" tour of the city.

A Priest Sheds Light on the Past

It was Tuesday evening around 6 p.m. and we were getting ready for our Audience with the pope the next morning. I had already picked up our tickets at the Office of the Apostolic Palace a few hours earlier. As usual, the Audience with the pope was scheduled for Wednesday morning at 10:30 a.m.

If the weather is nice, the Papal Audience is held outdoors in St. Peter's Square. If it is rainy, it takes place in the large Audience Hall, behind the colonnade of St. Peter's Square. Because the weather forecast was calling for a sunny day, we were scheduled to be outside. Our group was just returning from a tour through Rome, when our priest, Father Giuliano, came up to me on the bus and said:

"Arthur, I need to talk you. It's important."

"Of course, Father, what's up?"

"It's about Doña Aurora. She's not doing well."

"What? She was walking around with the group all day and I didn't notice anything wrong. What's the matter with her?"

"Let's get back to the hotel first. Then we can talk about it."

I was curious to hear what our priest had to say.

Our group was staying at the Hotel Michelangelo—probably the best location in Rome, just a short walk from St. Peter's Square and close to a lot of other tourist attractions. From the hotel entrance you can see the famous cupola of St. Peter's Basilica, which looks so close you wouldn't guess that the Via di Porta Cavallegeri is still in between, separating the hotel from the Vatican.

We walked into the hotel lobby and sat down.

"Arthur, on this trip you have been taking such outstanding care of Aurora. You have been so loving to her. All of us can sense that the two of you care for and enjoy one another. That's why I'd like to ask a favor of you. As you know, Aurora's children gave her this trip to Europe because to be able to stand face to face with the pope has always been a lifelong dream of hers. I've been watching you, Arthur. You're a real pro and know Rome so well. You've been to this town often and I'm sure this isn't your first Papal Audience. And Giovanni knows his way around Rome and the Vatican even better. Listen, would it be possible to get Aurora as close as possible to the pope?

There it was again, that touchy topic. And I had thought it had died a quiet death. On the one hand, this pope issue irritated me. On the other hand, I admired the stubbornness with which Aurora was sticking to her guns, now recruiting allies as well.

"Thanks a *lot*, Father... Now *you're* turning up the heat, too," I remarked, thinking to myself, "Am *I* the priest around here or is *he*? Does he think *I'm* a curia cardinal or something, with the clout to pull strings at the Papal Audience? I'm just a tour guide, not a staff member of the Vatican." The priest interrupted my train of thought when he added, "Let me see, what exactly does it say on our tickets?"

I handed him our yellow tickets but they didn't help much. Nothing on them indicated anything about seating arrangements or proximity to the pope. It was illusory to think that we would somehow be able to get close to him. These Papal Audiences are jam-packed, sometimes with as many as 5000 people attending. People push and shove. You can be grateful if you even get to see the pope at all. In fact, some attendees don't even see a thing.

"Father, listen," I interjected. "Let's just drop this whole thing. These Papal Audiences are totally unpredictable. Just you wait and see."

Father Giuliano, the son of Italian immigrants, was about fifty-five. He was from Chicago, spoke Italian fluently, and--language-wise—had held his own pretty well on the trip. Not only had he done a marvelous job of providing pastoral care to our flock, he was also a very good organizer. That is why I was all the more surprised that *he* was asking me to do something that was next to impossible. I looked at him and he grinned back sheepishly. "What now?" I thought.

"Arthur, I want to tell you a story. If you still feel the same way when I'm through with it, we'll drop the whole matter, OK?"

"Father, I'm pretty sure you're about to tell me some tear

jerker, but let me say this right now: Your story is not going to change anything."

"Just hang on, Arthur, just hang on."

He hailed the waiter and asked for a bottle of red wine and two glasses. The waiter brought Father Giuliano's order and, after a sip, the Reverend launched into his story.

"Arthur, Doña Aurora was born in the Mexican town of Chihuahua in 1931. In the local language *Chihuahua* means "a dry and sandy place." Situated in the desert and surrounded by mountains, Chihuahua today has a population of about 700,000. As you might know, Chihuahua was also the boyhood home of Pancho Villa, the notorious Revolutionary, whom many Mexicans today still revere as a kind of Robin Hood. As is customary among the peasants of that culture, girls are married off at an early age. Aurora was married off at sixteen. By the time she was twenty-one, she already had five children. Just picture that! She basically had to raise those five children by herself because her husband worked in a copper mine and was rarely home, toiling hard to put food on the table for the seven of them. Tragically, when Aurora was twenty-two, he was killed in a mining accident. Things like that happened pretty often back then. Apparently the shaft in which he was working with the other miners was poorly braced and caved in. That horrible accident cost Aurora's husband and a few other men their lives.

Aurora's world collapsed along with that mine shaft. Not only was she now on her own at the still young age of twenty-two, she also had to raise the children, plus feed them and herself. This soon proved to be an insurmountable task. At first, Aurora tried cooking and ironing for rich folks in the provincial capital, but that just didn't pay well enough. Everything she tried seemed to hit a brick wall. Working and children are just incompatible--at least when you're a single parent.

The only solution to this predicament, as far as she could see, was for her to emigrate to the United States, the same conclusion that millions of other Mexicans have reached over the years. More precisely, she wanted to move to California, the "land of milk and honey," and start a new life. Of course she'd have to work there, too, but at least she figured she'd be making much more money than in Mexico. With the *real* money she'd earn, after a while she'd be able to send for her children and then they could all be together in California.

From her new vantage point, Aurora's sole purpose in life was now her children. She was no longer interested in men, let alone marriage. "My *children* are my life," was her new motto. How had she reached that conclusion?

Well, her marriage with José hadn't exactly been a bed of roses. Sure, he had been industrious and had gone to work regularly, but he had also loved his tequila. In fact, there were even rumors that the fatal accident wasn't a "normal" work related accident, but that he might have been drinking on the job. But Aurora shrugged off those old stories. José had not been a very good husband, true, but he hadn't been a particularly *bad* one either. He had hit her only once—really rare for a Mexican man. They *all* beat their wives, Arthur, whether they are young or old, rich or poor. That's simply a part of Latin America's *machismo* culture. *Every* Mexican man does it. In fact, a guy who *doesn't* beat his wife is considered a wimp. But, as far as Aurora was concerned, that one time José had hit her was one time too many. Something inside her shattered when that happened. Their relationship had never been quite the same after that. She simply had not been able to forget it. For that reason, remarrying was now out of the question.

Thank God, Aurora still had her mother who was still quite young and took Aurora's children in without any complaints. Her own children were already grown and had left home, and besides, she was a widow and lived all alone in the village, in a poor adobe hut. As far as the children were concerned, Grandmother had now become the most important person in the world. *Abuela* (granny) was always there for them when they needed it. Put another way, without her mother's help, Aurora would not have made it with her five young children.

The fact is, Aurora's children really *were* in good hands with their grandmother. Aurora could be certain that they would be well taken care of. So the young widow started preparing for the daunting challenge ahead, immigrating to *los Estados Unidos,* so she and her children could lead a better life.

As many others before her, Aurora would have preferred to take the shortest route to the U.S. That would have been via El

Paso, Texas, a city right on the border. But the wide road is also the road most frequently traveled. Even in the early 1950s, the United States had beefed up law enforcement in areas where illegal border crossings could be assumed. That is why Aurora chose not to go due north to El Paso, but rather west, toward California. Besides, another advantage California had was that her brother-in-law Juan, José's brother, was already living there.

So Aurora's trek began, over precipitous cliffs and rugged mountains, through steep canyons and across endless plains. Back in 1953, the railroad line across the state of Chihuahua had not yet been built. That wasn't until 1961. Only *then* was it possible to more or less comfortably travel the four hundred miles (650 km) to California. Today that railroad has eighty-six railroad tunnels, thirty-eight bridges, and countless switchbacks for the trains traversing the rough mountain ridges and steep canyons of western Mexico.

For Aurora, the only means of transportation were her own two feet and—when she was lucky—occasionally the back of a donkey. No wonder that by the time she had finally reached the Pacific Coast a few weeks later—with only a few tortillas to provide her nourishment—she was at the end of her rope.

Every person trying to get to *los Estados Unidos* was as dirt poor as she was—poor and hungry, yet yearning for a better life.

The group of immigrants she had joined included a few good-looking young men who had not failed to notice the spunky young *Mestiza*. She most certainly would make this tough trip more bearable, some of them thought, and they would have done anything for her, if only…

But that was completely out of the question for Aurora because she now had only *two* things on her mind: *los Estados Unidos* up ahead and her children back home. Anything else was out of the picture.

Eventually she reached the Pacific Coast. Aurora made relatively good time because toward the end of her journey she was sometimes able to hop the freight trains running north and catch a ride. Once, while riding the rails, Aurora witnessed how another young woman, trying to climb onto the train, was pushed off by a rude young man. Losing her grip, the female hobo somehow got caught under the rail car and was run over by the train. No one noticed the incident and the cars just kept on rolling. Aurora never found out what became of the other woman.

Traumatized by incidents such as these and practically starving to death, Aurora finally limped into Tijuana, a seedy bordertown teeming with "low life." In order to safely make it across the border, she would have to hire a *coyote,* one of the tough and sleazy young men who make their money smuggling illegals across the border and who profit from the economic disparity of the two cultures. Scoundrels of this sort can be found pretty much wherever Third World countries butt against prosperous nations. *A coyote* would not be cheap, Aurora knew, but even back home she had heard that there was no getting around their services.

That is why, during her journey north and west, Aurora had preferred to risk starvation rather than dip into the savings she would need for the *coyote.* Several times during her journey her savings had almost been robbed, but Aurora had sewn her money into her clothing so cleverly that the robbers hadn't been able to find it. Familiar with the harrowing tales of fellow Mexicans who had made it into the States, she knew she would need that wad of cash at the very end of her journey. For illegals who didn't have enough money to pay the *coyote*—and there were several such pitiful travelers in her group—the gates of paradise would remain closed. Aurora was determined she would not share their fate. Thankfully, as the border was coming into view, she had enough money to pay her "escort."

Illegal immigrants usually sneak across the frontier at night. So it was with Aurora as well. The *coyote* managed to smuggle her little group—three men and one woman— across the border. A relative of the *coyote's* was waiting for them on the Californian side and drove them to the next large city, San Diego. There she called her brother-in-law, Juan, who was able to take her in for a while.

Juan found her a stint with a farmer near Fresno almost immediately. But even though she was now in the "land of milk and honey," she still found herself doing back-breaking work in the fields. Luckily, Aurora was not afraid of hard work. She was young and the prospect of being paid cash every evening and being able to send that money to her family quickly made up for her toil.

On the other hand, it didn't take Aurora long to discover that "wetbacks"—as they were called back then—were often being caught by immigration officers. This ongoing cat and mouse game between the illegals and the Border Patrol was simply a fact of life. Occasionally, the Border Patrol raided the shacks in which the illegals were staying, but sometimes the illegals were able to dodge their arrest and thus avoid being deported. In all of these incidents, Aurora's agility and cleverness kept her one step ahead of the authorities.

One time, the only thing that saved her was sheer luck. The Border Patrol had conducted a raid and picked up illegals right in the fields, hauling them directly to Fresno county jail. Before long, those laborers were deported to Mexico. Aurora was only able to escape deportation that particular day because she had been sick and had not been able to report for work.

But the illegal aliens also had ways of defending themselves. They exchanged information and tried to organize themselves. Aurora was very popular among her peers. They respected her, admiring her tenacity and the fact that she stuck to her principles and was able to tough it out alone. Her morals and Christian ethics made Aurora a role model for young and old alike.

One day Aurora's group decided to pack up and leave California. They were tired of the low wages, hard labor, and the fear of being picked up by the Border Patrol. They all agreed that Chicago, Illinois, would provide better opportunities. Before long they had reached the Windy City and had found a place to stay in Pilsen, the Hispanic neighborhood on the Lower West Side.

But Aurora couldn't find decent employment as quickly as she had hoped. Any jobs she *could* land, such as washing dishes in run-down dining halls, were simply too depressing.

Fortunately, after a few weeks she stumbled across a family looking for a maid. These well-to-do people lived in a large house on Lake Michigan's "Gold Coast," which, as you probably know, is one of Chicago's wealthiest neighborhoods. They hired her as a maid, cook, and nanny—all rolled into one. Their children were still young—and very spoiled, too. The youngest girl was especially snooty, determined to show our heroine at every opportunity that Aurora was "only" the maid. The girl often refused to do what she was told. Whether it was school work or little chores around the house, the little girl more often than not refused to obey. It was in moments like these that Aurora thought of her own children and how dearly she missed them. Desperately homesick for them, she sometimes wept when she was alone. Her children tugged at Aurora's heart so badly that she sometimes couldn't even eat. Aurora prayed to God intently during that period, begging Him for a reunion with her children.

By the time her first year in Chicago was up, Aurora had already been working in the United States for four years. During this time she hadn't seen her children once. Arthur, you can imagine how tough that must have been for her. But even though President Eisenhower's "Operation Wetback," which had been launched in 1954, was continuing to make life difficult for illegal aliens, God apparently heard Aurora's prayers because around 1957 she somehow got her status legalized.

Her first order of business now was to fetch her children. The first one she brought up north was her oldest son. Then she got the other four children as well. Only seven years after illegally entering the United States, she had finally made it. Not even thirty years of age, Aurora was now living in the United States as a legal immigrant. Her days of hiding were over.

Her employment situation continued to improve and, by now, Aurora and her family had become well known and quite popular in their neighborhood. She managed to work for several families simultaneously—as a seamstress for one family, as a maid for another, as a cleaning woman for another, and as a nanny for yet another family. Even her children were able to find odd jobs here and there and were thus able to contribute to the family income. And so, slowly but surely, Aurora and her children were beginning to live the "American Dream."

This went on for many years. Over time, all of Aurora's children had become real Americans. In fact, they were having trouble speaking Spanish without an American accent. All of them went to school, with the two boys even going on to college and becoming academics. The girls learned a profession, too, and today have children of their own. Aurora is proud of all of them."

At this point, Father Giuliano took a break from his long narration. By now, we were already on our second bottle of red wine. After a moment, I noted:

"That certainly was a long story and it touched my heart, to be sure. But why are you telling me all of this?"

"Oh, I forgot to mention that Aurora's children know full well to whom they owe their happiness and affluence: to their mother. So when Aurora turned seventy this year, her five children decided they wanted to make her dream come true. Arthur, do you know where I'm going with this?"

"Yes, sir, I do… But it won't change a thing. Even if I *wanted* to help her with that papal visitation, it is not within my power to get her up close."

"Arthur, don't underestimate yourself. You have the heart of a lion and, besides, you *love* challenges like this, am I right? In fact, I think you're secretly looking forward to this challenge to show us what you can *really* do."

I couldn't believe it. The man was turning this whole issue into a matter of personal honor. He was piquing my pride—a pretty clever psychological move. He had a point: I *was* fed up with all of those teary requests and most certainly didn't want to appear to be a roadblock for the happiness of this fine woman. After deliberating a moment, I decided it was time to raise the white flag.

"OK, OK, you've convinced me. Listen, I'll give it a try, but don't blame me if it doesn't work!"

"Don't worry, Arthur. I trust you completely."

The Private Audience of Doña Aurora

As I went upstairs, I thought to myself, "What kind of fool are you anyway? How in the world could you get suckered into a thing like this?" By the time I had reached my room, I had almost worked myself into a state of despair. I wanted to—yes, I even *had* to—help this wonderful woman, but I knew that I didn't stand much of a chance. For several minutes I was lost in thought, trying to think of a way to untie this knot. There had to be *some* way...

But my mind was locked. So I finally kneeled by the side of my bed and started to pray.

"Dear Lord, you know the anxiety in my heart. It isn't for my *own* sake that I want to help this poor woman. I just want to help make this dream of hers come true. It might well be the last and biggest dream of her life. But I just don't know how to go about it. Please help me. Send me an idea, give me a sign!"

I got up, sat on the side of my bed, and held my head in my hands, agonizing over this matter. A few minutes later the phone rang. It was Giovanni, our Roman tour guide.

"Hi, Arthur. I need to discuss something with you about the Papal Audience tomorrow."

Could this be it, the idea I needed? Of course, *Giovanni* was the solution! No one knew the ins and outs of the Vatican and how to get what you wanted, better than he did.

"Giovanni, you're a godsend!" I cheerfully cried.

"What's up, Arthur? How can I help you?"

"I'm not quite sure yet, but we need to give this a try."

"Give what a try?"

I quickly went over Aurora's bio with him and shared her wish.

"Giovanni, we need to find a way to get Aurora up towards the pope."

"Arthur, give me a few minutes. Let me see what I can do." Then he hung up, leaving me to my thoughts.

Less than fifteen minutes later my cell phone rang. It was Giovanni.

"Hey, Arthur. I think I've got a solution. Can you get to St. Peter's Square tomorrow by 8 a.m.? I'll meet you there and take you to the Polish nuns. They'll lend you a wheelchair. Have Aurora sit in that wheelchair. The two of you wait there about forty-five minutes. At around 9:00 you simply wheel her up to the door of the basilica. The Swiss Guards will wave you on through and then the two of you position yourselves way up front with the disabled, right up front, facing the Holy Father."

"Giovanni," I cried into the phone, relieved. "This really sounds exciting, like some kind of CIA operation. But listen, are we allowed to do this? What if they find us out?"

"You just can't let that happen. It's that simple. You've got to

57

play your roles perfectly: Aurora is a wheelchair user. You are her assistant."

"You know, Giovanni, as clever as I think this solution is, I'm not sure whether it is ethical. This isn't doing the right thing. Aren't we stealing some disabled person's spot?"

"It's your call, Arthur. You need to make up your mind. We don't have a lot of time to hem and haw. You need to tell me right now if you want to go through with this or not."

"OK, for heaven's sake, let's do it," I said, feeling somewhat uneasy. I guess there *was* no such thing as a perfect solution here. Well, I *had* found a way to resolve this issue, although it was already giving me a belly ache. Now we just had to pull it off.

So *that* was how we were going to go about it. Why hadn't I thought of that myself?

This weird and slightly unorthodox solution might just work after all, I thought to myself. In those Papal Audiences John Paul II always sits facing the people squarely in the middle of the first row. To his rear left are the cardinals, bishops, diplomats, bridal pairs, and other guests of honor. To his rear right are the invalids, the physically challenged, and wheelchair users. They have priority seating and the Swiss Guards always let them through—after a quick security check. As clever as this solution was, if you thought about it, it *did* reveal a gap in the Vatican's security system. "I hope one of those nut cases doesn't get this same idea one of these days," I thought to myself. Then I fell asleep.

After a short and restless night, my travel alarm clock started beeping at 6:30 a.m. I took a shower and went down to breakfast. But I wasn't hungry. In fact, I was so tense I could only get down two cups of coffee. I was becoming increasingly fidgety and could hardly wait for the event to begin. At 7:45 I picked up Aurora and we silently walked over to St. Peter's Square. I had briefed her on our "Operation Wheelchair" the night before and she had immediately agreed. As long as she got to see the Holy Father up close, she didn't care, she said. On our way to the Polish nuns, I again reminded her what she was to do—and *not* do.

"Aurora, whatever happens, *do not* get up once you are in that wheelchair. You're disabled, remember? I'm sorry we have to play these games, but there is simply no other way. If they figure out you aren't really disabled, we'll both wind up in prison. *Comprendes?*"

"*Si, Señor,*" she replied quietly, grinning impishly. "It'll all work out, you'll see."

Getting the wheelchair from the nuns turned out to be a cinch. They didn't even give Aurora a second glance. Apparently, all you need to do is request a wheelchair for an old lady. Then we waited for an hour. I cannot recall the last time sixty minutes went by so slowly. Finally, the church bells of the basilica rang nine times, my "starting gun" to resolutely wheel Aurora to the entrance of St. Peter's Square. From there we turned right, heading towards where the Papal Audience was to take place and making a beeline for an empty chair in which we assumed the Holy Father would be sitting.

Next, we passed the Swiss Guards who conducted a listless security check. After all, who would assume a wheelchair user would be armed or in possession of any dangerous materials? That over with, I energetically wheeled our Mexican lady toward the empty chair. I navigated Aurora to the front row and sat down behind her. We were finally where Aurora had wanted to be—way up front! It was simply incredible. Somewhat teary-eyed, she gratefully looked up at me from her wheelchair. Everything was lining up picture perfect, even to the point that this particular Wednesday morning in October was a wonderfully sunny day—almost like summer. Aurora and I had no problem whatsoever waiting the following ninety minutes, now that everything was in place.

Finally, the big moment arrived. You could tell from the ripples of excitement rolling through the crowd that the pope was approaching. John Paul II was being driven straight toward us in his *papamobile*. It stopped quite near us and then he exited in a dignified manner with the help of his assistants. Coming ever closer, he was then moved in a specially designed vehicle toward his gorgeously appointed throne—that empty chair—which was less than ten feet (3 m) away from where we were sitting. Every single one of us, myself included, was gripped with emotion. We all got to our feet. So did Aurora, popping out of her wheelchair like a jack-in-the-box, so excited that she had apparently forgotten what we had discussed. I quickly leaned forward and shoved her back into her seat.

"Aurora, for heaven's sakes!" I hissed between clenched teeth. "Sit down! Remember what we talked about? Do you want us to wind up in prison?"

"*Perdone, perdone,*" (Excuse me, excuse me), she replied miserably. She immediately sat down and I let out a sigh of relief. Made it!

John Paul II began the Papal Audience with a reading from Psalm 67.

"May God be gracious to us and bless us and make his face shine upon us,

that your ways may be known on earth..."

In his message the Holy Father interpreted the psalm, and then greeted the attendees in the traditional way, each group in their native language. Whenever a particular language was spoken, various sections of the crowd responded with cheers and applause. I checked my watch. One hour had already passed. Next, the pope would be greeting select attendees personally. The first people to receive this special greeting were already getting up and walking toward the pope. I got up, too, and started wheeling Aurora over to the pope's throne. Because we were sitting in front, Aurora and I were also among the first to have the privilege of his personal address.

When it was our turn and Aurora was finally about to have her dream come true-- meeting the pope face to face—something awkward happened. While I was mumbling in German "May the Lord bless you, Holy Father," I saw that Aurora had once again gotten up from her wheelchair and was reaching for the pope's hand, trying as hard as she could to kiss his ring. Rocked by her emotions, our Mexican friend was once again overlooking what we had agreed upon. Instantly, the pope's bodyguards intervened and tried to stop her. The bodyguards seemed as taken aback as I was. Wanting to avoid a scene at all costs, I had to think of something fast. Almost panic stricken, I cried out in my very best Italian:

"*Miracolo, miracolo, può di nuovo camminare!*" ("A miracle, a miracle, she's walking again!").

At the same time, I rammed the wheelchair into the back of Aurora's knees, causing her to plop into her seat. Then in a mad dash, I wheeled her away from the pope, toward the exit and toward the rest of our group.

As I was hustling her away from the Papal Audience, Aurora sheepishly turned around to me and whispered, "Will they throw us in prison now, Arturo?"

I was much too excited and angry to answer her right then and there.

After the Audience was over, I returned the wheelchair and then strode back to the hotel with mixed feelings.

Over lunch there was only one topic among tour group: Doña Aurora's "Private Audience." Everyone wanted to know how we had pulled it off. But my lips were sealed. I glanced over to Father Giuliano who grinned back at me. Only he and I knew what had led up to this.

Aurora was beaming from ear to ear. With God's help, her impossible dream had come true. She had a sparkle in her eyes for the rest of that trip. And, as far as I was concerned, that beautiful smile more or less made up for the bumpy visitation we had just had.

The next day we took a day trip to Pompeii and surrounding areas. But I didn't register much of it--my mind was still reeling from the events of St. Peter's Square.

After ten long and eventful days it was finally time for the tour group to depart. I accompanied them out to Rome's Leonardo da Vinci airport and said goodbye to each and every traveler. When it was Aurora's turn, she gave me a big hug, a kiss on my cheek, and then whispered:

"Gracias, muchas gracias, mi amigo."

I mentally flew back to Chicago with her. What would she tell her children? The truth? Or would she proclaim to everyone that she had, in fact, kissed the pope's ring? I don't know. But I must admit, just the thought of our little adventure fills me with quiet joy, to this very day.

Unfortunately, I never heard from her again.

Adios, Aurora!

About half a year later I once again traveled to Lourdes. I was still struggling with the sin that Aurora and I had committed toward the pope. And so I went to private confession and poured

*out my heart. The Polish priest who was in the Confession booth
that day told me: "My son, what you did was most certainly not
right. In fact, it was a lie. But you did so out of compassion and
in order to make someone else happy. But if the Holy Father had
known what you were trying to do, I'm pretty sure he would have
laughed and been sympathetic to your predicament."*

*Even today, whenever I think of St. Peter's Square, I can't help
but chuckle as I recall Doña Aurora's "Private Audience."*

On the Beneficial Effects of Conversing with God

"We are only a prayer away from God." This simple yet beautiful quotation by Mother Teresa has always impacted how I feel about prayer. So when adversity strikes in my life, or when I don't know to whom to turn—more times than I would care to remember—I try to retreat to a quiet place and humbly turn toward my Creator. In His Sermon on the Mount, Jesus reminds us:

"But when you pray, go into your room, close the door and pray to your Father, who is unseen. Then your Father, who sees what is done in secret, will reward you" (Mt 6:6).

Christian prayer has various labels, such as meditation, devotion, reflection, intercession, or supplication. But the prerequisite for Christian prayer is faith in Christ, which is created by the Holy Spirit, who helps us and guides us in our prayer.

What Christians call "prayer," other religions might call "reaching in or up, toward an inner or Higher Power." Every major religion of the world views this "reaching in or up" as central to its faith.

Whereas in some religions, "reaching in or up" might seek to attain a higher level of consciousness or is viewed as a practice to awaken "inherent inner capacities of strength, compassion and wisdom" (such as in Buddhism), Christian prayer is a personal relationship with God, with believers conversing immediately and directly with the Trinity (and not with a generic "Higher Power," as in many other religions).

Prayer provides Christians with a daily application, giving us the opportunity to communicate our thoughts, wishes, and needs to our Creator.

This conversing with God can free us of our fears and pressures.

Prayer is, of course, also our way of expressing to Him our thanks for all His eternal and earthly blessings—not only for our salvation on account of Christ's work on the cross, but also for His blessings of Our Daily Bread, family, friends, resources, and all the other things He has provided for us terrestrial sojourners.

Interestingly, for some theologians, prayer is somewhat of a paradox: After all, isn't God's will destined and thus unchangeable? If this is so, how can we alter His will by means of our petitions?

As with so many other divine issues, our 4.5 pounds of grey matter are not able to comprehend this profound mystery. While we realize from Scripture that God is omniscient and that He knows from eternity everything that will happen, Scripture teaches that every single thing in our lives is not "predetermined."

The best way to resolve this apparent paradox is to trust God's promises about the power and value of prayer in Christ's name, yet also to obey Scripture by praying faithfully and frequently.

Furthermore, while prayer sometimes is a petition before God, in that we request Him to help us, our neighbors, our loved ones, or sick people--we must always see these petitions within the larger context of "Thy will be done," as is indicated in The Lord's Prayer.

So, in order to give our souls something to grab on to, we weak humans--wandering through life, unsure of ourselves—continue to strive for this unio mystica (mystical union), this basic trust. Believers simply want to be sheltered and received in the realm of the triune God—in a world of trust and love. And prayer is the medium to connect believers to this other realm.

Christian prayer recognizes the glory of God, which transcends all understanding. Prayer does not begin in our questions, requests, or petitions. Rather, it begins in and is filled with Christ Crucified—without whom our conversation with God would not be possible in the first place.

***

Many years ago, I took a long trip through India—fascinated by the country, people, and the diversity of religious forms that you encounter on that subcontinent.

Traveling with a Tibetan tour guide, we were having trouble one day scaling the steep mountains. We rested in front of a *stupa*, a mound-like structure containing Buddhist relics—a common feature in the Himalayas.

This particular *stupa* was small and not particularly interesting—weathered from many years of wind, snow, and sun. We had no way of telling whose bones it contained, but on its worn limestone face we recognized the well-known Buddhist mantra, *"Om Mani Padme Hum."*

A few feet away from the *stupa*, we noticed a weathered stone slab, onto which were scrawled several lines in Sanskrit. I asked my Tibetan tour guide to translate, to which he replied:

"Of course, I *can* translate this inscription, but it will sound quite strange to your European ears."

"Go ahead, Gendün," I told my companion with a grin. "I think I can handle it."

He stepped up to the stone slab and started to translate:

"'It quarreled with that thing and said, 'Everything, even the lowliest, most inconspicuous, ignorant thing of all can do something, even if it is only to pray.' But that thing, indignant about the phrase 'even if it is only to pray,' said that it was arrogant and proud, since prayer is the most noble thing one can do.' Then the third thing spoke up and said, 'While the two of you are arguing about philosophical things, I will do it,' and began to pray. And all turned out well.'"

"Does that make any sense at all to you, Arthur?"

"Basically it does, but who is that strange *It* speaking to *That thing*? And what is that *Third thing* taking the initiative? Why doesn't it refer directly to *Him*? And why do they use the neutral term *That*? It would seem obvious that this inscription is about prayer, but *who* is praying here and what is it about?"

"It's like this, Arthur," replied Gendün, pointing his middle finger like an arrow at my torso. "The unknown author of this verse is referring specifically to every creature--humans, animals, plants, and everything else that has life in it. *Every* living thing is a gift of Creation. Not just human beings. In Buddhism, we have the right and the ability to address our Creator. So animals and plants can pray, too."

Something clicked in my mind, and I started to reflect on this. I recalled how Ps 148 states, "Praise the LORD from the earth, you great sea creatures and all ocean depths, lightning and hail, snow and clouds, stormy winds that do his bidding, you mountains and all hills, fruit trees and all cedars, wild animals and all cattle, small creatures and flying birds." (Ps 148:7-10).

Then I remembered how in the Book of Revelation "The four living *creatures* said, 'Amen,' and the elders fell down and worshiped." (Rev 5:14)

St. Francis of Assisi and his loving relationship to nature came to mind, as did St. Catherine of Genoa who lovingly talked to trees, plants, and flowers and how these creatures obeyed God as if they were living persons.

I thought of Dr. Dieter Volkmann, a plant researcher from the University of Bonn, Germany, who years ago claimed that plants can see, hear, smell, taste, and feel—a statement that caused a bit of a stir in Germany at the time. Volkmann reported on experiments he had conducted in a vineyard in beautiful Montalcino in Tuscany, Italy, with biologist Stefano Mancuso. The two scientists had discovered that wine actually grows better when regularly exposed to classical music because music apparently causes the grapes to grow larger and sweeter, which, in turn, produces superior wine. In laboratory experiments, moreover, Mancuso had been able to prove that corn seedlings actually turn towards a source of sound and grow faster at certain frequencies. In particular, the tips of the plants' roots are apparently able to process acoustic signals.

Quietly observing me as I was contemplating all of this, Gendün finally stated, "Just accept it, and don't overcomplicate things. Creatures can communicate with their Creator at their own particular level of consciousness."

It would seem that in India, prayer *is* much more and can *effect* much more than I would have imagined from my European upbringing. After all, modern Western civilization is heavily influenced by rationalism, that is, the concept that *reason* is the source of all knowledge. We Westerners instinctively balk at the idea of seeing and feeling—not to mention *praying*—plants or animals.

As I continued to reflect on that inscription, I recalled other instances of pre- or perhaps post-rationalist thinking I had heard about over the years.

A friend of mine, Bill Evans, is a heart surgeon from Madison,

Wisconsin. For many years, Bill has been treating patients struggling with serious cardio problems. He once told me that there are a number of studies trying to determine whether heart patients who pray about their heart condition or who are the recipients of such prayer might have a *better* chance of recovery than those who have nothing to do with prayer.

Similarly, an American cardiologist, Dr. Mitchell Krucoff of Durham, North Carolina, has done studies on seven hundred and fifty angioplasty patients, splitting them up into two groups of three hundred and seventy-five patients each. Dr. Krocoff had people pray for one of the groups over a period of three years and concluded that more than ninety percent of that group was recovering significantly better than the people in the group for which no one had prayed.

Furthermore, Dr. Peter Findeisen, a German physician and the Director of the Bad Bevensen Retreat Center, recently published an article indicating that prayer speeds up patients' recovery because it strengthens their immune system.

These examples are just the tip of the iceberg of research proving the beneficial effects of prayer. In other words, the power of prayer goes way beyond what we rationalist Westerners are normally prepared to accept.

Here is yet another example of prayer:

I once met a ninety-two year old lady in Valinhos, Portugal. "Valinho" is the Portuguese word for a small, hilly valley—typical of the landscape around the village of Ajustrel, near the pilgrimage site of Fátima, where the bare hills are baked by the sun of the Iberian Peninsula.

Almost every time I had been to the area of Fátima, I had noticed the same old woman dressed in black. Whenever my pilgrims and I were walking toward "Loca do Cabeço" (where the angel had appeared twice to the seer children), I spotted this woman slowly making her way in the opposite direction—toward the beautiful white marble monument of the Blessed Virgin—which was erected at the spot where she appeared to the children on August 19, 1917.

Every single time, this old lady had been praying the rosary, seemingly lost in thought.

I had always wondered what she was doing there, but never had the courage to address her. So one day I plucked myself up and went over. As usual, she was dressed in mourning clothes—typical for widows in Southern Europe. Her white hair and black scarf made it difficult for me to guess her age. She could have been eighty or even older.

With my pilgrims almost out of view, I stepped up to her. She was sitting on a stone wall, continuously moving her fingers over a black rosary.

"Senhora, please excuse me. I've seen you here frequently and have noticed how intensely you pray the rosary. Are you from around here?"

She studied me for a few seconds and then answered in a soft voice. "Yes, I am, young man. I come here every day and pray the rosary. I've been doing this for twenty years now." As she was speaking, I noticed her friendly toothless smile and weathered hands.

"That long?"

"Yes, that long."

"May I ask how old you are?"

"I turned ninety-two this year. My name is Maria Jesus Santos de Oliveira. As you can see," she murmured, looking down at her clothes, "I am a widow. My eight children are all grown and out of the house. Some of them live in Lisbon, some in Santarém. One of my sons even lives in America."

"Who takes care of you?"

"No one. I live all by myself. Sometimes one of my nieces comes to visit. She cooks for me. But most of the time I am alone."

"Were you born around here?"

"Of course; where else? I'm from Moimento, a little village near Ajustrel. I've been to Lisbon a few times and to Coimbra, too, but otherwise I've lived here my whole life. There is always a lot of work to do. My family is related to Lucia in the third degree. Do you know who she was?"

"Yes, of course. She was one of the child seers of Fátima," I replied.

"Well, she was a distant cousin of mine. I still remember her. The last time I saw her was in 1987, when our family visited her at the Carmelite cloister in Coimbra. At that time, she was already seventy-two. My husband was still alive at the time. We had a little farm and led a very modest life. We are simple people, *senhor*. Back in my day, no one in our village was really able to read and write. Our daily bread was the work of our hands."

She paused, glancing down at her rosary, then out towards the horizon—apparently lost in thought. "When I saw Lucia in Coimbra, I asked her what an uneducated woman like I am could do. I, too, wanted to do something wonderful as she had done."

"And what did she tell you, *senhora*?"

"Lucia said I should pray—*daily*. She actually *directed* me to pray the rosary every day. 'You can basically pray for everything,' she said. 'All over the world there is such great suffering. You can pray for peace in the world; you can pray for good crops, you can pray for the souls lost in Purgatory. There is nothing for which you *cannot* pray.' At that point, I was determined to pray for all the poor people in this world, but especially for all the poor souls in Purgatory.

So every day, as I walk from my village to the monument, I pray the rosary for all the people on this earth. It's about three kilometers [= two miles] each way. Then I pray the rosary on the way back. I walk this distance in the summer and in the winter— whether it rains or shines, whether it is calm or stormy. Six kilometers a day. For the past twenty years. And I've been praying for you, too," she said, looking up with a bashful and toothless grin.

For a while neither of us knew what to say.

Wanting to break the uneasy silence, I asked, "May I take a picture of you?"

"Why not? But I have a request of you. Take the picture in front of the monument of the Blessed Virgin."

"As you wish," and we started to walk to the monument. I took my little digital camera out of its case, she struck a pose, and I snapped a few pictures.

I thanked her. Then we say goodbye, and I hurried over to my group, which by now was barely visible in the distance.

I always have that picture of Maria Jesus near me. Sometimes, when I am especially humbled, or when I feel I might collapse under the load of life, I think about that old lady and how she walks six kilometers every day—at the age of ninety-two—praying the rosary for everyone in the world.

And then I tell myself, "That old woman just won't quit. She draws new strength from prayer every day."

This gives me courage.

Saint Olaf

Whenever I go to Assisi, I like to buy some of those simple St. Francis crosses and just take them along. You'll find them at every street corner. They cost only 1 euro (approx. $1.40) each. I've been doing this for a number of years now. I'll give these crosses to the group of pilgrims that I'm traveling with. Everyone gets a cross. I believe these crosses protect them and will give them joy their whole life long. The first time I saw Olaf, I immediately noticed his homemade yet beautiful pictures of saints, which he sells on the street for 1 euro each. So I thought to myself, "Why should I only buy these good luck charms in Assisi? This is how I got to know Olaf a bit better.

***

Olaf Wand didn't originally come from Frankfurt am Main, where I met him in the pedestrian zone a few years ago. He hails from Breitenworbis, a quaint little town south of the Harz Mountains in what used to be East Germany. Breitenworbis is located between Göttingen and Nordhausen, about where the Harz Mountains start softly rolling towards the horizon. This is where Olaf was born in 1970. This little town with a population of 3,000 lies within the region of Eichsfeld, which at that time was still demarcated by a death strip, patrolled by Border Police who would shoot to kill. What *unites* this region, however, is its strong Catholic faith. Over the centuries, the people of this region have endured their share of suffering because of their faith. Ever since the Reformation, which was sparked not far from this area, the people of the region of Eichsfeld have been stubbornly hanging on to their old faith—to the point that, over time, the area became a Catholic island, as it were, in a sea of Protestants. And, of course, living out your Christian faith was not exactly easy in the days of German Democratic Republic (GDR), either. But the people of the region of Eichsfeld are a very particular breed: tough, persevering, and stubbornly sticking to their ways. The same was true for Olaf's family. Going to Holy Mass every Sunday, baptism, Holy Communion, confessions—hanging on to all of this in the face of government despotism was a tough row to hoe. But they bore the burden because it was worth it to them. Olaf's family were farmers. His parents ran a dairy farm, one of the many "agricultural co-operatives" ("LPGs") typical of that country.

At fifteen Olaf ended his school career, as all young people did who wanted to learn a trade. But he didn't have the faintest idea which trade to choose. All he knew was that he did not want to go into farming: that was the one thing he knew for sure, because his family had been farming for three generations without much success. So in 1985 he began as an apprentice in the textile industry, figuring he could become a weaver and learn how to make beautiful clothes. But he always clashed with his superiors. Frequent run-ins, the pressure to conform to his surroundings, what he considered to be a boring lifestyle—all of this combined led to his dropping out of the program after only one year. Before long he tried his luck as a skilled laborer. But he didn't complete this apprenticeship, either. So between 17 and 18 he decided to work on his father's co-op after all. Even twenty years later, he recalls those months with a shudder: "A complete disaster." After a huge blow-up with his father, he finally left his family home on the spur of the moment and hit the road.

For some strange reason, he felt drawn to the punk scene, which did, in fact, exist in the waning days of the German Democratic Republic—even in Breitenworbis. He was impressed by the way these people moved from one place to another, by the way they dressed, by the way they didn't give a hoot for anyone. They did whatever they wanted! And so he joined their ranks. People called them "layabouts," which they really were, too. But at the same time they were also seekers, young people seeking a purpose in their lives. Problem was, they just didn't quite know *what* they were looking for. All they *did* know was that they weren't going to be stuck between the rock of East Germany's dreary, working class culture and the hard place of self-denial.

Even after the Wall came down, nothing changed for Olaf. He was still living on the streets. There was something cool about it; it made him special. This went on for a number of years until Life finally started knocking on his door with the message that it was finally time to get real. Sooner or later everyone has to settle into a "normal" life. But unfortunately, Olaf had so removed himself from normal life that it was impossible to return to it. So an apprenticeship was now totally out of the question for him. For one thing, there were not enough openings. Besides, he was already too old. Take a regular job? Jobs were as rare in Breitenworbis and its surrounds back then as they are today. Besides, he still had that issue about easily rubbing people the wrong way. He clashed with this person, was at loggerheads with that person... So he tried a lot of things, but everything fell flat.

He couldn't—maybe he didn't even *want* to—settle into a normal, working-class life: beds in the back room, fussy babies in the front room. Who knows, maybe all it would have taken would have been for him to meet the right woman. But he hadn't found her. The young women who wanted to get ahead in life now lived either in Leipzig or in the West. But they most certainly had fled Breitenworbis. Besides, Olaf had his problems with women anyway. They didn't appreciate his flare-ups, his unpredictability, his hot temper. They were afraid of him and avoided him. So, eventually he just left them alone and moved on. He was a loner.

Go West, Young Man

By now it was 1997, seven years after reunification, when—just like so many people before and after him—Olaf could no longer resist the great undertow pulling people to the West. And so the day finally came. He grabbed his few possessions, said goodbye to his pals, and started walking west. He had no idea which way he was drifting. Needless to say, he couldn't go to Berlin or Leipzig, they simply weren't "West" enough. So he headed for the city located as far west as possible—Frankfurt am Main, which some people call "Mainhattan." His eyes bulged the first time he saw downtown. Those skyscrapers, the traffic, all the people racing about...They seemed to be chasing towards some secret destination. *His* goal, on the other hand, was enticingly simple: all he wanted to do was find work. That couldn't be so hard to do, in such a rich town... He wasn't asking for much, just enough work to get by. The first thing he did was to find a place to stay—at the

Catholic Church. They agreed to let him stay a few weeks, so he could take his time and find a job. This wasn't bad at all. And besides, they even gave him one warm meal a day.

Those first few days in Frankfurt Olaf was still in high spirits, checking out one business after another, asking for work. But there were no openings, at least not for someone without any skills. That was his first lesson. Next, he tried the classifieds. Bright and early one morning he purchased some newspapers, a *Frankfurter Neue Presse* and a *Frankfurter Rundschau*, and studied the want ads. He called dozens of employers. But every place he called, they wanted a formal job application, complete with credentials, a passport picture, etc. How in the world would he be able to provide that? Finally, he resigned himself to the sad fact that Frankfurt am Main, as well, would give him only a bit part in the play of life.

From that point on, he limited himself to want ads looking for janitors or gardeners. But that was not even the worst of it. Frankfurt had turned him into a day laborer for all kinds of dubious companies, which barely managed to pay him the agreed upon amount. Some even "forgot" to do *that*. If only he had one German mark for every time they had forgotten to pay him! Some people recommended that he go to the social welfare office to apply for subsidies because he had come from the East and all that. But that was out of the question for Olaf: No hand-outs. No, sir. So, by day he moved furniture, ran errands at construction sites, or was the messenger for a printing company. And by night he managed to wind up with a few German marks in his pocket. For a while he helped clear out apartments. With the help of colleagues, his job was to clear out as fast as possible old and very often dilapidated apartments after the tenant had died, and at breakneck speed get the space ready for the next move-in. Boy, was that tough work! Mercilessly dump anything superfluous, whether it was reusable or not. Ouch. That was something Olaf had yet to experience—destroying things of value.

Bogged Down in a Swamp of Drugs

They got together every night—he and his kind. In the summer they sat around in parks, in the winter in smoky bars—just drinking. It just turned out that way. Besides, everybody did it. There were people like "Peter" from Hamburg and "Manfred" from Kassel, "Schorsch" from Mainz, and "Elfi" from Offenbach: now *she* was a pip, a regular clown when somebody treated her to a beer. They had a lot of things to share. The reunification of Germany had trickled down to this level as well. The money he worked so hard to earn during the day flowed down his throat by night— down his and *others'* throats, to be more precise. Sometimes as beer, sometimes as schnapps. By the time he dragged himself to his quarters, usually at midnight, his pockets were empty. More often than not, he was broke the next morning, with not even enough money to buy a roll for breakfast.

When Olaf saw bums peacefully drinking their beer, he would ignore them. Ignored—at first. As for the other guys, for the most part younger than Olaf and his buddies, guys with long, scraggly hair, haggard, and looking absolutely terrible, Olaf ignored them too – at first. Sometimes he saw them messing with syringes. Some of them did cocaine or speed. When you see things day after day, over time you get used to them, you lose your fear of them. People had always warned him about drugs. But now he didn't really think they were that bad any more. Day after day, these guys offered him drugs. No, thanks. No, thanks. No, thanks. Until, one day, he stopped and said "OK," and took them up on their offer. Even though at that time alcohol was still his preferred *modus operandi,* he popped some of their pills, but the effect was actually more disappointing. But then he tried cocaine. Well now, *that* was a different story. Cocaine gave him an instant rush, making him feel so strong, so good. All of a sudden he was able talk to other people. His life didn't feel so bleak any more.

It was from that point on that drugs had gained a permanent place in his life. Joints, cocaine, speed, alcohol. That's all he needed. During the day he had his hands full, trying to make enough money to dive into his dream world at night—a world that distracted him from his desperate monotony. Although he didn't realize it, he soon became a regular in the drug scene. And a horrible, downward spiral began. Olaf needed more and more money for drugs. At the same time, he was becoming more and more dependent on them. This went on for many months. The only people he now dealt with were junkies. His life had hit a dead end and had become hopeless. Every morning he knew the kind of work awaiting him and already started yearning for quitting time, when his friends and his drugs would gently take him into their arms. Olaf was headed for his doom, soon to experience the same fate as hundreds of young people in Frankfurt and elsewhere. At the end of the line, someone finds them lying on the floor of a dismal public restroom—with a needle stuck in their arm. Desolate, dirty, and dead. What kept Olaf from this fate was his fear of needles. He could barely tolerate getting a shot at the doctor's office, but to inject *himself* with a needle? No, he was terrified of that.

One day it dawned upon him that he was stuck in a prison, within himself. And a feeling welled up in him: "I've got to get out!" But the dull rhythm of his life, the drug scene, his dependency, and his despair conspired: They wouldn't let him find a quick solution. Day after day he tortured himself with this problem: "How can I escape this kind of life?" No longer did he want to be a day laborer or waste his life with drugs.

Olaf Is Saved

Funny enough, memories of his parents now started to float into his consciousness—images of his childhood in Breitenworbis... of his school days, too. But, in particular, memories of his pious mother tortured Olaf, his dear mother who had taught him so many prayers... Olaf dreamt about her as well. One day, when the pain in his soul was absolutely unbearable, he knelt down and, in a simple prayer, asked Jesus to help him. Over the next few weeks, these prayers became more frequent and more intense. Only a few days later, while cleaning out yet another apartment, he found a wooden rosary. He took it, although he had scruples about stealing. But it had come at just the right time, right on cue. Late that same night, he took the rosary and began to pray:

"Glory be to the Father, and to the Son, *and the Holy Spirit.* I believe in God, the Father Almighty..."

Once again, he saw images of his childhood. His home. His parents. It was especially the memory of his mother that he couldn't seem to shake. When was the last time he had heard from her? Years had gone by. How she had always cared for him... No distance had been too great for her, there was nothing she wouldn't have done for him. And what was he *doing* with his life? All of these thoughts flooding his mind gave Olaf the courage to face his problems.

A few days later—once again, with the rosary in his hands and collecting his thoughts for prayer—Olaf heard a voice. Loudly and clearly it told him: "Be reliable!"

Now what was *that* supposed to mean? It took a while for him to understand the deeper meaning of this message. This went on for several weeks. Whenever he was praying the rosary, he always had to mull over that "Be reliable!" message. He couldn't seem to concentrate on anything else. It was as though his brain were locked. Well, *of course* he wanted to be *reliable*. Yes, he did want to be a reliable person. Away with the junkies, away with the drugs! No more lies, no more swindling big stuff or little stuff! Truthfulness, genuineness, and, well, reliability: These things were pulling at him strongly.

Reflecting on those weeks, Olaf told me that it was without a doubt his daily prayers that had given him the strength to turn that corner. It was the realization that he was not alone: *that* was what gave him strength. He had clearly felt the presence of the Creator—that was his great consolation. And little by little, he found his way back to a normal life.

One day he even dared to look for some different kind of job. And, wouldn't you know, he landed one! Well, OK, it was only a cleaning job, but so what? Anyway, he now showed up every evening in the fancy *Zeilgalerie* mall in downtown Frankfurt to clean an electronics store. Here he had peace and quiet. The rooms were heated. And he wasn't earning *that* badly, either. He actually got by with the money he earned there and was even able to afford a modest apartment.

Very close to downtown Frankfurt's *Zeilgalerie* mall is the *Liebfrauenkloster* (Cloister of Our Dear Lady), where Capuchin monks and Franciscan nuns reside. This oasis of quiet is located amid the hustle of Burger King and bustle of the IMAX Cinema, twin pillars of capitalism. By coincidence, Olaf stumbled across this place of refuge. In the middle of the cloister stands an altar to Mary, on which at any given time hundreds of candles are lit.

Visitors and tourists from around the world light them—as did Olaf on that particular day. In fact, it was at this very spot that he learned to enunciate and offload his worries.

Olaf noticed that the burning candles were completely exposed to the elements, not being protected in any way. In fact, many of the candles had been extinguished. Since he paid hard-earned money for his candles, he knew that other visitors as well would appreciate it if their candles were actually burning—and not blown out by the wind. So he started to relight candles and place them on the altar. He came every day to take care of the altar to Mary. He removed wax from the candlestick holders, cleared away burned-out candles, and put the finishing touch to his clean-up work every evening by sweeping the area in front of the altar. Needless to say, it was only a matter of time until someone noticed him. One of the monks in the cloister observed Olaf's work and kept a watchful eye on the young man. And it didn't take long for the monk to approach Olaf and officially make him caretaker of the altar to Mary. Olaf now had a permanent task at the cloister and they regularly gave him a tip, which he could use all too well.

Olaf Loses Something Old, Gains Something New

There are certain stages in everybody's life. Stages of calm some-times abruptly shift to times of great change. Why this is, the individuals usually never get to know. This was certainly true for Olaf. For the very first time he now had the opportunity to turn his back on street life and the drug scene. Both were over and done with—at least, that's what he thought. His life was once again free, almost without a care. Everything seemed to be moving towards a normal, ordinary life. He was in the process of integrating into society. But, looking back, it is obvious that at that particular point in his life, Olaf was not really prepared to meet the challenges yet to come. The anger and hatred of street life were still bubbling in his blood. One day Olaf had a falling out with his manager. This led to a petty argument about a customer, who felt that Olaf was not friendly enough in his job. The manager shouted at Olaf in the middle of the *Zeilgalerie*, rather than in a discreet corner of the store. The whole thing blew up when Olaf blurted out, "You know what? You can shove it!" and then stormed off. From that moment on, he was without work. That was in 2000.

Everything he had built up so carefully was now in one single moment destroyed. Now what? It took quite a while for Olaf to deal with this blow and once again focus on the future. About the same time, all the newspapers were reporting on the Holy Year and the big party the Pope was planning in Rome. On top of that, a World Youth Day was being planned in that city as well. Drawn by the catchy slogan "Party with the Pontifex," tens of thousands of young people from around the globe were going to be celebrating Masses with Pope John Paul II. So Rome had to be Olaf's next destination as well. He just had to go. He had to see the Pope. If Olaf could only see him, that would somehow give him insight into what step to take next in life. But there was one problem: he didn't have enough money to take the trip. While he *had* been able to scrape by on his meager earnings, he had not been able to *save* any money—and most certainly not enough for a long trip like that.

But no matter. Olaf was not able to shake off the beckoning of the Eternal City. For days he deliberated about how to pull off this trip. Then it dawned upon him: he would choose the simplest way—and *walk* there. After all, in centuries past, a lot of people had done that. In fact, pilgrims in particular had found a deeper meaning to life by walking to Rome to cleanse their lives. Even Luther had hit the road. Why couldn't he, Olaf, do the same? So, on March 28, 2000, with a little bundle on his back, he began his long trek to Rome. After a difficult and austere hike through Southern Germany, he traveled across the Resia Pass and through Southern Tyrol. But he still had that long journey through Italy ahead of him. After two draining months, he finally reached his goal. He had made it, walking over 800 miles (1,300 km) in 60 days.

Olaf marveled at Rome, much as he had at Frankfurt. But how different this city looked! Here everything was ancient, and so much was related to the Church. There were hundreds of churches, ringing bells, ancient buildings, bridges, piazzas, fountains, and hordes of people. It was the tourists he noticed most. But, for right now, all this glory didn't help him one bit. It was almost the same story as when he had arrived in Frankfurt. Once again—no place to stay and no money. But at least in Rome it is pretty easy to spend the night someplace for free, in church facilities, cloisters, and hostels. Food is cheap, too.

Olaf Finds a Way to Survive

Those first few weeks, his senses feasted on all the sights and sounds. Every day brought new images and experiences, and new people to meet. It was so easy to make friends here. And everybody was of the same mindset, so it was easy to communicate—despite language barriers. One morning, as he was once again about to leave a cloister where he had spent several nights for free, the abbot gave him a beautiful picture of Christ. Olaf tucked it away without giving it a second thought and moved on. He barely scraped by in the Eternal City, which, aside from free church-connected lodging, can also be very expensive.

When his last savings were used up and he had his back to the proverbial wall, he came across that picture of Christ. He studied it for a long time, touching it, turning it this way and that. He was just about to put it away, when he had an idea—an idea that was to change his life: What if he were to sell this picture? But he only had one copy and, besides, who would buy a picture of Christ from him anyway, in Rome, of all places? Well, he could probably make a few lira off of it, though probably not much more than that because you could buy variations of that particular picture in any souvenir store. Still, his dogged determination never to beg overcame this obstacle as well. Just as he had resolved not to go to the social welfare office back in Frankfurt, he put any thought of begging out of his mind.

But he still had to think of something. So he took his last 50,000 lira, not a lot of money back then—just about $35.00 (25.00 euros). He went to a photographer and asked him to make as many copies as he could for that amount of money. And, sure enough, he got 100 copies. Even today, Olaf beams when he recalls that moment. *What a feeling, when he held those 100 pictures in his hands. He was so certain he was doing the right thing.* Rome has over 1,000 places of worship: churches and cloisters. And that's exactly where he went. He rang doorbells, showed them his pictures, and offered them his pictures in broken Italian, charging 1,000 lira each (70 U.S. cents or 50 euro cents). Within a few days, he had sold all 100 pictures. In a short period of time he had managed to double his capital! Now what? He did the same thing all over again and once again doubled his investment. Now he was able to live for awhile in Rome without worrying about money.

In July, 2000, after experiencing Rome for two whole months, Olaf once again felt Germany tugging at his heart strings. So he hitchhiked back and managed to get to Frankfurt in only nine days—a distance that had taken him two months to walk. As soon as he returned, he went straight to the Cloister of Our Dear Lady. As a matter of course, he immediately took up his old duties at the altar to Mary. It took him a few days to get into the swing of things in Frankfurt, but soon afterward he managed to get a steady job. What joy! And even back at the *Zeilgalerie!*—this time at the *Mövenpick* restaurant. His was hired to clean the dishes, but when they saw he was doing a good job, they soon let him make salads, sell ice cream, and even run the cash register. He actually enjoyed it, and his life soon eased into a nice rhythm. Olaf was able to work at that restaurant for three beautiful years. Things went well. No stress, no arguments, no fusses. During the day Olaf worked at the restaurant, in the evenings he went to the cloister and took care of "his altar."

In fall of 2003, his employer decided not to continue the restaurant's lease with the *Zeilgalerie*, because the rent was too high. Companies sometimes like to use "restructuring" issues like this to "drop ballast"—dark days for any employees deemed to be superfluous. Olaf was not the only employee who got a pink slip, but this time he actually got severance pay. Even though it wasn't really a lot of money, it was still a pretty decent sum: he'd never had that much money before. That was the good news. The bad news was, of course, that he was once again unemployed. But this time he had something new: a feeling of hope. By now, he was mentally prepared for such reversals. Somehow they just seemed to be a normal part of his life. By now he had learned that work is by no means all there is to life. His meaning of life and the strength to hold the course came from somewhere else: from his faith, which had grown considerably in the past three years. His life was no longer on the edge.

Now he looked back to his time in Rome, recalling how he had been able to stay above water financially during that time. He picked up his picture of Jesus and had to chuckle. Could this be the secret for the rest of his life? It was hard to believe. Sure, Rome had thousands of tourists and hundreds of churches, all of whom gladly purchased pictures of saints. But how could this work in Frankfurt, a banking city? But an inner voice told him to try those religious pictures nonetheless. So he bought little squares of particle board, which he worked into thin wooden plaques. Then he pasted beautiful, color pictures of Catholic saints onto them, adding well-known Bible verses. In loving detail, Olaf made dozens of these pictures, even whole collections of related pictures. On *Liebfrauenberg* square near the cloister, he set up his shop at a little table, offering his pictures to people who were on the way to the cloister. One euro per picture. From the very start his business went really well. Well, not well enough to get rich on, but that wasn't Olaf's goal, anyway.

He has been doing this for four years now. You can see him every day, standing at his table or sitting on a little stool. In front of him stands the original picture, the abbot in Rome had given him. He talks a lot to people now, too. Sometimes, when the weather is bad, when rain, storm, or snow might damage his pictures, he'll take the day off. But in the whole year, he doesn't take too many days off. People in the neighborhood know "their Olaf." He's a part of Frankfurt.

Sometimes when I'm downtown, I'll visit Olaf. As far as I'm concerned, he's a fixture, just like the Main River. We chat a while. He tells me of his plans, how business is going. And I order more pictures that I can give to my pilgrim friends on my travels. A while back, he told me that he wanted to travel to Rome again, but this time not necessarily on foot. This time he wanted to fly. And so he did, treating himself to a plane trip for Easter 2007.

I think he deserves it.

The Final Journey of Dennis Yosick

Everything that lives, resists death. This is an iron-clad rule of life. Where I am, there death is not, and where death is, there I am not. Everyone alive is afraid of his or her own death. Everyone – even if they claim the opposite. Pondering our mortality makes us uneasy. That is why we deny death – the great equalizer – and its immense power. But there does come a time when we have to look at death squarely in the eye, whether we regard it as that Pale Rider or as a friend – even if we don't "get it" until the very last minute. After so many years of thinking about death, there is one thing of which I am most certain. The most important and most difficult exam we have to pass on our trip through life is to work out an amicable relationship with death, maybe even learning to greet death joyfully when our final hour arrives. That brings to mind a philosopher who once said: "You haven't really grown up until you start reckoning with death. From that point on, your perception of time changes, including your dependence on earthly things, and any bitterness about all the things that have gone awry in life. Once you include death in the building blocks of life, you will actually become more liberated, albeit only if you use this new-found relationship to establish a relationship with God".

As I write these lines, I am reminded of a book that I recently read entitled "The End is My Beginning," written a few years ago by Tiziano Terzani, the well-known Italian author, who wrote down his thoughts and feelings during the last weeks of his life. With noble, yes, even stoic wisdom, Terzani described how, over time, death came ever closer and how he was able to regard it as a friend, finally even accepting it. Although suffering from intense pain, Terzani rejected any medication whatsoever, greeting death fearlessly and courageously. In fact, he even invited death to hurry up, to take him to that place he had not yet reached and from which none of us has ever given an account. "The only new thing I have yet to be exposed to," Terzani on his deathbed told his son, "is my own death. I've never seen it, I've never experienced it. Where will my trip go? I can hardly wait." Every one of us dies his or her own death, just as we all live our own lives. But just how that death will look, how we will accept it and what we will make of it—that is in our own hands.

"I'd love to meet such a courageous person," I thought to myself as I read that book. Problem was, I doubted whether any such person existed, apart from Terzani. But just a few months later, in May 2006, my vocation acquainted me with just such an unusual and impressive individual. His name was Dennis Yosick and his widow has allowed me to relate the story of his last journey, exactly the way it happened.

***

Once again our location is Lisbon, the city to which I feel so connected and where so many of my pilgrimages begin. The date was May 18 and it was unusually warm, in fact warmer than many summer days in Germany. As is my custom, I arrived in the city on the Tejo River one day early, so as to get back into the mood of Portugal and to mentally prepare for the 10-day journey, which I assumed would be demanding. Relaxing in a little *bodega* in Barrio Alto, I went over our route for the umpteenth time and reviewed it to see whether we might have forgotten anything. I also took the time to go over the list of travelers. As a tour guide, it's always a good idea to know with whom you're dealing and where your travelers come from. After all, you want to avoid any slip-ups and make the trip as pleasant as possible for your guests. The next morning I was scheduled to pick up fifty-two travelers at the *Portela*, Lisbon's airport—all of them pilgrims from the American Mid-West. While I was relaxing in the *bodega*, sipping my glass of red wine, they were already in the air, having taken off from Chicago's O'Hare. The travel agency had informed me that this particular program was going to be extra special. The pilgrims entrusted to me were about to travel in the footsteps of José Maria Escrivá de Balaguer, the legendary and canonized founder of Opus Dei. This organization was founded in 1928 by Escrivá as a so-called "prelate"; an order-like faith group for Catholic lay people. Its purpose was to provide religious education and pastoral care to students and employees, enabling them to lead God-pleasing lives at work and at home. As such, all Opus Dei members are called to strive for holiness in their lives. Born in 1902, Escrivá led the Rome-based organization, which today boasts some 85,000 members in more than 65 countries, until his death in 1975. Escrivá was canonized by Pope John Paul II in 2002. What made this all very personal for me was the news that a few of the pilgrims winging their way to me were members of Opus Dei.

From a different angle as well, this trip promised to be special because the travel agency had booked only 4-star luxury hotels for our group in Portugal, Spain, and France. Of particular interest to these pilgrims were the places where Josemaría Escrivá had worked, namely Torreciudad, Barbastro (the place of his birth) and Saragossa. This was where he attended university, was ordained and lived for many years. The cities of Logroño, Madrid, Ávila, and Segovia intrigued the pilgrims, too.

The next morning I was right on time and ready to pick up my group of pilgrims. At Arrivals, the first thing that caught my eye was a wheelchair with four equally-sized wheels that was being pushed through the glass exit door. In it sat a man who looked at me with hollow, tired eyes. He was wearing a strange brown suit—the kind you normally find in the tropics—and a large-brimmed hat. His hat was plopped awkwardly on his emaciated head that in fact looked more like a skull. The man's face was only partially visible because half of it was covered by a white linen facemask, like they use in hospitals. This traveler was being pushed by one of our travel agents, Juan Landa. Operating out of Madison, Wisconsin, Juan and his wife Erin run a travel agency by the beautiful name of "Mater Dei (Mother of God) Tours." The Landas have carved out a special market for themselves: Catholic pilgrimages. Of all the travel agencies I know, the love and care these two people embody, as they accompany their guests around the world, is unique. Further back I spotted Father John Grigus, the leader of the group, who had already been waving from afar.

John Grigus is a widely traveled Franciscan friar whom I know from many trips we have taken together. Trailing behind him somewhat hesitantly was Father John's little flock, clearly somewhat fatigued from the flight. John and I greeted one another like long-lost friends and he introduced me to the group. I tried to cheer everyone up with a few jokes, but my efforts fell on deaf ears. Apparently the travelers were distressed about the sad figure slumped in the wheelchair—one of their fellow travelers. After we had exited the terminal, we started to board our motorcoach. At this time I introduced the group to our Portuguese driver, Joáo Manuel, who was already loading the many heavy bags and suitcases onto the bus. Not surprisingly, our departure was delayed because travelers still had to go to the restroom, while others already wanted to exchange their dollars into euros. In the mean time, the rest of the group was busy choosing their seats on the motorcoach. I was standing by the door up by the driver, helping people on board where necessary. Out of the corner of my eye I saw the man in the wheelchair coming my way. I turned towards when he addressed me in a thin, wispy voice:

"Arthur, that's your name, right? Hey, can you help me get on board?" He stuck out a thin, almost bony hand and said, "My name is Dennis, Dennis Yosick, and this is my wife Emilia," a lady who looked about forty years of age. In this marriage, it seemed evident that Dennis was the one calling the shots. Emilia appeared to be from Latin America. She had a kind, attractive face and seemed to be a pleasant person.

"Welcome," I replied in a friendly voice. "That's right, my name is Arthur. I'll be your escort and will be accompanying you on our entire pilgrimage. Pleased to meet you." I grasped his cold hand and returned his handshake very gently. I shook his wife's hand, too. Dennis tried to look relaxed, but the best he could do was to give a pained expression: "I hope you won't regret it," he said, a comment I didn't understand at the time. Then without any prior notice, he popped up from his wheelchair and all of a sudden was standing in front of me on shaky legs. I attempted to help him but he pushed my hand aside, exclaiming, "It's OK, Arthur, I'll manage." Swaying back and forth, he approached the steep steps of the motorcoach, looking like he was going to climb up. But after placing his foot on the first step, he turned around towards me with a pleading look in his eyes. Without hesitating, I simply picked him up and carried him on board.

"Lord, how light this man is…," I thought to myself. In my whole life I had never seen a sixty-year old man who was as slight as a child. Without tensing his muscles a bit, he rested in my arms and let me place him in a seat, but not without first showing me which seat he wanted.

"Arthur, I'd like to sit near you. I don't want to miss a thing."

"Whatever you like. Here, this seat behind me is still available." As I let him gently slide from my arms, I noticed that he had a strange "padding" in his pants that didn't at all fit to his emaciated body. Recalling my old mother, I knew what that padding was: Dennis Yosick was wearing adult diapers. I must admit that this revelation scared me. "What in the world is this man, who is obviously very ill, doing on such an arduous trip? In ten days we're going to cover over fifteen hundred miles (2,500 km) in three countries. But as yet I kept my thoughts to myself and went back to work. I sat down next to the driver, picked up my mike, and greeted all the guests. As we were slowly pulling out of the bus parking lot and heading toward the *autoestrada*, I pointed out to the group what we would be seeing and experiencing that day.

On the way to Fatima I had the driver pull over, so we could take a little break in Santarem and have a Mass of Thanksgiving. After the service we didn't waste any time getting back on the road because it was obvious that everybody was, by that time, pretty much "maxed out." Our plan was to get to Fatima and checked into the hotel as quickly as possible. Portugal's colorful spring landscape was rushing past us, but somehow, I was not captivated by the scenery. What intrigued me more was the old man sitting behind me, the man wearing adult diapers and who looked like his days on earth were numbered. He seemed composed, but, whenever I happened to look his way, also quite exhausted. I must confess that I had mixed feelings about him. On the one hand he did trigger my compassion, but on the other hand, I was also struggling with the big picture: How could they possibly be taking such a seriously ill man on a journey like this? What if he collapsed before they made it back home again? But, finally, my curiosity won the day. What was his story? What was he doing here? Besides, it was undeniable that this gentleman possessed a certain charisma. Yes, there was no doubt about it. Somehow this individual intrigued me. There seemed to be a mystery surrounding his soul, a mystery that I would soon be determined to solve. And solve it we will, just you wait!

Whenever I turned around and glanced at him, his deep-set eyes seemed to be saying: "Right now you're thinking about me. I realize it and I know exactly what you're thinking!" And I thought, "He knows what I'm thinking?" That look, which was characterized by deep suffering, seemed to penetrate everything and read my every thought. There was no doubt about it, this Dennis Yosick had an extremely strong personality and was used to getting what he wanted. Over time, my discomfort—and my frustration—would metamorphose into fascination. His charisma would change the feelings deep down in my soul. Before long, I decided I wanted to get to know him better and help him wherever I could on this trip.

We arrived at the Hotel Fatima in the town of the same name. Our check-in was as fast as lightning because everyone just wanted to get to his or her room and crash. An hour later we all met for our first dinner as a group. The hotel staff bent over backwards for us, preparing a welcome menu with several courses. Most of the travelers took a liking to the fine Portuguese red wine, which also resulted in their turning in early for a good night's rest. Consequently, the richly decorated banquet hall was soon vacated, with only a few stragglers remaining in the restaurant. Dennis, his wife Emilia, and his mother-in-law were among the few people still downstairs chatting. Just as his wife was about to wheel him out of the dining room, he had her stop for a few minutes so he could have a short but intense dialogue with Juan, our travel agent. By this time, Father Grigus excused himself, waving us all good night. After a while, Dennis and his family retired for the evening as well.

Juan and I were now the "Last of the Mohicans." Juan looked my way, smiled, and came over to my table. I could tell he had something weighing heavy on his heart. Juan was originally from Cuba. Many years ago, he fled to the U.S. with his parents and somehow wound up in the travel business. I've known him for several years now and we have always gotten along very well. In fact, we've become good friends, which might also be due to the fact that we communicate in his mother tongue.

"Arturo," which was how he usually addressed me when opening up a conversation, "Arturo, I need to talk to you."

"Juan, let me take a wild guess…I'll bet this has something to do with Dennis, right?"

"You got it, amigo. I could imagine that you might be irritated, maybe even shocked that we brought along such a severely handicapped man on this trip."

"Why would you think that?"

"Dennis told me."

"That's weird. I haven't spoken a single word about this with Dennis."

"Dennis notices everything. He has a sixth sense. He told me a while ago, that he needs to talk to you. But this evening he was just too bush-whacked. He wants to talk to you and tell you something about himself. Maybe he'll even do that as soon as tomorrow, once he has regained his strength somewhat. He asked me to tell you that."

"Hmmm, I don't really get it," I said pensively. "My behavior towards Dennis was absolutely correct. In fact, I even went the extra mile for him. I was helpful and polite. He didn't complain about me, did he?"

"No, Arturo, not at all. On the contrary, he said some really nice things about you. But he knows fully well that he isn't "your average traveler." He realizes how sick he is. Listen, if he wants to talk to you, that's a good sign. It shows that he likes you. So just wait for him to approach you."

"OK, chief," I said with a grin.

"Oh, Arturo, there's one more thing." He hesitated and then looked straight at me.

"You bet there is, Juan. I'd like to know from you why in the world we are taking a terminally ill person on this trip."

"Yes, you're absolutely right to want to know. Besides, I need your help in this regard, so you have a right to know why we brought Dennis Yosick along." By this time, I felt greatly honored that Juan had placed such great trust in me, so my attitude softened considerably. Besides, I was more than curious to hear what he had to say.

"Well, I only met Dennis personally last year. That was at a

89

recital of the Choir of the Archdiocese of Chicago that we both attended. Emilia was there, too. He and I had been corresponding for some time because Dennis was interested in a pilgrimage. He was especially eager to visit Lourdes and Torreciudad. In fact, he has wanted to visit Torreciudad ever since he was a youth. As you know, Torreciudad is a center of Opus Dei and both Dennis and his wife are very involved in Opus Dei. In fact, several years ago Dennis even became an active member. So we agreed to meet in Chicago to talk about him taking a pilgrimage. Dennis went on and on about the Shrine of our Lady at Torreciudad, which he only knew from pictures. As far as he is concerned, it is the most beautiful shrine in the world. Outside of Spain, Torreciudad is practically unknown. Even most travel agencies don't know about it. That is why you'll rarely find any that offer trips there. Most agencies just stick to the classic pilgrimage program: Fatima, Santiago de Compostela, Ávila, Lourdes, Rome, and Assisi. Well anyway, we all got to know one another better in Chicago. We talked about the church choir with which Dennis and Emilia would be performing on stage that same evening. By the time they parted, they had signed up for a trip to Torreciudad and even made a down payment on the spot—even for his mother-in-law whom they definitely wanted to bring along. Up to that point, I hadn't noticed anything unusual as far as his health was concerned. So far, so good.

"Yes, but Dennis is obviously seriously ill. How did that come about?" I interjected impatiently.

"Hang on, *amigo*; I was just about to tell you."

"A month ago Dennis tried to call me. He was calling after office hours, so he left a voice message. The next morning I listened to the message and he said that, unfortunately, he would have to cancel the trip because of some unexpected bad news. Of course I called right back and then he told me he had been diagnosed with lung cancer. They had just found out. On top of that, the doctors told him that he had a very aggressive strain of cancer and wouldn't have much longer to live. They told him he had apparently contracted the disease over a period of many years, probably on the job. We're dealing with asbestos here, Arturo."

"Asbestos?" I answered, stunned. "You keep hearing about it

all over—in the States and here in Europe, too. I hear it is a very painful death. Why is this happening so frequently?"

"Well, I guess it has to do with the long time between when you start inhaling those microscopic particles and when the disease actually breaks out. The whole thing can take twenty years or more."

"How come you know so much about it, Juan?"

"Dennis is not the first person I know who has contracted this disease, which they also call asbestosis or asbestos lung cancer. So I looked it up on the Web and read up on it. As early as 1970, physicians determined that asbestos fibers can cause cancer. But it took almost ten years until countries first started banning asbestos. In the U.S., it was not banned until the late '70s. In Germany it wasn't banned till 1993. So, sadly, by now Dennis' cancer had already reached such a stage that his doctor made him change his mind about taking such a long trip. We were in constant touch by phone and Dennis told me he wanted to wait for the results of some extensive clinical tests before he definitely canceled the trip. About three or four days later he called me back. Although those additional tests had confirmed the terrible initial diagnosis of his doctor, Dennis said he was nonetheless determined to take the trip. "I'm going" – that was his final word on the matter.

"That man has got a strong character and knows exactly what he wants. What did his wife say?"

"As far as I know, Emilia left this whole thing totally up to him. I asked him a few days later whether we should really book this pilgrimage and whether he was absolutely certain about it. "Of course!" he answered dryly and to the point, even adding that there wasn't a doctor in the world who could stop him from going. And then he said something else that has been giving us a royal headache ever since. His doctor told him that if he was going to take this trip, then he should definitely take along an oxygen tank."

"Oxygen—why?" I asked surprised.

"I talked this over for a long time with Dennis. The disease he's got is not just plain lung cancer. He's got what they call pleural mesothelioma, a malignant tumor of the pleura, the lining around the lung. The pleuron is a very thin membrane surrounding the whole lung and chest cavity. A doctor I know explained this to me in great detail. You've got to think of it like this: The lining around the lung is a thin, lubricating layer that lets us breathe. Without it, our lungs would collapse and we wouldn't be able to breathe at all."

"I see…and that's why Dennis is having trouble breathing?"

"That's not the only thing. He sometimes has these coughing attacks and always has chest pains that sometimes become unbearable. This tumor spreads around the entire lung extremely fast and then, well…'

Juan's cheerful expression had vanished. You could tell this whole thing was getting to him personally.

"How long do you think Dennis will live?"

"Dennis has really got bad luck. This is one of the most aggressive tumors known to man. This cancer is incurable. Who knows how much longer he has to live—maybe one or two more months…"

Glumly we both took a sip of wine—there wasn't much left in our glasses—and thought of Dennis. But Juan wasn't finished yet. He still wanted to keep on talking, even though this topic was obviously hitting a raw nerve for both of us.

"Well, the doctors recommended he take along an oxygen tank and most certainly a wheelchair, because he'd be getting weaker day by day. He could probably only survive the strain in a wheelchair, they said. Now the ball was in our court. Getting a wheelchair was easy…the problem was that oxygen tank. As you can pretty well imagine, every airline in the world would have a problem with that. This goes beyond 9/11 and fear of terrorist attacks. The deal is that these oxygen tanks are under extreme pressure and you can never be totally certain that they are really screwed shut tightly. Cabin pressure is constantly changing during take-off and landing… So you can imagine what would happen if one of those tanks leaked and exploded. That would put the whole plane at risk. As you can imagine, our airline requested all kinds of technical and medical details from us. They wanted to know what they'd be getting into. Then we had to wait several weeks for their reply. They finally said "No," as we had expected.

Air France's medical department informed us that taking along external oxygen would pose too great a threat for everyone involved. In the worst case they would have to be prepared for an emergency landing, which would be horrendously expensive. So they just declined. Period."

"How did you manage to pull it off anyway?" I asked excitedly.

"No one wanted to assume responsibility. The only thing I could do was to get Dennis to forget about the whole trip. So I called him up and explained the situation and asked him to please understand that we couldn't get a single airline in the world to take that risk. I appealed to his sense of responsibility and begged him to consider that he wouldn't be the only passenger on board. But he stuck to his guns and said, "I'm going." Every single time we discussed it that was his final word. Then I worked on Emilia to get him to come around. That didn't work either. Emilia told me, "Juan, you've got to know that Dennis doesn't give up that easily. He's a mule. When he makes his mind up about something, he follows through with it." After yet another talk with Dennis, I got to experience his stubbornness first-hand. While I was still trying to use diplomacy and reason to get him to give up this trip, he cut me off and practically shouted into the phone, "I am going on that trip! So let's just forget that stupid oxygen. No more blabber. That's it. End of story." I lay low for a few days and hoped he would come to his senses. Then I called him again. By now he was a bit more reasonable and said, "Juan, look. I've got to go on this pilgrimage. For me this is not just a normal trip like for everyone else. I need this trip to bring closure to my life because my faith demands it of me. Besides, the doctors just *recommended* that I take along oxygen. It was just a recommendation, Juan. My whole life long I have never paid attention to recommendations. I make up my *own* mind. I've got to go on this trip, even if it kills me." That was his last word on the matter.

"Now I understand this situation a lot better," I replied contemplatively. "This man is here because he has religious convictions. He's going to die soon anyway, but he needs this closure for spiritual reasons."

"That's it, Arturo. God knows, I've dealt with a lot of believers in my life, but I've never known someone with such strong faith."

"What happened then? Did you just forget the oxygen and take a gamble?"

"Bingo. A few days later I saw Dennis and Emilia at a presentation about the pilgrimage. I always do these presentations before large intercontinental trips, so the travelers can be adequately prepared. For the first time our whole group was together that evening. In the meantime, Dennis had become noticeably weaker. He was already wearing that facemask to protect him from infections. Amazingly though, even though he might have been physically weak, his energy permeated that whole meeting. He was absolutely euphoric. That same evening I informed the whole group about the situation because they had a right to know what they were getting themselves into. Of course I also told them about the risks of crossing the Atlantic with a terminally ill man and admitted there was even a chance we would have to make an emergency landing on some island. And Arturo, you know what? I didn't think this would be possible… No one, not one single person in that group declined to go on the trip and no one demanded that Dennis drop his plans. We all left that meeting happy and content.

As far as I was concerned, that meeting confirmed my opinion. I didn't want to fail one of my customers; I didn't want to prevent him from fulfilling the final dream of his life. On the contrary, I was determined to do everything I could to make this trip possible for him. The only thing that would have stopped me from taking Dennis along would have been the other travelers. If they had refused to take Dennis along due to safety concerns, he would have been crushed, but Providence spared us that debacle. In fact, I think it's some kind of divine Providence that we are all taking this trip with him. Do you understand? Not only do we have a terminally ill man traveling with us, but we are actually conscientiously taking along a man who is about to die because he wants to take this trip from the bottom of his heart.

The next time I saw him was yesterday, when we were boarding the plane. Just between you and me, I was shocked. I could hardly recognize him. He's just skin and bones. Emilia told me he used to be a strong, muscular man and used to weigh about 165 pounds (75 kg). Now he barely weighs 110 pounds (50 kg) and he's still losing weight. He hardly eats anything. All he does is drink fluids. He is in great pain and lives on medication. But nevertheless: He survived the flight with flying colors. And we were petrified of that flight, I can tell you...and we weren't the only ones. During the flight I regularly went over to see how he was doing. He didn't move a muscle in his face; he just gave me a "thumbs up." You know that, Arturo. We Americans love giving the "thumbs up." There's something positive about it. Well, and now we're here. We can only bring this trip to a happy ending if you help us, Arturo. We need your help."

Juan had taken almost an hour to give me all the necessary information about Dennis. For about the past half hour, the waiters in the restaurant had been nervously looking over to us because we were the only patrons left. Presumably they wanted to go home. Now he's finally done, I thought. But after a short break, Juan kept on talking.

"Arturo, I pray for Dennis every day. I pray for his healing. I pray for a safe trip home and that Dennis would find fulfillment on this trip, even with his almost intolerable pain. You need to know that he's on extremely strong meds--he takes morphine tablets to fight the pain. Emilia always makes sure he takes his meds on time. I know I'm asking a lot of you. This is not a run-of-the-mill trip. I want Dennis' last journey to be a terrific experience for him. He really deserves it.

We both fell silent. Dejected, we finished our glasses. It was already past midnight and most of the lights in the dining room had been switched off. Lost in thought, we said good night, shook hands, and promised to all take special care of our friend Dennis.

I took the elevator up to my room and had a night cap, dwelling on this long conversation. "There are such strange destinies in this world. If I had not seen Dennis with my own eyes, I would hardly have believed a story like this," I thought to myself. I switched off the light and prayed intensely for Dennis, asking the Lord to help my new friend on this obviously divinely inspired journey.

I was restless all night long—pursued by thoughts, images, and dreams having to do with Dennis and his special mission. Could this man handle the strain? How would we react if he just collapsed somewhere out in the country? To be honest, we didn't have a strategy worked out for that particular scenario. Rather, we were totally dependent on divine Providence for the success of this trip. Yes, that was what we were hoping for and what we were basically trusting in. As it turned out, only a few days later our faith in divine Providence was to be severely tested.

The next morning, all the nightmares that had racked me had evaporated. The weather was perfect, too. Bright sunshine greeted us and made our breakfast a happy occasion for all. Gone were the worries about Dennis, disease, and death. My thoughts turned to the schedule of the day. We discussed the day's program at the large breakfast buffet and everyone was in a great mood. There was only one catch: Dennis did not show up.

Our city guide, an expert on Fatima, was already waiting for our group at the front desk at 9 a.m. Shortly afterwards we began our walking tour of the city, visiting the various locations of the appearances for which this pilgrimage town is famous. In the meantime, Dennis and his little family had joined us as well. We took in the Cova da Iria and the basilica where Lucia, the oldest of the three shepherd children of Fatima, was interred. Lucia was a nun of the Carmelite order and died in 2005, laid to rest next to her cousin Jacinta. Lucia was 97 years old. Next, our motorcoach took us to Ajustrel, the hometown of the three children. There we visited the homes where they were born. It had warmed up considerably and some of the travelers were already starting to droop. Nevertheless, we continued on foot to Valinhos, taking the same route the children took in 1917 at the time of the appearances. Dennis seemed to be hanging on pretty well. Emilia was pushing his wheelchair and practically everyone in the group was lovingly helping Dennis get in and out of the bus at the various stops. Apparently they did not regard Dennis as a burden. Intuitively they all knew what was at stake here.

Today an impressive marble statue stands in Loca do Cabeço, where the angel of Portugal appeared to the children twice. We assembled at this spot and prayed together. Then from a book I recounted what the angel had told the children at that time.

"When the angel had appeared to the child seers, he said: 'Have no fear! I am the angel of peace! Pray with me.' He knelt, bowing his forehead down to the ground and let the children repeat these words three times:

"My God, I believe, I adore, I hope, and I love You! I ask

pardon of You for those who do not believe, do not adore, do not hope and do not love You!"

Then he got up and said: 'Pray in this way. The most sacred hearts of Jesus and Mary hear your requests.'"

When I had finished my reading, I was gripped by emotion but noticed someone to my left. It was Dennis, standing straight as an arrow, clean and neatly dressed in his safari outfit. Protected from the sun by his broad-brimmed hat, he patted me on the shoulder with his emaciated right hand, smiled, and exclaimed:

"Arthur, I thought you were our big expert on Fatima around here. But it looks like you have to read from a book." Today, for a change, he was not wearing that hospital facemask so you could see that there was a rakish grin on his face. Apparently he was feeling better, what a relief. I didn't mind his little dig. On the contrary, it was an indication that he was in good spirits.

"I like your sense of humor, Dennis. I'm glad you're in good shape today," I replied sincerely. His eyelids twitched ever so slightly, suggesting that he had registered what I had said. When he wasn't talking, Dennis was able to express more with his facial expressions than some people are able to communicate with their voices. As such, he was able to utilize the lines on his forehead, the corners of his mouth, his eyebrows, his eyelids, and even his ears as communication tools.

The morning had been pretty tiring and the travelers were still struggling with the effects of jet lag, so they all appreciated having the afternoon off. Personally, I was looking forward to a long siesta on my hotel bed. But before resting, I decided to go over to the Chapel of Apparitions, the Cova da Iria, to pray the rosary for my deceased family members. Then I would sacrifice a candle and only then take a nap.

As I was just about to leave the chapel and return to the hotel, I recognized Dennis. There he sat all by himself, propped up in his wheelchair near the chapel. He was lost in prayer, his fingers moving over the beads of his rosary. I stood back to watch him for a moment. He was praying intensely and didn't take the slightest notice of me. After two or three minutes I was about to go back to the hotel. Before leaving, I turned around to look at Dennis once more and then he spotted me. He waved me over and asked me to join him. I quickly stepped up to him and was about to ask him whether I could help him in any way, but with one quick gesture he bade me to keep silent. *He* was the one who wanted to talk:

"Well, Arthur, I thought that as a good German you'd be spending your spare time hanging around in bars drinking beer, instead of hanging around with pilgrims. Don't you have anything to do?"

Of course I knew he was jerking my chain. This was apparently his way of getting closer to people. I guess everyone has his own style, so I decided to toss the ball back.

"You should talk! Here you are, sitting around at the place of apparitions, instead of taking a siesta." He seemed to enjoy this somewhat rough conversation. So with a twinkle in his eye, he kept on going.

"Well, my dear fellow, I will be needing *her* pretty soon," he declared, nodding towards the chapel. "You see, for me this is a whole different situation. But seriously, Arthur, it's refreshing to see a tour guide who takes his profession so seriously. That gives me pleasure," he said matter-of-factly.

As we were chatting, I moved his wheelchair from the hot sun over to the shade by some stairs, so I could sit down. "Yes, I am feeling surprisingly well today," he said, obviously relieved. After a moment of reflection, he added, "Earlier this morning in Loca do Cabeço, when you were talking about the angel and the child seers, I recalled a story that archbishop Fulton Sheen once told about the appearances of Fatima some fifty years ago. I've got to warn you though, Arthur, that this is *his* interpretation, not mine."

"You're sure making it exciting, Dennis. Don't worry, I'm used to a lot of stuff." I wondered what one of Americas' first television preachers had to say about Fatima. "Tell me, Dennis, I'd like to know what he said."

"OK, Arthur, I'll tell you. Archbishop Sheen claimed that there must be hidden meaning to the fact that the appearances of the Virgin Mary back in 1917 had occurred in a backwater Portuguese village, of all places. Strangely enough, this village was named after the favorite daughter of the prophet Mohammed. You need to know a bit of the history of that village. After the Battle of Santarem most of what is today Portugal returned to Christian rule. But a Muslim noblewoman named Fatima remained in Portugal. She converted to Christianity and soon married a knight. He became the village's feudal lord and named the village after his wife. There's another connection to Islam. In their visions, the three child shepherds that you mentioned this morning described the prayers of the angel who had appeared to them. You read it to us quite correctly. Do you remember?"

"No, I don't know what you're driving at."

"Look, it's so clear. The angel touched the ground with his forehead. The child shepherds did the same."

"I see, but what is that supposed to mean, except that Portugal was influenced by Islam for a long time."

"Well, I don't really understand the meaning myself, but Muslims do pray the same way that angel taught the children. That is food for thought, wouldn't you say?" he said softly and thoughtfully.

"I can tell you a story that will give you pause, too."

"Shoot."

"You've heard of the prophecies that the Virgin Mary told the child shepherds, right? There's also a link to Russia and the liberation from communism."

"Oh, I know about that, Arthur. You're probably referring to the prophecy of July 13, when she said the following, among other things—correct me if I get it wrong..." And at that point Dennis started to recite the entire prophecy from memory:

"When you see a night illumined by an unknown light, know that this is the great sign given you by God that he is about to punish the world for its crimes, by means of war, famine, and persecutions of the Church and of the Holy Father. To prevent this, I shall come to ask for the consecration of Russia to my Immaculate Heart, and the Communion of Reparation on the First Saturdays. If my requests are heeded, Russia will be converted, and there will be peace; if not, she will spread her errors throughout the world, causing wars and persecutions of the Church."

"There's more, Arthur, but I guess that'll do for now."

"Yes, that's exactly the one I mean, Dennis. You see, today Russia is in fact liberated from Communism, and the Virgin Mary's prophecy was actually fulfilled. But there is yet another connection between Fatima and Russia. Remember the wooden paneling in the interior of the Chapel of Apparitions?

"All I remember was that there was a magnificent wooden ceiling."

"That's the one I mean. A few years ago the old wooden ceiling was in deplorable shape. The wood was all moldy and in urgent need of repair. The senior pastor of the chapel was extremely concerned about the safety of the pilgrims. In fact, he figured that sooner or later they would have to temporarily close the chapel because of its state of disrepair and because they had no funds for renovation. The only thing the church could do at the time was pray. Some time later this pastor got a phone call from the Port Authority in Lisbon. One of the employees there wanted to know if his church might be interested in a delivery of heavy oak wood. The pastor was thrilled and wanted to know where the wood was. They told him that a Russian freighter had tied up in the port of Lisbon and wasn't able to pay the harbor dues. For that reason part of the cargo had been impounded and sold to pay them off. But over night the entire crew had bolted and so no one was left who was responsible for the remainder of the cargo. Lisbon Port Authority planned to auction off the cargo and the ship but they wouldn't be able to get rid of the wood. They'd give it away if someone came to pick it up. Not only that, they would help load the wood, too—good, heavy oak from the Russian taiga.

Thrilled and relieved that his problem was going to be solved, the pastor immediately agreed to pick up the wood. He asked a few people in his congregation to help him and before long he had dozens of volunteers to collect the wood in Lisbon. By the time the volunteers had unloaded the wood here at Fatima, the whole town had heard the story and a number of carpenters offered to restore the church free of charge. The old wood paneling was re-moved and professionally replaced by solid, Russian oak. Quite a few helpers wound up donating spare time to repair the ceiling of the Cova da Iria."

"That is one impressive story. There's one more example of the power of faith," Dennis replied. "I've never heard that story."

"You see, Dennis, I guess I'm a Fatima expert after all," I said with a chuckle. As far as I was concerned, our little chat was concluded. I was about to walk back to the hotel. But then Dennis said, "Oh, Arthur, hang on a minute. I wanted to chat with you anyway. I presume Juan has already talked to you."

At this point he made a little pause, as if wanting to take a deep breath before a long sentence. "When we met at the airport yesterday, you were pretty shocked about me, am I right?"

"Yes—well, I don't know if shocked is the right word, but I *am* worried whether you'll be able to hack this strenuous trip. This situation is new for me, too, even though I've been doing these pilgrimages for almost 15 years now."

"Go ahead and admit it, I don't mind—not at all. Since I've had this disease and have been confined to this wheelchair, I've gotten used to the fact that people are shocked about me. By now it seems pretty ho-hum to me. But to be fair, I'd be taken aback, too, if I saw a guy like me, strapped to a wheelchair and wearing a cowboy hat, face mask and with such a pitiful looking body. When people look at me, they see something they normally tend to deny: their own mortality. Whereas I have accepted the fact that my time here on earth has pretty much run out and that I'll be going home soon, these people deny any thought of their own death. In our culture death is taboo and they want nothing to do with it. But I don't worry about it. You see, I love to get in the thick of things, as long as I have the time. I'm the kind of guy you can't get rid of, even though I sometimes run the risk of generating a bit of friction or rubbing some people the wrong way."

"Hey, Dennis, don't worry about these things. You can talk about anything with me, even about death. Death doesn't intimidate me as much as it used to when I was younger. In fact, I think about it every day. The reason I reacted the way I did yesterday has more to do with the fact that I'm worried about how this trip will end, whether you'll make it and how the others would deal with a crisis situation. I want you to make it home alive, Dennis. At first I was upset that nobody had told me anything about this and that they had just dropped the bomb on me here. But in the meantime Juan has talked to me and now we're in touch about this. I've calmed down now."

While we were talking, I gripped the handles of Dennis' wheelchair and slowly started pushing him.

"Well, Arthur, by profession I am a plasterer. That's sort of like a bricklayer. Construction has always been my line of business. Even back in high school I supplemented my allowance with odd jobs at construction sites. Back then, it wasn't really about the money. I just wanted to find out what people do at construction sites. After high school I joined the U.S. Army because weaponry was another interest of mine. After I was honorably discharged, I worked as a plasterer again for a couple of years. I'll tell you one thing, Arthur, construction sites are tough, but it's honest work. You'll see right off the bat who's up front and who's not. Sure, you've got blowhards in that line of business too, just like you do anywhere. But there's no place where they'll be exposed as quickly as they will be at a construction site. The toughest job around…Pretty soon I realized I didn't want to be a small-time plasterer anymore. So I took college prep classes, lucked out, and passed the entrance exams. Then I went to a state university in Dayton, Ohio. For five years I studied constructional engineering, graduated near the top of my class, and then landed a job as an engineer."

Dennis had to catch his breath now. He wasn't used to talking that much any more, but was still eager to finish his story. After taking a sip from the plastic water bottle hanging from his wheelchair, he continued his story.

"My whole professional life I worked at the same company, United States Gypsum—USG. So I went to Chicago and started as a young construction engineer. Even back then, USG was one of the largest suppliers of building supplies, with almost 1,000 employees. These days about all they do is make various kinds of ceiling panels. Back then, though, they also made insulation board, plasterboard, plaster, mortar, etc. I really applied myself and worked my way up the ranks. Before long, I had risen to senior middle management. I was respected, people liked me, and I always stood up for the company. You see, even back in the 1970s there were rumors about asbestos. And it was no secret that our insulation boards contained asbestos. Asbestos is an excellent building material. Back then they even called it the miracle fiber because it is very sturdy, heat and acid resistant, has excellent isolation properties, and can even be woven. Thanks to these properties asbestos became a premier building material in shipbuilding, for building insulation, and even in the automotive industry.

Despite rumors that asbestos was hazardous to your health, I championed USG. Then the first asbestos lawsuits started hitting us and even then I went to staff meetings and stood up for USG. I was on their payroll for thirty-three years. And, God knows, I made good money, too. But I also witnessed how exposure to asbestos started making so many of my buddies sick. Some of them just accepted their fate and died, some of them filed lawsuits that took years and won settlements. Me? I was absolutely certain that nothing could ever happen to me. I guess I've got that attitude because I'm an outdoorsman. I've always been outdoors, I've always done a lot of sports, I ate healthy, never smoked—so how could anything happen to me? I didn't even catch colds in the winter. I was everybody's role model."

His voice started to fade and then he began to cough. Dennis had worked himself up a bit, so he needed a breather. He took another sip from his red plastic bottle.

"If you're too tired, Dennis, we can continue this conversation tonight or tomorrow," I suggested, trying to be compassionate.

"No, my friend, we're going to do this now. I want you to know what's up with me," he said with a new burst of energy. "So now you've just got to listen to me."

"Of course," I ensured him as I pushed his wheelchair. By now the hotel was slowly coming into view.

"So, some years ago I left USG. With my life insurance policy and two pension funds I was able to afford it. At that time, my health was actually pretty good. True, I had some coughing attacks in the morning and had trouble breathing when I went to bed, but I could handle it. A few months ago I saw a doctor because my symptoms had gotten worse. The doctor referred me to a university clinic and they diagnosed my disease.

"Yeah, Juan told me about that yesterday," I said.

"This is a really bad deal, Arthur. People don't recover from this disease. The average life expectancy for people in my situation is 16 months—tops. That means I've only got a few months left, if that much."

"I don't quite understand, Dennis. How did you manage to

inhale asbestos? I thought you were a middle management guy who worked at the office, not at construction sites…"

"True, enough. But you see, asbestos consists of very fine mineral fibers. You don't necessarily need to go to construction sites to come into contact with it. In my case, at the plant I had a lot to do with site managers who came into the office for meetings. Even *those* contacts can be sufficient for you to inhale asbestos if they occur over long periods of time. Those fibers linger on your clothes, your hair, and they fly around in the air. When you breathe, they stick to your lungs and your body is not able to break them down. They accumulate in your lungs and often lead to serious lung diseases. Get the picture, Arthur?

"Yes, Dennis, that's plenty. I get it.

By now he was obviously exhausted and desperately needed rest. Fortunately, by that time we were very close to the hotel. I pushed him into the elevator and took him up to his room where Emilia was already waiting for him. Then I retired to my room for some respite.

After dinner we had all planned to attend the big Procession of Lights, held every evening in the large square right in front of the basilica. Our whole group wanted to go. I've attended these processions many times so I was content to just watch from the hotel window.

Even from far away, it is moving to view that endless sea of lights, to hear the pilgrims singing hymns as they amble across the square. On the spur of moment, I decided to go down after all and join the thousands of people, each of whom was holding a light. As I was about to leave the hotel, I saw Dennis, sitting all by himself in his wheelchair holding a candle. He was painstak-ingly moving his lips, no longer able to sing along with everybody else. He was following the procession in his mind. I quietly joined him and asked him if I could help him. He just waved me aside with a tired gesture. He was obviously having trouble speaking but seemed composed and at peace. Later I found out that he was suffering from extreme pain that particular evening. A moment later, I bumped into Emilia near the hotel, and she explained to me that Dennis just wanted to be alone. She just stood there, keeping an eye on her sick husband.

After two nights in Fatima, we bade that town and Portugal farewell. We were now on our way towards Spain. Traveling northward, we passed the famous university city of Coimbra. Then we turned northeast, crossing over into Spain. Next stop: Salamanca. When you enter the city, which is divided by the Rio Tormes, you cross an ancient Roman bridge. First-century master builders constructed it out of heavy stone blocks, enabling it to survive the past two millennia. Over six hundred and fifty feet (200 meters) long, this architectural wonder spans the Rio Tormes. It was by the bridge that we took a short break for a photo stop. Before everyone got off the bus, however, I made a PA announcement and asked all the travelers to stay close to the motorcoach. We were only going to have a 15-minute photo op, I stressed. With that, I sent them off.

The bridge is particularly beautiful at night, when each of its twenty-six arches is illuminated. Salamanca is the oldest university in Spain, boasting 8,000 students even in the Middle Ages. Today 40,000 students are in attendance and it is these young people who give the city its upbeat pulse. Taking advantage of the spectacular view of the city from the bridge, our group took lots of pictures. We didn't want to actually drive *into* the old town, since our goal was Alba de Tormes near Salamanca, the burial place of St. Teresa of Ávila. The weather was particularly gorgeous that day, with the sky an intense—almost unreal—blue and the landscape a golden yellow. The scenery reminded many of our travelers of Florida or California.

After about fifteen minutes I was already positioned in my seat next to our driver who had already started the engine to get the A/C up to speed. But when you travel with all kinds of people, problems and misunderstandings will occur—that's just the way it is. After I had finished counting heads on the bus, it quickly became clear that one traveler was missing. We soon figured out who it was: Jenny, an elderly lady from Madison, Wisconsin. Her husband was calmly sitting next to his wife's empty seat. He hadn't even noticed that she was missing. "I guess she must have gone across the bridge," he casually suggested. So we waited. After ten minutes there was still no trace of Jenny, so Father Grigus and I decided to look for her. Unfortunately, we were also tight for time because the shrine of St. Teresa at Alba de Tormes was scheduled to close at 5 pm. Latecomers are not admitted, so we would miss the day's highlight if we didn't get there in time. Understandably, this made for some unhappy people on our motorcoach. Since travel agencies sell trips with a clearly defined program, we tour guides are required to run a tight ship. If an event is listed in the program, the itinerary has to be kept. Otherwise the travel agencies can be sued—justifiably so.

Father Grigus and I quickly crossed the Roman bridge, searching for Jenny on the other side of the river. We saw neither hide nor hair of her.

"What now?" I asked John Grigus.

"Keep on looking, what else? We've got to find her."

Just past the bridge there is a small rise on which the cathedral of Salamanca is built and which, even today, draws many tourists. "I don't think Jenny could have walked that far," I was thinking to myself. But Father Grigus and I apparently reached the same conclusion because, without expressing it, we both started hoofing it to the cathedral—not the most pleasant thing to do in that heat. Once inside the cathedral though, we were greeted by pleasant cool air, which compensated us for the strain and heat of 95 degrees (35C) Fahrenheit outside. I felt sorry for Father Grigus in his heavy, black Franciscan cassock, which was obviously uncomfortable. As we were discussing how best to look over this maze of a church, Jenny casually strolled toward us. I managed to keep my cool, although it was not easy. How in the world could she mess up our schedule like this? But I didn't say a "peep." After all, there was a priest standing next to me, whose job it was to take care of such things. Father Grigus took her by the arm and stepped aside with her. I couldn't hear what they were saying—and wasn't supposed to either. All I saw was Father Grigus pointing somewhere with his right arm. I assume that he really laid down the Law. After a few moments we quickly returned to the bus. What I always admire about Father John is his warm and calm manner--always the right approach when things go wrong or get stressful. The man is always calm, has a distinguished way of speaking, and doesn't have an angry bone in his body.

We quickly got back to our motorcoach and I asked the driver to pick up the pace the rest of the day. Fortunately we were able to maintain our schedule, so there were no repercussions from our little episode with Jenny.

As far as Dennis was concerned, I was always keeping an eye on him. Juan and I had a mutual agreement to watch out for him. Even as early as breakfast, he was the primary object of our concern. "How did he sleep?" and "How is he doing today?" were our most frequent questions.

That evening in the hotel Juan asked me, "Arturo, have you noticed that Dennis hardly eats anything?"

"Yes, I have. Emilia shared with me that he has hardly eaten anything since they left Chicago. He usually is in tremendous pain. Eating is a major problem for him and causes him even greater pain. What kind of pain killers does he use?"

"As far as I know, he takes morphine tablets, but I'm not certain, Arturo. Poor Dennis. I guess there's nothing we can do to help him."

But Juan and I were not the only ones taking care of Dennis. The whole group had obviously taken it upon themselves to help him wherever possible. In fact, the men in our group were almost fighting over who would push his wheelchair next, who would get him across the street or lift him onto the motorcoach. The women wanted to be close to him as well. They were always offering him cool drinks and didn't mind being turned down by him all the time. Despite his pain, Dennis even cracked a joke here and there. One day he told me:

"Hey, Arthur, if I had known I'd be fussed over by so many ladies and that so many guys would want to carry me around like on a royal divan, I would have rehearsed for this trip. This isn't too bad."

I grinned at him, thinking what a relief it is—for everyone concerned—when people are able to handle divine trials and tribulations gracefully. It makes life so much easier.

By the next morning the weather had cooled down considerably and we were scheduled to visit the medieval castle of Ávila. At 9:00 o'clock our city guide was ready for the two-hour tour. This time Dennis was joining us. He looked rested. Emilia was pushing his wheelchair but was struggling with the bumpy cobblestones. Pushing her husband's wheelchair was becoming very tedious for her and she was trying hard not to lose sight of the rest of the group. Since all I had to do at the moment was to keep the group together while the city guide was leading the way, I decided to relieve Emilia. As soon as I stepped up to Dennis, he started kidding around with me—always a good sign.

"Well, well, our Commander in Chief, how nice."

"Hi Dennis, how are you doing today?"

"Thanks for asking. But I am messed up beyond repair"," at which we both laughed. It was moments like these in which he and I really bonded. When Dennis was in good spirits—which he always was when he was more or less pain-free—he sure was an amusing guy. He must have been a fun guy to be around way back in his healthy days... Once the city tour began, we couldn't really chat anymore. We checked out various palaces and court-yards, walking more than 1.5 miles (more than 2.5 km) along the Romanesque city wall with its many towers and gates—even the cathedral and the synagogue from the Moorish period. Dennis did not want to enter every building. In fact, the longer the tour took, the more lustless he became. So more and more frequently, he and I just sat outside, waiting for the rest of the group. I didn't fail to notice how Dennis was becoming more and more silent and frustrated. Finally, he stopped saying anything. When we arrived at the "Torreón de los Guzmanes" directly in front of the "Plaza del General Mola" the group entered by themselves the inner courtyard, while we were waiting outside. Dennis suddenly tried to get up. I started to help him but he pushed me away vehemently. Whenever he reacted like this—and I had already become familiar with these situations—there was no sense in trying to stop him. Dennis was even more thick-skulled than me. Finally, using every last bit of his energy at his disposal, he was able to pull himself up to a standing position. Now he was standing right in front of me on shaky legs and I really wondered what he was up to. Step by step he wobbled my way, stood right in front of me for a mo-ment, raised his head—and ultimately collapsed in my arms. I was caught by surprise and had trouble keeping balance myself. So I caught him and held on to him, feeling how tightly he was holding on to me. Instinctively, I did the same thing and hugged him back. I could tell how this did him good. I guess it gave him a feeling of comfort and even some "one-on-one" with another human being—something terminally ill people don't get very often. So Dennis and I stood there, just clinging to one another, which probably caused the tourists walking by do a double take.

All of a sudden I noticed a shudder go straight through his body: Dennis started to cry. Before long, he was sobbing as freely as a child. I felt his tears, which he didn't hold back, running down my neck. At that moment I didn't know what to do. I froze, still hugging him tightly. Then I heard this pitiful voice in my ear:

"I'm just a burden for everybody, good for nothing. Why didn't I stay home? What have I done?" Then he started to sob once more.

And then something happened that threw me for a loop: I started to cry, too. I don't know how long we were both standing there in front of the Dávila Palace, embracing one another and sobbing, but it must have been several minutes. After a while we both calmed down. I was the first one to regain composure and started to speak:

"Dennis, you know that's not true. You've seen yourself how everyone around here is taking such good care of you and wants to help you. Doesn't that mean anything to you?"

He finally let go of me and I of him, whereupon he stepped back and looked me in the eye.

"Dennis," I maintained, "surely you know that everybody loves being around you and that we all love you."

Straight as an arrow, he stood in front of me, thinking about what to say. But it took a while for him to find the strength to speak.

"You're right, Arthur. Everybody is so good to me. That's why I am so moved." If I hadn't been in such a crying mood at that moment, I probably would have laughed out loud. Dennis and his good ol' black humor…

Then he dragged himself over to his wheelchair and collapsed in it. He was exhausted and probably feeling empty. Suddenly I had what I thought was a bright idea. I suggested that we have our picture taken. After donning sunglasses to hide our weepy eyes, I located a tourist standing in front of the castle who was also waiting for someone, just like us. I asked him in sign language if he could take a picture of us, then I stuck my camera in his hand and made "take a picture" gestures. Then I went back to Dennis. We heard the click. That particular picture is now one of my all-time favorite photographs. I still have it. There I am standing behind Dennis, posing in his wheelchair. That picture is still hanging on my bulletin board next to my computer. I presented Dennis with the picture in my camera's display—one of us sitting, the other one standing—and both of us wearing shades. Even if you studied it closely, you wouldn't notice the powerful atmosphere that, only minutes before, had moved both of us to tears of emotion. When Dennis saw the picture, he almost doubled over laughing—well, at least as far as his wheelchair would let him double over.

"Hey, Arthur, you look like a real gangster. Why am I not surprised?

"Look who's talking, Dennis, you don't look any better...."

"You know, we look like *The Godfather* and his bodyguard." Sure enough, Dennis was right. That's exactly what we looked like: *The Godfather* and his bodyguard.

Once again, we shared a heart-felt laugh and our guffawing echoed down the narrow alleyway.

And then, as if they had been summoned by a bell, the first members of our group started returning. A few moments later we continued our city tour. What had transpired between Dennis and me would most likely remain our little secret.

Emilia now took my place pushing the wheelchair. Dennis was probably in need of some medication or something to drink, all of which she kept with the wheelchair. While dropping back to the end of the group, I was reflecting on a conversation I had had with Emilia, in which she shared with me that Dennis Yosick, the successful construction engineer, had married his *first* wife many years ago. That marriage had been blessed with two boys, the younger of whom already had one son of his own. One day Dennis pulled out his wallet on the bus and showed me two pictures of those two young men of whom he was very proud. But after about 20 years of marriage, —his sons were 14 and 18 years of age at the time that first wife had died of cancer of the colon. The pain of losing his wife almost killed Dennis, now a single dad and all alone with two teenage children. But he made it, thanks to his personal strength and his faith. During this period Dennis dedicated himself even more to the mission of Opus Dei, an organization that gave him support and hope. In some way Opus Dei became part of his now much smaller family. Dennis hired caretakers and in the evening cooked for his sons and himself. "With my cooking skills, it's a miracle I didn't poison them," he told me.

Barely three months after the death of his wife, about the time his life had calmed down somewhat, the older son, Tim was diagnosed with a congenital disease. Every method of treatment failed and the only way his life could be saved was with an operation, which, however, left the boy a paraplegic and confined to a wheelchair. Not only was Dennis now responsible for two minors, but one of them was also severely handicapped. As Emilia had explained, it took Dennis a long time to bounce back from these twin blows. They caused him to struggle with life in general and with his Savior in particular, leaving him to wonder why *he* was being dealt one severe blow after another. Dennis felt alone and deserted. It was only his faith that gradually brought him back to a normal life.

Dennis came from a deeply religious family. His mother, who was a converted Lutheran, raised her four girls and 5 boys in the Catholic faith and ran a tight ship. The girls attended a cloister school and two of them even became Franciscan nuns. His 4 brothers remained committed to the faith throughout their lives, even though they all chose secular vocations. As such, it came as no surprise that Dennis during this greatest crisis of his life would seek consolation and encouragement in the arms of the Church. He joined Opus Dei in 1979, a move that further strengthened his faith in God. Years later he met Emilia near Chicago in a church choir. They immediately fell in love and got married a few months later and by that time his worst crises were already over—or so he thought.

But back to our pilgrimage. The highlights of that day were our tour of the Diocesan Museum. Father John showed us where the relics of St. Teresa, the most famous daughter of the city and whose image is omnipresent, were placed after her death. A mystic and teacher of church history, St. Teresa was elevated to sainthood by the Vatican and went down in history as Teresa de Cepeda y Ahumada (1515-1582), also known as Santa Teresa de Jesús or as Teresa of Ávila. The various Carmelite cloisters she founded are a witness to her exemplary and sanctified life. St. Teresa was canonized in 1622 and every year hundreds of thousands of pilgrims visit this little town in her honor.

Viewing all these sacred objects, Dennis became very emotional. He actually got out of his wheelchair and laid his chest, arms and head on the marble table, which is now an altar, and prayed intently to Saint Teresa. Later he told Emilia who was standing next to me, "I felt how she took me in her arms. I'm on the right track. Of that I am sure."

Before moving on, we also visited Sonsoles, which is located near Ávila. Many pilgrims come here to visit the chapel of the Virgin Mother, as did in 1933 José Maria Escrivá, the founder of Opus Dei. During the lengthy wars between Christians and Muslims the image of the Virgin Mother had been hidden to protect it from defilement. Many years later it was accidentally discovered by shepherds. According to tradition, when they came across it they said, "Look at her beautiful eyes! They look like suns!" ("Son soles!"). That particular afternoon in Sonsoles it was hotter than blazes. Every step we took was a struggle. We looked for shade wherever we could and drank as much as we could hold. One look at Dennis quickly reminded me how tough this must all have been for him.

Months later, while talking on the phone to Emilia, she shared with me that whereas this pilgrimage had indeed been necessary for Dennis, it was also extremely strenuous for him. Just changing his clothes every day, washing, and attending to his personal hygiene must have been agony—not only for him but for Emilia as well. Not to mention, managing his pain with strong medication on an almost hourly basis was presumably anything but pleasant. On top of all that, his throat was almost constantly irritated, he was short of breath, not hungry (despite all the delicious food they served us), driving on bumpy cobblestone roads was painful for him, and he had great difficulty entering and exiting the motorcoach. All of this would have made the trip intolerable for most any of us. I often reflect on how and why he survived that trip. I think the reason he did was because this journey wasn't just any old tourist trip but rather a pilgrimage in the true sense of the word. Its whole purpose was that it *had* to be strenuous and full of hardship. For Dennis, taking this trip was more like doing penance: He was offering his misery and suffering to the Lord as a sacrifice and with his whole heart. This pilgrimage enabled him to cleanse his soul. And this, in turn, was the only way he would be able to face the future, guiltless.

For these very reasons Dennis never complained and never really discussed his suffering. His attitude and behavior were exemplary. Everyone knew how sick he was and that he could die any day. Death had him in its clutches and had left its indelible mark on his face and body. Everyone could see it. So could Dennis. He had long since given up any sliver of hope of somehow escaping death's iron grip. The only thing keeping him alive was the thought that he still might be able to bring this pilgrimage to a happy ending being alive. He regarded every day he was still able to experience as a gift and as divine Providence. In this way he made the most of what he had left, looking forward to a gracious reception at his final destination.

Fascinating Ávila had kept us busy for two days but now it was time to move on to Torreciudad. On the way there we passed Madrid, the capital of Spain, which most in our group had never visited before. Around noon our bus drove us into Spain's capital, sizzling in the sun. Relaxing in our climate-controlled motorcoach, our tour of the city, which I conducted over the PA system, was quite pleasant. That same afternoon we drove on to Sigüenza, a medieval city in Guadalajara province, located some seventy-five miles (120 km) northeast of Madrid. That was as far as we wanted to go that day. Situated in a terraced landscape, the small town with a population of just under 5,000 sat baking in the late afternoon heat. The predominant color was dusty brown. The first thing we noticed was a striking castle, towering on a hill over the hamlet. This was the Alcazaba, a national historic site of Spain, built in the 12th century. The castle was recently remodeled and turned into a luxury hotel—the well-known Parador of Sigüenza.

We spent one night there. The creature comforts of this luxurious hotel, situated in a forbidding arid landscape, more than made up for the discomforts of the previous few hours.

The next morning we returned to our motorcoach refreshed and full of energy. Our journey now led us northward, with Saragossa our goal. At a population of 660,000, this is Spain's fifth largest city and also the capital of the state of Aragon. Crossing the wide Ebro River on the Puente de Piedra, which leads into the Old Town, is enough to take your breath away. Standing on the bank of the Ebro, the Basilica del Pilar with its many spires immediately catches your eye. Built in honor of the Virgin Mary, this is Spain's largest Baroque building and also the city's landmark. In the interior of the basilica is a column (*pilar* in Spanish), which marks the first apparition of the Virgin Mary in history. In front of this impressive building is the Plaza del Pilar, a huge square adjacent to the Catedral de la Seo, the oldest church in Saragossa. Here we took a lunch break and viewed the basilica, a must-stop for every tourist. Of course we also wanted to view the beautiful statue of the Madonna, which the Spaniards call Nuestra Señora del Pilar. In the 17th century this monumental church was built around the pillar. According to legend, on February 2, A.D. 40, Mary, the mother of God, appeared to the Apostle James the Elder on this very spot to encourage him to continue spreading the Gospel. Commemorating the very first apparition of Mary, this event is commemorated annually on October 12 at the patronage festival of the Virgin del Pilar. On this day, carpets of flowers, beautiful bouquets, and a nineteen-foot (six meter) pyramid of flowers are presented in honor of the Virgin Mary in a moving ceremony.

The closer we got to Torreciudad, the more nervous Dennis became. When we left Saragossa the next morning on our way there, Dennis was once again sitting right behind me on the bus. Even though he wasn't feeling too well—you could tell because from time to time he was silent, just struggling with his physical pain—he was still quite talkative, almost fidgety. Sometimes he wanted to get up, sometimes he pointed wildly at something whizzing by outside. At one point he nudged me to ask me something:

"Hey, Arthur, you always know everything, right?"

"Well, I have taken this trip several times, but obviously I don't know everything."

"OK, then can you tell me when we'll get to Torreciudad?"

I glanced at my watch and called out something in Portuguese to the driver who nodded with his head.

"A good hour more, Dennis."

We had many such short conversations as we approached the Barbastro Mountains in the Pyrenees, heading to the place where José Maria Escrivá was born on January 9, 1902. For about the past half hour our fully-loaded motorcoach had been grinding its way up a steep mountain pass, taking us past a beautiful reservoir over half a mile (1 km) long. Its turquoise water was most tempting in the shimmering afternoon heat.

"You know what that gigantic reservoir is, out here in the middle of these mountains, Arthur?"

"I do happen to know that, Dennis. The Rio Cinca, which comes down from the mountains, is dammed up in this reservoir. The Rio Cinca is a tributary of the Segre, which has its source in the Pyrenees. This reservoir is called El Grado and it's almost twelve miles (twenty km) long. Tourists come here just to scuba dive in its beautiful indigo water."

"Good grief, why do they need such a large reservoir out here?"

"They need water for drinking and for agriculture, too. Agriculture plays an important role in Spain."

"This scenery is simply mind-boggling. These mountains, the reddish-brown earth, and that strange deep-blue water... Somehow this all reminds me of "Lord of the Rings," part one. There is this one scene where they're riding along a body of water. This is so stunning—like in a dream."

Then he just sat silently for many minutes, just looking out the window.

Dennis later told me that Torreciudad was the highlight of his trip. Not only because this place is the Spanish epicenter of Opus Dei, but also because of the huge and magnificent shrine to the Blessed Virgin Mary, which Dennis had wanted to see for half of his lifetime. I was happy for him and also thankful that the Lord had blessed us with such wonderful weather. Just before we reached the peak, where the portal of the sanctuary is located, we picked out the old hermitage. It was on our left, some 400 yards (more than 400 meters) below the old church, at the very spot where the miraculous image of Our Lady of Torreciudad has been venerated for centuries.

In 1904 a little boy named José Maria Escrivá was miraculously healed at this location. An insidious illness had afflicted the two-year old—a dangerous infection that was incurable, according to the doctors of that day and age. Every attempt to heal him had failed. In fact, the Escrivás' family physician, Dr. Camps, had already given up any hope of saving the life of the cheerful lad. That last night before the healing the family doctor had even confided to the father of little José Maria: "He probably won't live through the night." But the boy's parents were devout Christians and prayed all night long, fully trusting God and beseeching Him to heal their child. The boy's mother, Dolores Albas, promised the Mother of God that, if he were healed, she would take José Maria on a pilgrimage to the chapel of Torreciudad, located on one of the mountain ranges in the foothills of the Pyrenees.

The next day the doctor made a house call at the Escrivá home. As he was stepping into the house, he asked, "When did the child die?" Overjoyed, the father replied, "He didn't die! In fact, he seems to be completely healed!"

By the time we had finally reached the mountain range, we could see the newly built church. There was even special parking lot for motorcoaches, so it was easy to find a parking spot. Dennis wanted to be one of the first off the bus. We came to a footpath, which led past illustrations of the Joys and Sorrows of St. Joseph. The path leads from the left rear corner of the square, downhill to the old chapel, where it takes you to the first point of the Stations of the Cross.

St. Josemaria Escrivá was the impetus behind the construction of the new chapel at Torreciudad. His initiative and the support of Opus Dei made it possible for this house of God to be built in the middle of the wilderness. Escrivá had the new church constructed in the hope that it would aid in the veneration of the Blessed Mother and would help spiritually renew believers as they receive the sacrament of penance. Today, Opus Dei looks after Torreciudad and its center of Social Education, located next door.

The focal point of Torreciudad, which was designed by architect Heliodoro Dols, is the pilgrimage church. Its large and famous alabaster altarpiece was sculpted by Juan Mayné. The altarpiece consists of three elements: The tabernacle at the top, the crucifixion scene in the middle, and—at the bottom—the miraculous image of Our Lady of Torreciudad, the Queen of Angels, which was painted in the 11th century. This Altar depicts eight sculptured scenes of some of the most important events in the life of Mary: The wedding, annunciation, visitation, adoration of the shepherds, the flight to Egypt, the carpenter's workshop in Nazareth, the crucifixion of the Lord, and the coronation of Mary by the Holy Trinity.

As soon as we got off the bus, Monsignore Javier de Mora, the director of the sanctuary, greeted us in the large parking lot. After a short break so the travelers could refresh themselves, Monsignore Javier proudly showed us through the sanctuary. Demonstrating an obvious love for details and a passion for this house of God, he pointed out the construction of the church, its two chapels, and the sanctuary itself. Father John Grigus celebrated Mass in the church of the sanctuary and, finally, we toured the visitor center.

The whole time I kept watching Dennis from a distance. Up to this point he had braved his way through the program, but now he was starting to look frayed at the edges. His face, as least as far as one could see behind his facemask, was red and bloated. He also seemed to be perspiring more than usual. After Mass he waved me over. We waited a while until we were certain that no one would overhear us.

"Arthur, I'm at the end of my rope. I've tried everything. I've even been clenching my teeth, but the pain won't quit."

"How can I help you, Dennis? What can I do for you?"

"Arthur, I need new pain relief medication. I've almost used up the meds I brought from the States."

"What do you mean, Dennis?"

"Look, these past few days I've been taking more of my pain relievers than I had planned because the pain is so intense. This is also because of the chemo that I did right before our trip. At first I didn't want to do chemo. I don't believe in it. My time is up, plain and simple. No therapy in the world is going to change that. But my wife and the doctors urged me to do chemo. So I finally gave in. I spent a week in the hospital. After that I felt simply awful. I didn't think it could get any worse. My doctor told me that if the pain got too bad, I could double the dosage—no problem. Well," and then he paused and threw up his hands, "Well, I used up my pain killers this morning."

"But Dennis, why didn't you say something this morning in Saragossa? It would have been easy to find a doctor and lots of pharmacies there"

"Do you think we can find a pharmacy out here?"

"No, to be honest, I don't."

"Oh, by the way," he added with a pained expression, "I've also run out of diapers."

I didn't say what I was thinking and I didn't really mean what I said next. But I had to calm Dennis down somehow: "Dennis, I'll try every trick in the book to help you. You can count on it. I'm certain our Spanish friends will help us work this out."

He didn't say a word but just looked at me with sad eyes, squeezed my hands, and let his head droop.

"Dennis, tell your wife and our group that I have to run some errands. I'll be back."

I turned around and walked over to our driver. Our group was busy buying souvenirs and taking pictures. First I talked to Joáo Manuel and asked him what we might do. He recommended that we drive back a bit to El Grado, the town that we had passed on the way to Torreciudad. El Grado was the town after which they had named the reservoir. We took the bus to a desolate village in the foothills, 6,500 ft (2,000m) above sea level. But as we were turning off from the main road and onto the little main street of the village, our driver saw that we wouldn't make it around the bend. I got out to help him negotiate the turn. After a few minutes we had to quit this attempt. There was no way we were going to get into the actual center of El Grado, at least not in such a huge bus. So I left Joáo Manuel onboard and set off on foot.

The village street was devoid of human life, so I knocked on the door of the first house I saw, asking for a pharmacy. No luck. After a while I finally found someone able to help. I couldn't believe what the lady had to say. Stepping out onto the street, she pointed to a mountain beyond the village and told me that there might be a pharmacy *up there*, about a mile or a mile and a half

(1-2 km) away. A small car would make it up there but down in the village no one owned a car, she stated. I got the message: Whether I liked it or not, I would have to hoof it up that steep and unpaved road in the broiling noon sun. Now if I had been a slim and trim young man who knew his way around those parts, that might have been a nice little challenge. But I *didn't* know my way around and I'm not exactly slim, trim, nor young, either. I immediately thought of the 235 lbs. (107 kg) of body mass that I would have to propel up that mountain and back. As I was contemplating that, I followed a dirt "road" that was less than ten feet (3m) wide and which wound its way up the pretty steep mountain. There wasn't a single tree up there that could have given me some shade and a bit of respite. At least I was wearing my Adidas athletic shoes, as I always do on such trips. You live and you learn…

About forty-five minutes later, after the last curve, I saw a large estate surrounded by a number of sheds and stables. This had to be the pharmacy. What if it wasn't? I hurriedly walked the remaining three or four hundred yards (meters) until I was certain. Gasping, perspiring—and happy—I spied a silver sign announcing a *farmacia*. Before entering, I wiped the sweat off my face and allowed a few minutes to catch my breath. It was already past *siesta* time, so I was hoping that somebody might be around. I pushed down the door handle. Yes, the door was un-locked. An old-fashioned bell rang, which was a good thing, too, because it turned out that I was the only person in the sales room of this village pharmacy. It reminded me of the pharmacies of my childhood in Würzburg, Germany, Almost ten feet (three meters) tall and holding a myriad of jars of various sizes, dark wooden shelves and cabinets dominated the room. They were identified by Latin labels. A beautiful old cash register held sway on a counter that was maybe ten feet (several meters) long and looked like it might have been made of marble. "What luxury, way out here! I wonder for whom?" I thought to myself. I was just about to call out impatiently, when a middle-aged man stepped into the sales room thorough a back door. I noticed that he had quickly donned a white lab coat before he entered the room, so as to greet me professonially.

"Señor, how may I serve you?"

He was of medium height, about fifty years of age, and sported a sizable paunch. He wore a large mustache and expensive metal-rimmed glasses.

I was a bit embarrassed and didn't want to come right to the point about the painkillers, so I first asked for the diapers.

"Diapers," he repeated, straightening his eyeglasses. "Yes, I think you're in luck. I do carry diapers. You see, up here on the mountain we're more than a pharmacy. We're also a drugstore, department store, beauty salon, and much more. That's why we carry diapers, too. How many do you need? And, more importantly, what size?" When he heard they were for an adult man, however, he looked doubtful. "Let me take a look." He left me standing there and went in back to check his stock. I could hear him digging around in his storeroom. After a few minutes I heard his muffled voice: "Once again, you're in luck. I've got a whole bag that size. I can't believe that we've got these at all. No one has ever requested them." He returned to the sales room lugging a huge plastic bag and slammed it on the counter. "But you'll have to purchase the whole bag. These are one hundred adult diapers. I hope you get down the mountain with them. But I'll quote you a good price."

This plethora of diapers caught me by surprise and I pictured myself walking over one mile (two km) down the mountain with the huge bag. But what could I do? "Well, at least the bag isn't heavy," I said. He was about to ring up my purchase when I stepped up closer.

"Oh, there's one more thing before you ring up my purchase. I need some pain relievers."

"Is Aspirin OK?"

"No," I said quietly and slid the American prescription across the table. Dennis had given it to me before I left. He picked up the prescription and started to read. Once again, he fidgeted with his metal-rimmed glasses. I held my breath and didn't dare say a word. Suddenly he stopped, put the prescription down, and stared at me. "I am a pharmacist, sir," he stated in a dignified manner. "I do not supply junkies. Don't you think that for one minute!"

"Listen, I'm a tour guide and I urgently need this medication for a very, very sick traveler who is at Torreciudad right now." His black eyes locked on to me.

"OK, *you* listen to *me*, sir. Do you have any idea what you are asking me to do? The medication in this prescription is for a person in a hospital and clearly not for someone on a bus trip. So don't give me those fairy tales."

"Please, believe me. This man is from America. He is suffering from cancer and did chemo two weeks ago. He just *had* to take this trip to Spain. And now he's run out of morphine on this trip. Please help this poor man. This medication is not for me. It's for this man racked with excruciating pain. The prescription you are holding was written by his physician just before the trip."

"I find this all very hard to believe," he said, having calmed down somewhat. "But even if I wanted to, I don't even have this exact medication. The only thing I have is a drug with a similar effect that the hospital down in the valley occasionally orders from me."

"Please, please, at least give me *that* medication! I'm begging you!" The pharmacist took another look at the prescription and then went in back again. If I wasn't totally mistaken, I had won, I figured. When he returned, his wife was accompanying him. Presumably she was supposed to help him make the right decision. Before they could speak a word, I said:

"May I make a suggestion? Let's take your car and drive those few miles down to Torreciudad and I'll show you the patient. Then I'm sure you'll give me the painkillers."

They both looked at one another with baffled expressions. The elation I had just felt was starting to take a nosedive—into hope-lessness. "Lord, please help me!" I was praying silently, "Help me to get this medication now!"

The pharmacist and his wife must have felt my naked despair. They looked at one another, whispered something, and nodded to me."

"OK, you've convinced us. But I need to ask you to translate the directions for the patient so he'll get the correct dosage. If he uses this medication incorrectly, the effects might not be sufficient."

I promised to do everything he said and obediently paid 100 euros (some $150.00) for my purchases, took the tablets and the huge bag of diapers, and hurried on my way. I was so thrilled that

I didn't notice how silly I must have looked with that gigantic bag, advertising *Adult Diapers* in bold letters. Going downhill was considerably quicker and in less than half an hour I had reached Joáo Manuel who was still dutifully waiting for me on the bus.

"Joáo, I did it!" I called to him from afar. He jumped out, took the awkward package off of me, and shared my joy. I quickly hopped aboard and we rushed back to Torreciudad.

A short while later Joáo pulled our motorcoach up onto the Torreciudad parking lot. I immediately asked some people from our group who were standing around where Dennis was. Someone said he was sitting in the church at the altar to the Blessed Virgin. I most certainly did not want to enter the sanctuary with my huge bag of diapers. So I peeked through the huge crystal windows of the nave and spotted Dennis sitting in front of the altar, motionless and lost in prayer. He was all by himself. It took a few moments for me to realize the deeper meaning of this moment. Dennis had reached the finish line of his painful journey. He was now at the center of his faith. His whole life long he had dreamt of this artistic and timelessly beautiful altar to Mary. This was the focal point of all his yearning. What he had up to now only known from books, travelogues, and slide shows was now standing directly in front of him. But it was probably even much more than that. I would presume to say that only at that precise location was he able to open up to his Savior and to enter into a dialog with Him. Only there could he come clean with his life and find closure. He had to. I stood there, very moved. I wanted to let him complete his heartfelt prayer in peace and quiet. So I walked back to the motorcoach and let Juan know what I had been doing the past two hours. Then I doubled back and re-entered the sanctuary. Dennis was still sitting motionless in front of the magnificent altar, that I now had an opportunity to observe myself in a moment of repose. I settled back in a pew and was soon lost in prayer as well. Probably more than thirty minutes later Dennis finally came to himself and turned around. Then he saw me and an imperceptible smile crossed his lips.

"Hey, Arthur, are you already back? Thank you, my friend. Did you really get the tablets?"

"Yes," I said. "I did...not exactly the same kind, but they seem to be close enough."

He stretched out his hands again, squeezed my hands really hard, looked at me without saying a word, and nodded. His eyes were moist. "Arthur, if you only knew what this means to me."

He let go, wiped the tears from his eyes and peered into mine: "Arthur, this past hour I brought my life to a close. Do you understand what I'm saying?"

I nodded wordlessly.

"In my prayer I lit that spark. Now I can just let the rest of this journey come to a close, in deep contentment and peace. Arthur, I saw it."

"*What* did you see, Dennis?"

"I saw death, Arthur…my own death. At first it looked horrible but after a while it changed appearance. In the end it looked very peaceful and tempting. Yes, Arthur, my life is drawing to a close. But I'm not scared anymore. Now I know that everything will turn out well. I'm just going on ahead of you guys, that's all."

Now I had tears in my eyes, too. I placed both hands on his shoulders. Both of us understood the situation. It was coming down to the wire.

I took Dennis back to the motorcoach where our group was waiting for both of us. Then we drove on a few more miles to our hotel, the Tezal. Tezal is a green type of granite that is common in this part of Spain. On the way to the hotel my thoughts were once again with Dennis. That spark he was talking about was probably the prayer he had prayed while I was observing him. I suddenly realized that I had unknowingly witnessed a precious moment, in which the spark of prayer had grown into a roaring flame.

That evening Juan surprised us with the news that he had ordered a terrific dinner for us in a deluxe restaurant in Barbastro. He asked us to wear evening clothes for the occasion. This news was greeted with applause by one and all. We retired to dress elegantly for the luxurious dinner. Juan shared with me that he had organized the banquet in honor of Dennis: "I'm curious to see how he'll react. He loves gourmet restaurants. He always makes those jokes about being a lousy cook but I'm certain he likes to eat well. I wanted to make him especially happy, so from the States I made reservations at this special restaurant. It was even awarded a star in the Michelin Gourmet Guide. What do you think?"

"What a terrific idea, Juan. I hope he'll be able to come along. A little earlier he was still in great pain." And so we parted, both of us a somewhat worried but hoping that the Spanish analgesics would have some tangible effect by the evening.

An hour later, at 8 pm, everyone was dressed in fine evening clothes and waiting downstairs in the lobby. The motorcoach was ready to take us to Barbastro. The entire group was there—except for Dennis and his family. We waited for a while, and then I went to the front desk to call his room. Emilia picked up the phone.

"Hello," she said in a deep voice.

"Emilia, it's me, Arthur. Please come on down. We all want to go to dinner now."

"Oh, Arthur, I completely forgot about the dinner. Dennis is not doing well. He's in pain and I'm sure he won't eat anything. Please go on without us."

"That's too bad. We wanted to dedicate this evening to the three of you, to Dennis in particular. But if that won't work, then we'll have to go without you. That's really too bad."

"Yes, that's too bad, Arthur. I guess it can't be helped."

"May I at least bring some of the delicious food back to you? Maybe you'll be hungry a bit later."

"Yes, that's a fine idea. Thanks, Arthur."

"OK, I hope Dennis will be feeling better soon. See you later." I hung up and went over to Juan, breaking the sad news. "Well, there's nothing we can do," he said, shrugging his shoulders. I waved the whole group over to me, so we could board the motorcoach in an orderly way. The dinner *was* in fact extraordinary and, from a culinary point of view, certainly the highlight of our trip." Sadly, though, none of us could really get into the swing of things or relax. Conversation was muted. Dennis was there in spirit; there was no denying that. I asked the staff to give us samples of each course and put them in a "doggie bag," which we were going to take back to Dennis and Emilia. After only two hours we silently returned to our hotel and went up to our rooms without much ado. Now I only had one more thing to do. From the front desk I called up Emilia to let her know that dinner was on its way. It took a long time for them to get the phone. I immediately regretted disturbing them unnecessarily. Apparently both of them had already been sleeping and here I was waking them up with my phone call...

"Hello," I heard a sleepy voice say on the phone. "What's up?"

"Emilia, it's me. I'm sorry I woke you up. I've got the food."

"Oh, yes, the food. Thank you, Arthur, but we're not hungry anymore. Just tired."

"I understand, Emilia. I'm sorry. Well, see you tomorrow. Good night."

The food I brought from the gourmet restaurant eventually wound up with the Columbian night watchman who thanked me effusively. I went to my room deep in thought and lay down on my bed. It had been an eventful day. I was physically exhausted but my mind was still churning. Only after I had said a prayer for Dennis, asking that his pain might be relieved, was I able to let go and, with some effort, fall asleep.

The next morning Juan wanted to join us in doing the Stations of the Cross before we departed for Lourdes. So bright and early we went up the mountain where the Stations of the Cross are located. Once again, Emilia took Dennis up to the altar to Mary, to which he bade farewell for the last time. An hour later we were all sitting on the bus, on our way to France. Dennis seemed to be much calmer than the previous day—at least that was the impression he gave. At any rate, I knew why. Once we had crossed into France, I turned around and asked him, "Well, old pal, you OK?" He didn't say a word but gave me two thumbs up.

Now we were heading down a mountain. Barely an hour had passed and we could already make out the little town of Lourdes down in the valley. You could see churches and steeples and even the little river Gave de Pau, fed by the melting mountain snows. This little town is 1377 ft (420 m) above sea level and was a sleepy little village until 1858. Today it boasts a population of 15,000, features hotels with a total of 30,000 beds, and reports six million overnight stays a year. This tremendous interest is generated by a series of events that took place from February to July 1858, and which enchanted all of Christendom. During those months the Blessed Mother appeared to fourteen-year old Bernadette Soubirous eighteen times in the Grotto of Massabielle, near the river. On Thursday, February 25, 1858, three hundred people witnessed as

Bernadette, directed by the Blessed Mother, discovered the bubbling springs. Used by millions of people a year for drinking and bathing, these waters are responsible for countless miraculous healings. In the 145 years since this town has been a place of pilgrimage, at least 6,500 cases of miraculous healing have been recorded here, although the Church officially recognizes only sixty-six of them. The last miraculous healing was that of Jean-Pierre Bely, a man suffering from multiple sclerosis, who came to Lourdes in a wheelchair in 1987. After attending Mass he had a "feeling of being released," as he described it. Case in point, on his journey home he was able to board the train without any help.

When we drove into town around noon, Dennis said to me, "Boy, is it crowded here." "You bet," I replied. "This place is hopping in May. It's an especially good month for pilgrimages to Lourdes." The first thing we did was check into our hotel, the Saint Saveur, which is located very conveniently right across from the entrance to the Compound of the Basilica of the Rosary. Processions of Light take place at Lourdes as well—every evening at 9 o'clock—and are even grander and more impressive than at Fatima. But sadly, Dennis, who I had hoped would join us, was no longer able to participate—not even in his wheelchair. We had only been traveling for six days but in his condition he must have felt like we had been traveling for weeks or months. He was now drawing on his last bit of strength. Apparently he had used up much of his stamina at Torreciudad. Nevertheless, he had an intensely peaceful look about him, radiating a magical serenity that nothing could shake. While our group of pilgrims was eagerly soaking up everything, especially moved by the locations where Saint Bernadette saw the appearances, Dennis stayed at the hotel. He was quietly sitting in his wheelchair when I visited him that first afternoon at Lourdes.

"Dennis, have you done the baths yet?" It took a long time for him to raise his head and look at me incredulously. Then he slowly said:

"Baths? Why should I do the baths? No, Arthur, I'm not interested in those baths."

"Excuse me? You don't want to do those healing baths?" His answer couldn't have been more cut and dry:

"No."

I must admit that I was at first stupefied. After all, Millions of people from all over the world, some of them with incurable diseases come to Lourdes every year for that very reason. They are brought there in wheelchairs, even in rolling beds, with the vague hope of being healed. That is what I had been thinking of. But I didn't mention it.

"Arthur, you're judging me just like you did at the beginning of this trip. Don't say a word. I can tell by that look what you're thinking."

The more I thought about it, the more I realized he was right. My thoughts had been wrapped around myself, not focused on him.

"Arthur, I don't need any miraculous healing. I *am* healed. I told you at Torreciudad: I've brought my life to a close. I am going home reconciled. The Mother of God has determined the path that her Son has already prepared for me. I am going in peace."

His long, thin fingers reached for my hand and he squeezed it as hard as he could.

"Arthur, my dear friend. I regard it as a late blessing in my life that I had the privilege of meeting you. You're a good guy. I wish there were more people like you. But you need to let me go my own way now, the way the Lord has destined for me. Don't be frightened when I tell you that the coffin is the cradle of life. Death is liberating. I know what I need to know. This trip will soon be ending and the other trip, the Big One, will soon begin."

With that, he let go of my hand and turned away. He already seemed to no longer be of this world.

On our last evening at Lourdes I handed out, as always, my little presents, those Pictures of the Saints that I always have made by Olaf, my friend in Frankfurt. I gave one to Dennis, too. When I came up to him at the table, he took the picture of the saint, carefully holding it in his hands, looked up to me, and winked. He didn't say a word. What should he have said anyway? I already knew what he meant.

The next morning our motorcoach drove us to Pau, where a few years ago they built an airport just for pilgrims traveling to Lourdes. Here our trip came to an end. Once we all had our baggage and had said goodbye to our bus driver, we went over to Departures and checked in. Fifty-two passengers were scheduled to fly to Chicago; only one was on his way to Frankfurt. The time to say farewell had come.

Believe me, these moments are always the most difficult ones for me. Pilgrimages are hard work, but you get to know people pretty well during those few days. You eat together, pray together and, yes, you sometimes even cry together. These are bonding experiences. And so, with a heavy heart, I went from one person to the next, shook hands, hugged people, gave a word of encouragement here and there, wrote down my address in countless notebooks, and received a number of business cards. At the end of the line I was drawn to Dennis. There he sat in his wheelchair, motionless, once again wearing that horrible facemask and his broad-brimmed hat. I leaned down to him, pressed my cheek to his and whispered into his ear:

"Good bye, my dear friend. When you get there, give my regards to the Man Upstairs. I'll be joining you before long. Make sure they let me in."

When I straightened up, he shook both my hands. His face didn't show any signs of sadness. Rather, it was beaming with a kind of relaxed and relieved joy. I turned away, took my suitcase and started wheeling it to the gate. After walking about fifty feet (ten to twenty meters) I stopped, turned around, and waved to Dennis. He waved back, raised his right hand and gave me a thumbs up.

Thumbs up.

Yes, Dennis, thumbs up, Dennis. Go with God, Vaya con Dios!

Four weeks later, in July 2006, I received a letter from Father John Grigus. He told me that Dennis Yosick had died peacefully on June 29, 2006, the Day of St. Peter and Paul. Juan and his wife Erin attended the funeral. They were also present when the coffin was closed.

A few weeks later I received thus letter from Emilia, Dennis' widow. She wrote me the following:

Dear Arthur,

Please forgive me that I haven't gotten back to you until now, but I understand that Father Grigus has already informed you about the passing of Dennis. After these strenuous months I needed a few days off, so I only now have returned to the empty house in Chicago. Yes, it is lonely without Dennis. I miss him very much, even though death was a relief for him. The committal took place with very few people attending. A few relatives, a few former coworkers, Juan, Erin, and a few neighbors were there. I still go to his grave every day and talk to him.

After we had returned from the pilgrimage, our physician prescribed him stronger medication. The old prescription didn't work that well anymore. Besides, he wanted to try something else to help Dennis. But Dennis refused everything. He gave everything over to God and our Blessed Mother, as was his custom... But at the very end his pain must have been intolerable, despite the medication. One day he told me: "I must have done something terrible that I have to endure such pain." I told him that he is not suffering for his sins but for the sins of us all. He just accepted that comment and didn't mention it any more. He simply accepted his suffering as the will of God. Only a few days before his death he told me that he didn't know how much longer he would be able to bear that cross. Thank God, it didn't go on too much longer. Dennis insisted that I take him to the hospital. He told a friend of ours he did not want to die at home because I would be alone and he wanted to spare me that strain. He died quietly while I prayed the Chaplet of Divine Mercy with him at 5:15 am on the Feast of St. Peter and Paul. He had fallen asleep peacefully. May God have mercy on his soul.

Farewell.

Sincerely yours, Emilia Yosick

Every time I enter the dining hall of the *Saint Sauveur* hotel at Lourdes—and that is at least five times a year—I can't help looking over to the corner where Dennis sat at our farewell dinner, when I was handing out the pictures of the saints. I always get goose bumps because I can just picture him sitting there, waiting his turn. Faithful Dennis!

Angels' Voices at Dachau

*Most of the trips that I organize turn out the way they were origi-
nally planned. But sometimes things take a different turn. Every
once in a while—out of the blue—a normal trip can take a totally
different tack.*

*I'd like to tell you a story about how the entrancing voices of
a choir created a magical moment at a very powerful location.
What began as a routine trip turned into a journey that brought
two nations closer together.*

* * *

Roman Catholic Church choirs are quite popular in many countries around the world and in the United States as well, where they
enjoy an excellent reputation. In fact, almost 500,000 Americans
find a deeper meaning in life by devoting some of their spare time
to a local choir. Church choirs draw immense crowds. It would
be an interesting exercise for all of us to contemplate why this is
the case.

In the summer of 2007 I was standing at Arrivals at Frankfurt's
Rhine-Main airport, waiting to pick up a men's and women's
choir from Madison, Wisconsin. Twenty-nine men and women
were scheduled to go on a two-week tour of southern Germany,
Switzerland, and Austria, and to give concerts in select churches.
A group of practicing Catholics who enjoy each other's company
and love to sing, the Madison Diocesan Choir is one of the most
prestigious Catholic choirs in the United States. These gifted choristers from every level of society meet several times a week for
rehearsals at Madison's Bishop O'Connor Catholic Center, where
they also perform. On this particular trip they were expanding
their horizons, planning to pay the Old Country a visit. In fact,
they had even engaged a special concert agency in England to co-
ordinate their performances on this, their *Alpine Voices Tour 2007*.

Their plane landed earlier than expected. Apparently tail winds
had given them an extra boost. Being a tour guide for so many

years, I have learned to "roll with the punches," and so I was already standing by. The bus scheduled to take us to Köln (Cologne) was ready to roll as well.

The first few hours of such trips with people coming in from transatlantic flights are always a mixed bag of exhaustion—and the sheer joy of arrival. And so, as our motorcoach headed towards the autobahn towards Cologne, some choristers fell asleep within minutes, whereas others were already engaged in deep conversation about their first impressions of the trip. By early afternoon we had arrived at the metropolis on the Rhine. The impressive sight of the twin spires of Cologne's famous Gothic Kölner Dom (Cathedral of Cologne) coming into view silenced every conversation. All you could hear now was muted ooohs, aaahs and some muffled mumbling all the way to the hotel. It seemed that the sight of that cathedral made a deep impression on them.

There is probably not another city in the world where the residents have formed such a deep relationship with their main place of worship as have the people of Cologne with its population of over one million. The Kölner Dom, one of the largest cathedrals in the world, is the heartbeat of this city. Having escaped the war relatively unscathed and sticking out of a sea of rubble, in the spring of 1945 the cathedral's twin steeples loomed into the sky like a huge memorial. To the civilian population, which by then had survived hundreds of air raids, this towering ruin seemed to be sign from heaven: "What goes around, comes around..."

Now, in the early 21st century, the Cologne Cathedral--at 500 ft (157 m) the second tallest cathedral in the world--is arguably the center of Catholicism in Germany.

After a quick break at our hotel, I got the choir to the church on time. That particular day was a Saturday. Accompanied by the mighty cathedral organ, this was to be the Madison Diocesan Choir's premiere performance in Germany. As we stepped into the long nave, which seemed to go on forever, we saw that the wooden pews were already full of people. I know my way around that cathedral pretty well, so I led my little flock directly to a side gallery near the main altar. Considering the enormity and majesty of the sanctuary and the high expectations of the many believers in attendance, some of the choristers were feeling a bit apprehensive. I wanted to give them the opportunity to rehearse a little, something Patrick Gorman, the director of the choir, had asked me to try and arrange. He wanted them to be able to rehearse at least one or two hymns "to limber up their voices," as he called it.

I started to walk over to the sacristy to discuss the logistics of the concert with the head sexton, but was prevented from doing so. About half a dozen sextons, all wearing red silk albs, and then a number of cathedral staff blocked my access. I was dumbfounded. Didn't these people know that an American choir would be singing here in just a few moments? It certainly seemed so… We tour guides are usually a persistent bunch. We've *got* to be or else we'd rarely accomplish the task at hand. So I tried turning on my good ol' charm—and I guess my persuasiveness saved the day. A few minutes later, I had managed to work my way through to the head sexton and asked him whether he would please allow the choir to rehearse for a few minutes.

"*You've* got nerve," he snapped at me. "Today is Saturday and we'll be having Confession shortly. I would think you would know that there must be absolute silence during Confession." Waved his arms wildly, this rude and impatient gentleman demanded that I immediately clear the choir out of the gallery. I guess I must have come on a bit too strong, which triggered his heated reaction.

"And besides, our Rosary devotion starts in fifteen minutes," he added, now having calmed down a bit. "Please bring your choir over here to the sacristy. From here you'll walk up to the organ that is located under the roof. Your people will be singing up there. There's a rehearsal room up with musical instruments in it." I bit my tongue to keep from blurting out something that I might have regretted and led the group through the sacristy to the gallery of the "Swallow's Nest organ," also known as the "Langhaus Organ". It wasn't until later that we discovered that we could have taken an elevator up. So we dragged ourselves up the many stone steps, up through the narrow and stuffy stairwell. "This trip is getting off to a *great* start…" I thought to myself. The first impression my tour group was getting was anything but friendly.

The Rosary devotion was still going on when the organist finally arrived. This was where he went about his daily work—way up here, three stories above the congregation. Thankfully, this gentleman was a horse of a different color, greeting us in a very friendly way—the epitome of good cooperation. It just goes to show that you can accomplish a lot more with a smile on your face and a song in your heart than when you crack down on people with the Law. The Divine Service started at 6 p.m. sharp. Three priests served Holy Communion, accompanied by the dramatic sounds of the massive organ and the festive voices from Wisconsin.

Their first hymn was somewhat halting, but by the second one they had apparently gotten over the snags we had run into earlier. The love with which these people sang filled the entire sanctuary and seemed to impress one and all. In fact, Glenn Schuster, the choir's organist, was even allowed to play two hymns at the organ, even though he had never practiced on it. For him, this was a special moment--one that he holds dear and for which he thanked me profusely. "Don't thank *me*, Glen, thank the cathedral organist. *He* was the one who made this all possible," I replied.

After the service I led my *Alpine Voices* back to the hotel. They were now at ease but still somewhat bushed. *Rheinischer Sauerbraten* with potato dumplings, red cabbage, and freshly drawn *Kölsch* beer let the day end on a more or less happy note after all. The next day, our local guide, Gertrud—a real "classic" from Cologne—showed us her city and all the things that make it special. We visited three museums—the Wallraff-Richartz Museum, the Romano-Germanic Museum and, finally, the Chocolate Museum. That last one in particular was most appreciated, since visitors get free samples of the chocolate made on-site.

The next morning we drove along the Rhine to St. Goarshausen, where we boarded a riverboat. I figured that taking a river cruise would be a fun way to show my guests this most magnificent stretch of the Rhine. On the way to our point of departure, we stopped for a while at the famous Loreley Rock, a steep shale pinnacle that soars 420 feet (130 m) over the Rhine River far below. The view was breath-taking and their digital cameras were going full blaze. After a few minutes I had to prod them along because we had a tight itinerary to keep, which, among other things, included lunch in Rüdesheim. That same afternoon we still wanted to make it to Freiburg im Breisgau. The Black Forest is one of the nicest areas in Germany, both as far as climate and the landscape are concerned. "So far, so good," I thought: "After that initial bump, up to now our trip has been as harmonious and the camaraderie as close as you could ever wish for."

This tour group, a choir of practicing Catholics, was on its very best behavior. They were curious, yet modest, took part in every Mass and every Eucharist, and were respectful toward everything new. As far as I was concerned, these people were most impressive "ambassadors of the faith." They shared with everyone their gift of sacred song, which I personally was beginning to "get into" more and more each day.

From the many conversations I was having with their choir director and with them, I knew that their main goal was more than just singing hymns. These people were on a personal mission. They had a message for their listeners. From childhood on, we sober-minded central Europeans learn to communicate mainly through language. So when we hear hymns, we mainly focus on the words. But we seem to have lost the insight that music, and singing in particular, "speaks" its own language. Music is simple, natural, direct, and universal. Everyone can understand it. If you understand music correctly, it goes straight to your heart. It can convey joy and love but also difficult feelings such as grief and mercy.

The longer I was traveling with this choir and the more I was becoming familiar with their hymns, the more I began to incorporate this new channel of communication. Famous violinist Yehudi Menuhin once called music "a form of communication, a universal mother tongue." What a beautiful way to express this concept! Each day I was starting to comprehend this mystery a little bit better, as I was slowly being drawn into what these twenty-nine men and women singers were attempting to convey.

By 8 p.m. that evening we had arrived in the quaint town of Freiburg, a city proud of its tradition of freedom and its renowned university. The next day our choir was scheduled to give an *a cappella* concert in the Münster, Freiburg's cathedral. The night was peaceful, perhaps also due to the fact that we had all partaken of the fruit of the sun-drenched vineyards of Baden, which sent us off to dreamland rather quickly.

The next morning we had a bit of local politics to tend to. The city council and Lord Mayor of Freiburg had invited us to a champagne reception in city hall. After some chit-chat, they took us on a tour of the city. In contrast to Cologne, the choir was treated with the utmost respect, the citizens of Freiburg doing everything in their power to make the choristers' work as pleasant as possible. After the city tour we returned to the cathedral square, the Münsterplatz. A visit to Freiburg would not be complete without touring the Münster. This gorgeous Gothic sanctuary was built in the 12th century and its 380 ft (116 m) tall spire still dominates the cityscape. Some of the choristers wanted to tour the interior of the sanctuary and a few of the more daring even desired to climb the stairs to the top of the steeple. I declined, having done that years earlier—a little hike that required quite a bit of fortitude, I might add. You have to scale some five hundred steps up a winding staircase while hugging the wall to let oncoming traffic by—or you'll cause a traffic jam. While ascending the staircase, you peek out little open windows and can see the square far below getting smaller and smaller. No sir, no need for *this* old tour guide to try that one again…

Our plan was to let the angelic voices of our choir make the noon service in the Münster an unforgettable experience for the citizens of Freiburg. We got there on time and I joined the congregation, which had already filled up the cathedral quite nicely. I don't remember the minutiae of the service as such, but I *do* remember that it was interspersed by chorales and hymns, and that towards the end the service the choir gave a splendid rendition of *I Heard the Voice of Jesus Say.*

Even by the end of the first verse I was close to tears. Patrick and his choir sang with such intensity and force—penetrating the soul—that I could hardly stand it:

"I heard the voice of Jesus say, "Come unto Me and rest; Lay down, thou weary one, lay down Thy head upon My breast.' I came to Jesus as I was, weary and worn and sad, I found in Him a resting place, and He has made me glad."

It is strange how, on some days, a huge "musical instrument" such as a choir can produce tones that do not seem to be from this world. That's what happened on that particular day. I didn't know how and why, but it did. Their next hymn was *Teach Me Your Way, O Lord*. How could that second verse in particular fail to touch anyone?

"When fear assails my heart, teach me Your way.
When worries me besiege, teach me Your way.
Painful and joyful days, stormy and sun-filled days,
Let me in You rejoice, and hear Your voice

Their last piece was a musical version of Ps 116, after which they sang the *Litany of the Saints*. The concert was received with thunderous applause and I wouldn't be surprised if Freiburg will remember that performance for a long, long time to come.

The next morning we headed toward Switzerland. After passing Basle, the Alps starting coming into view. To the amazement of our group, the mountains seemed to eerily grow out of the horizon. Of course, many of our choristers were familiar with the Rocky Mountains, which are even higher, but somehow the Alps are different—not as widely spaced as the ranges of the Rockies. With their narrow valleys and all squeezed together in a relatively small area, somehow these central European mountains leave an even greater impression on the soul. To add to the mystery and magic, for so many Americans the Alps seem to be the stuff of fairy tales. Once we had passed Zurich, the peaks loomed ever larger. Soon we could make out the dark green water of Lake Lucerne (*Vierwaldstättersee*). Our destination was the town of Lucerne, which seems to dominate this magnificent lake. I had planned a two-day mini vacation for our group in this unique landscape. No sightseeing, no singing, just rest and relaxation—with plenty of shopping and delicious food.

On the other side of the lake lies *Bürgenstock*, a peak that a few years ago was transformed into one of the most prominent tourist spots in all of Switzerland. Up there tourists can choose between hiking paths, a cog railroad, or a paved road that will take them up to this vacation paradise. Up at the summit, three five-star hotels, an internationally acclaimed golf course, plus a number of world-class restaurants promise a most enjoyable stay. *Bürgenstock* is one of the centers of world-class Swiss gastronomy. Wistfully, I looked up and recalled how, forty-one years earlier, I had taken a hotel management class one unforgettable summer, before my wanderlust led me to the United States and then on to South America. Somewhere up there were memories of a wonderful season, full of ease and the joy of life. I walked back to our motorcoach feeling somewhat melancholy and pensive, not wanting to explain to the group why I was feeling so blue. So, to take my mind off the past, I launched into the history of *Kloster* (cloister) *Einsiedel.*

Kloster Einsiedel is an old Benedictine abbey dating back to the 9th century. Wanting to lead a pious and God-pleasing life, a monk by the name of Meinrad founded this hermitage in 835. Today some eighty monks live in this active cloister, which was established soon after the Meinrad era. The cloister also operates a humanist *Gymnasium* (a type of high school), well-known beyond the borders of Switzerland. A thousand years after the hermitage was founded, German immigrants established a Benedictine cloister, St. Meinrad Archabbey, in St. Meinrad, Indiana, which to this day is in close contact with the Swiss monks.

The road leading up to Einsiedel was tough going for our bus because a bad thunderstorm the night before had uprooted countless trees and even triggered a few mudslides. But the folk living up in these altitudes are accustomed to the whims of nature. They simply hauled out their shovels and brooms and in no time had swept the mud off the roads. In the center of *Kloster Einsiedel* lies an ornate church in the Baroque style, complete with frescoes and beautifully sculptured ornaments. We arrived just as the "Angel's Bells" (*Angelusläuten*) were ringing, which left no time for the choir to warm up. We filed out of the bus and walked over to the colorful Rococo altar. The *Alpine Voices* gave a majestic rendition of *Dixit Maria*, followed by *Praise Ye the Lord.* Once again, I had the privilege of hearing these now familiar hymns, but in this little sanctuary they sounded different from the cathedrals of Cologne or Freiburg. I submit that there is such a thing as a *genius loci*, that is, depending on the location, a kind of special spirit that melds with the art practiced at that particular place. Without microphones or amplifiers and just equipped with the power of their voices, this magnificent choir let us experience the magic of song. Pat, their director, was beaming, extremely pleased with their achievement. They had left an impression that would not soon be forgotten.

The little noon-day concert, which had barely lasted thirty minutes, gave us enough time to get to Munich that same day. There were many sights to enjoy along the way: Liechtenstein, Lake Constance (*Bodensee*), and the beautiful town of Bregenz, Austria, where we stopped for a bite to eat. That evening we reached Munich and I had to think of German author Thomas Mann who used to live here and who coined the phrase *München leuchtet* ("Munich shines"). Yes, even today that still rings true. Somehow this city *does* "shine." Munich has a special spirit that is hard to describe. The capital of Bavaria epitomizes a feeling of joyful energy, an atmosphere that you feel in the little side streets and in the beer cellars. I like visiting this city and I would even consider living there if it weren't so pricey. For this very reason many *Münchner* choose not to live in town but rather in one of adjacent counties such as Dachau. The next day we toured the city—a delightful blend of the traditional and cutting edge, of *Lederhosen* (traditional leather knickerbockers) and laptops. Without a doubt, Munich has managed to embrace globalization without losing its venerable traditions.

High-spirited and in a great mood, we continued on to Dachau that afternoon, a county seat only some 15 miles (25 km) northwest of Munich, right off the autobahn to Augsburg. I wouldn't be surprised if Dachau were better known in the United States than in Germany. The American travel agency that I worked with on this trip had included a visit in Dachau's former concentration camp on our itinerary.

The construction of this particular *KZ* or *Konzentrationslager* (concentration camp), as these camps are called in German, was ordered by Germany's National Socialist Party only a few days after Hitler took office on January 30, 1933, making Dachau the German Reich's oldest concentration camp. It is not of the same ilk as the gruesome death camps of Auschwitz, Treblinka or Sobibor in Eastern Europe. Rather, in the early years of the *Drittes Reich* (Third Reich), Dachau was built as a "re-education camp," a labor camp for the enemies of the NS regime: Communists, Social Democrats, union members, and even the homeless, all of whom were condemned to forced labor. Later inmates included practicing Christians, Sinti and Roma ("Gypsies"), Jews, Jehovah's Witnesses, Bible scholars, homosexuals, and common criminals.

These prisoners built roads, slaved in gravel pits or dug out rock quarries but were also put to work as skilled laborers. By 1942 the Holocaust had moved into full gear and doctors were starting to conduct medical experiments on the inmates. Human beings were now being tested on how well they could tolerate various levels of hypothermia, low pressure or high altitude pressure. The number of victims is not known, although it is estimated that between 30,000 and 50,000 people were murdered at Dachau. Amazingly, the concentration camp is located only about three quarters of a mile (1 km) from the center of the town of Dachau.

Today a well-paved county road goes right by the concentration camp for more than half a mile (1 km). When you contemplate the proximity of the town of Dachau to the concentration camp, it is hard to imagine that the local population did not know what was going on behind those walls.

By the spring of 1945, American troops were coming ever closer. In order to prevent their convicts from being liberated, the guards decided to flee with the majority of the prisoners, forcing them to march great distances. But even the strongest and healthiest of the inmates were so undernourished that hardly a single inmate survived those marches. Most of them just collapsed and died by the side of the road, where they were simply left behind, like trash tossed out a car window.

On April 29, 1945, the 45th Infantry Division of the 7th U.S. Army liberated the camp. What the American troops found was truly hell on earth. Indescribable suffering as far as the eye could see: hollow-eyed, emaciated human beings who barely had the strength to greet their liberators.

Several times a day the memorial shows a documentary in German and in English with actual footage of those gruesome scenes.

On our way to Dachau I prepared my group as well as I could for what I knew was awaiting them. In broad strokes I told them the history of Nazi Germany, the story of the Holocaust, and the Dachau concentration camp—at least as far as I was familiar with it. Over and over they interrupted me with questions that all boiled down to the same thing: "Why in heaven's name didn't the German people rise up against this dictatorship?" I wanted be as explicit as I could: "But we *did* attempt to overthrow Hitler!" It is ironic that Nazi propaganda has apparently succeeded in embedding itself in so many people's minds, in the sense that the many unsuccessful attempts on Hitler's life were concealed back then and are still largely unknown even today.

In actual fact, there were a quite number of resistance fighters—not just those with which many Americans are familiar, such as the famous *July 20 Plot* of 1944. For instance, there was the *Weiße Rose* (White Rose) group led by Hans and Sophie Scholl, siblings and confessing Christians. A few years ago an excellent movie about their resistance work came out: *Sophie Scholl—The Final Days*. Then there was the *Rote Kapelle* (Red Orchestra), a Communist resistance group. All told, over the years there were a total of *thirty-eight* attempts on Hitler's life. Even as early as 1921, some twelve years before he rose to power, unknown assassins attempted to kill Hitler in Munich. Apparently, even back then, some astute people could see the handwriting on the wall. Someone in a crowd in Tübingen took a shot at Hitler in 1923. Over the years there was a long and disappointing history of attempts to assassinate the tyrant. After every single one of them failed, it comes as no surprise that in his twisted mind Hitler thought he was "protected by divine Providence," as that madman once put it.

"When we get to Dachau," I told the choristers, "you'll see a prison cell that held a very special inmate for a number of years. His name was Georg Elser. In 1939 this man took a Herculean task upon himself: to rid the world of the monster Adolf Hitler. This attempt failed as well. But even today, Elser's act of bravery has hardly ever been adequately recognized. In fact, two out of three Germans have never heard of him.

Personally, Elser's act of courage has always impressed me. That's why I would like to share his story with you.

Georg Elser was a simple man, a watchmaker from southwestern Germany. An adamant opponent of National Socialism practically from Day One, not only did he despise Hitler's stiff-armed salute, he hated the entire system. In early 1938 Elser resolved to assassinate Hitler because he was convinced that his regime would unleash a terrible war. Elser's plan was to exploit an Achilles' Heel of the Nazis: their proclivity to celebrate important anniversaries of the "movement." To commemorate the 16th anniversary of his unsuccessful Beer Hall Putsch on November 9, 1923, at Munich's *Bürgerbräukeller*, Hitler once again wanted to give a speech at that very same location, as he did every year on that day. Right by the podium where the *Führer* was going to be delivering his speech there was a stone pillar. Elser's plan was to lodge a bomb inside it. The preparations for the assassination took almost a whole year. In order to acquire the necessary explosives, Elser took a job in a rock quarry. Once he had secured the explosives, he rented an apartment, which he turned into a workshop. Here he did various experiments with detonators. His nosey neighbors once asked what he was up to, but Elster satisfied their curiosity by claiming that he was an inventor. Months before the day of the assassination he started taking his modest evening meals at the *Bürgerbräukeller*. Every night he would wait for a good opportunity to sneak into a broom closet or the men's room just before closing time. When they had locked up for the night and the whole place was dark, Elser snuck out of his hiding place and started to hollow out the pillar behind Hitler's podium. This he did for a total of thirty nights, after which he had finally gotten the hole large enough that he could hide his bomb in it. Once that was done, he plastered the hole shut and painted it, so it would no longer be detectable. Knuckling down, Elser was able to complete his work by November 8, 1939, just one day before Hitler was to give his speech. A couple of times he had almost been found out and barely managed to escape detection. Like the clockmaker he was, Elser had timed the explosion with precision: The bomb was scheduled to go off on November 9 at 9:30 p.m.

So that evening everything goes according to plan. The bomb detonates in a mighty explosion. It devastates the restaurant, killing eight people, and injuring sixty-three, sixteen of them seriously. But Hitler escapes unscathed. You see, the *Führer* had decided to return to Berlin after the speech. But due to poor weather he had decided to take the train instead of a plane, so he shortened his speech by a few minutes, leaving the *Bürgerbräukeller* at 9:07 p.m. — exactly thirteen minutes before the bomb went off.

So that same evening Elser tries to escape to Switzerland but is arrested by border guards in Konstanz. They take him back to

Munich, then transfer him to Berlin where is interrogated by the *Gestapo.* Strangely enough, they do not execute him. They want to "save" him to stage a trial at a later date, which is why they shuffle him from one concentration camp to another over the years. When, in the spring '45, it became clear that Nazi Germany was about to lose the war, in the very cell you are going to see in a few minutes—they shot him in the back of the neck.

All the investigations by the Nazis at that time but also by German historians years later arrived at the same conclusion: This slight 35-year old would-be assassin carried out his attack single-handedly, without any outside assistance. To this day, Elser remains a tragic figure, even more than half a century after the war. No statues, no commemorative stamps, no Day of Remembrance—nothing. Only some fifty years after his death did people in Germany start to take notice of him. For example, German director Karl-Maria Brandauer made a very good movie on Elser and his largely unknown assassination attempt on Hitler."

By the time I had finished my story, we had already arrived at the Dachau concentration camp, turning onto the parking lot next to the memorial. Our choristers, who had earlier been in a terrific mood during our drive, had become noticeably quiet. People were now huddled in small groups, discussing what I had just told them. Maybe these personal statements do some good after all, I thought to myself. And even if all I do is to change a few prejudices some people might have.

To enter the concentration camp, you have to walk under a sign at the main gate declaring, *"Arbeit macht frei,"* ("Work liberates"), a slogan dripping with cynicism and cruelty. As soon as we walked into the exhibition, you could have cut the tension in our group with a knife. We looked at clothing, uniforms, and equipment from the Dachau concentration camp, a morbid place that attracts 800,000 visitors a year. After watching a documentary, we went over to the religious memorials located at the end of the camp, the so-called *Denominational Monuments*: a Russian Orthodox chapel, a Protestant church, a Jewish memorial, and a Catholic chapel. All of these memorials were quite small and modest. In 1964, a Catholic convent of the "Sacred Blood of the Carmelite" was erected right behind the religious memorials. Nuns now live here behind closed doors and for the rest of their lives pray for the poor souls of all those who were brutalized here and died. A chapel invites visitors to pause and pray, an opportunity of which we wanted to avail ourselves, kneeling and silently turning to the Lord. Then we all stepped outside. Intuitively the choir started to assemble and slowly, pensively started to sing. What happened next was one of the most intense moments I have ever experienced in my whole life. With incredible tenderness and respect, the choristers began to softly sing the *Prayer of Saint Francis: Lord, Make Me an Instrument of Thy Peace.*

> *Lord, make me an instrument of Thy peace*
> *Where there is hatred, let me sow love;*
> *Where there is injury, pardon;*
> *Where there is doubt, faith;*
> *Where there's despair, hope;*
> *Where there is darkness, light;*
> *And where there is sadness, joy.*
>
> *O Divine Master,*
> *Grant that I may not so much*
> *Seek to be consoled as to console;*
> *To be understood, as to understand;*
> *To be loved as to love.*
>
> *For it is in giving that*
> *We receive,*
> *It is in pardoning*
> *That we are pardoned.*
> *And it is in dying*
> *That we are born to Eternal Life.*
> *Amen.*

Strangely enough, this beautiful prayer by no means disturbed the quiet of the Carmelite convent. On the contrary, it enhanced the hush of this strange place in a mystical way--in a way that I wouldn't have thought possible. And once again I felt what I had been moving closer to that entire trip. When location and music are fused so brilliantly, as they were right there at the edge of a former concentration camp, something new is created— a kind of fourth dimension, far removed from place, time, and thought... something magical. Lyrics and melody exuded such intensity that no one was able to escape their grasp. One of our travelers, Tom Eichmann, an American of German descent (who, by the way, has nothing whatsoever to do with Nazi mass murderer Otto Adolf Eichmann), sang bass and his deep melodic voice kept on repeating the chorus.

After the last note of the hymn had faded away, we remained suspended in time—frozen like statues. No one dared move a muscle. The angelic voices of this choir had united us and I noticed that everyone had tears running down their faces. Then, after observing about two minutes of silence, these gentle people all hugged, wiped the tears from their eyes, and slowly trekked back to the bus.

What had happened here? Had we only heard a hymn? Or was there something more going on here? Probably both things at once. We *had* heard a hymn, but at the same time perceived something else: There *are* people who in their love remember the ineffable suffering of others and—may I even dare express it?—are willing to reach out to us Germans and to our descendants with the hand of forgiveness and reconciliation.

The remaining stops of our trip could not live up to the powerful emotions of Dachau. We visited Altötting, Germany's most famous pilgrimage site, then Marktl am Inn, the birthplace of Pope Benedict XVI, followed by Austrian cities of Salzburg and their capital, Vienna. But nothing was able to top Dachau.

After fourteen eventful days, the *Alpine Voices* returned to the United States.

As we were saying our goodbyes at the airport, Pat Gorman, their director, gave me several sheets of paper with handwritten notes on them—his impressions and thoughts during that impromptu concert in Dachau. These are his words:

"First, we prayed in the chapel. I knelt but had no words to pray. Leaving, I hope that God would grant me grace to know to pray. We gathered in the small convent courtyard to sing: I chose the 'Prayer of Saint Francis'! We sang a lovely unpublished setting by William Beckstrand. I hoped that the words and music would be respectful for all people of good will.

The Choir began rather tentatively. I briefly worried that they might falter, but soon I heard and saw that they recognized how special this was to stand feet from a Dachau guard tower and pray for peace and self-denial. Clearly the choir got stronger as the piece unfolded.

I looked at each singer while we sang – some had tears, others looked serious. But all looked profoundly moved.

When the singing ended there was only silence – no applause, no talking. All who sang and all who listened knew better. It was not a performance, but a prayer – for those who died, those who lived, and those who need to remember.

As I conducted, thoughts raced through my head. Could I have survived? Would I have resisted? What does Dachau and other such camps compel me to do today? Do I need to speak more critically and vociferously? About the war in Iraq? About ongoing racism and poverty? If places like Dachau are to mean anything, I probably should!

The choir went to Dachau and did the only thing they could – sing. I am hopeful that in some small way, the music of a group of Americans was pleasing to God and honored the memory of all who suffered in that horrible place."

Alfonso's Never-ending Death

In 1970, in a travel agency in Long Island, New York, I met a young lady from Colombia. Her name was Inez Piedad Amaya. It didn't take long before we fell in love and got married and moved to Bogotá, Colombia. At that time, my wife's sister, Fernanda Isabel, had already been married for several years to a certain Alfonso Valencia, thirty-one years old and a classic Latin American macho: brash, pompous, swaggering, and apt to look down on people. Whenever the whole family got together, Alfonso's showiness got on my nerves—big-time. When he was holding forth, everybody else shrunk to the role of potted plants or table decorations. His behavior upset me greatly, so I avoided him as much as I could. After a while, he noticed my reserve and actually sought out my friendship, and we gradually got to know one another better. As it turned out, there was a sensitive and intelligent person buried under all that bravado. Alfonso was beginning to fascinate me. In fact, over time, we actually became good friends. The following story took place exactly as I am about to tell you.

***

On September 21, 1980, a bright sunny day in Bogotá, Don Alfonso Valencia exited his luxurious penthouse. With measured step, he headed over to the elevator and rode down to the lobby of the well-guarded building, located in the prosperous northern part of the Colombian capital.

Exiting from the elevator, he scanned around for Juan, his uniformed guard, whom he had personally hired to ensure security. When he saw his employee, Don Alfonso calmly but decisively said, "Please give me the pistol, Juan."

"*Si, padron!*" the man replied obediently. The guard turned around, opened a cabinet, and unlocked a metal drawer. He removed a highly polished police revolver, a Smith & Wesson 38, which Alfonso had given the guard a few months earlier for safe-

146

keeping. Alfonso grasped the gun and flipped out the cylinder to make sure the pistol was actually loaded.

"Mmm, muy bien," he mumbled.

In South America a subordinate would never ask a superior *"Why?"* The absolute obedience customary in that culture would never permit such a question. So, Juan just snuck a peak at Don Alfonso as the *patron* turned on his heel and silently walked back to the elevator. Alfonso returned to his exquisite penthouse, which he had purchased for his family and himself a few years earlier for $800,000 USD. In addition to this penthouse, Alfonso also owned four other luxury apartments in the same building, which he rented out to well-to-do Colombians.

The *patron* opened the door to his residence and walked down the hall, decorated with exquisite works of art, as was the rest of the penthouse. As always when he walked down this hall, Alfonso glanced at the resplendent art work by Alejandro Obregón. Alfonso was proud of this famous painting, which he had bought from the master himself in the artist's Barranquilla home for $200,000 USD.

Alfonso strode into the bedroom that he shared with his wife Fernanda who had been staying with her parents for the past two days. He got undressed and entered the large bathroom, gripping the gun in his hand. He opened the shower cabinet that was embellished with gold décor, stepped in, and closed the heavy crystal doors. Then he stuck the barrel of the revolver deep into his mouth and pulled the trigger.

A few hours later, at 2 pm, Alfonso's 10 year-old daughter, Maria Fernanda, came home and found the bloody corpse of her father sprawled in the bathroom. He was only 41 years old. Alfonso had left nothing in his life to chance—most certainly not the time of his own death. Everything he had done had been well thought through and meticulously planned. Alfonso had never let anyone take the Law of Action away from him---not even in adversity and tragedy.

Rice

Who was this Alfonso Valencia?

Alfonso Valencia was born and raised in Bogotá, just like his father who had originally been a small-time farmer. Whenever people had asked his father what he did for a living, he explained that he was a "commerciante," a businessman whose exact type of business is unclear. Initially, Father was not fortuitous but he did manage to keep his family afloat with a steady flow of projects and dealings. Alfonso learned a lot from his dad. *Keep first things first. Stay practical. Be industrious, be determined, and keep at it.* Even as a young man, Alfonso had always wanted to hit it big. He didn't really know for what exact reason, but so many things in life have no explanation. His determination to get wealthy was a driving force, an inner power plant that never shut down. With an iron will to move up and beyond his modest background, Alfonso wanted to show the world he could make it. And he wouldn't quit until he had reached that goal. Eventually he did, in fact, reach that goal, even though he had to take several stabs at it along the way.

At the age of sixteen, Alfonso ran away from home. He and a friend worked their way down to Leticia, the southernmost town in Colombia. With a population of 35,000, Leticia in the mid 1950s was a medium-sized river port town on the Amazon, where Colombia, Brazil, and Peru meet. Back then, the livelihood of the population was still mostly dependent on rubber from the Amazon jungle, a one-time boom market whose demise was obvious even back then. Natural rubber was gradually being replaced by synthetics, which are a lot cheaper to produce. Leticia was well past its heyday. Today, the indians of Leticia live off fishing, the lumber trade, and now also tourism, which has become a key source of income.

Alfonso and his friend came into contact with the Ticuna Indians living in San Martin de Amacayacu, a small jungle village near Leticia. The young man's plan was to buy natural rubber from the Indians—or more precisely, to bilk them out of it. So they bought cheap mirrors, costume jewelry, and trinkets, which they tried to trade for the valuable raw material. But the days in which primitive natives could be duped with baubles and beads, were long gone. As such, the two would-be entrepreneurs had to admit that they had misjudged the whole situation and were forced to move on empty-handed. Alfonso and his friend parted ways and Alfonso returned home, to the City of Bogota, in 1955.

This episode taught Alfonso a lesson. He would have to plan his climb from rags to riches better. Rubber was no longer the key to success, that much was clear. The only path to riches in this dirt poor country would be in agriculture. At least that was what he thought. Two years later Alfonso made his second attempt. This time Alfonso headed for the center of Colombia's agriculture, a region known as the *Llanos Orientales* or Eastern Plains of Southern Colombia. This was an arid region southeast of the Cordillera of Bogotá. In those days, the *llanos* or prairies, as they are known in North America, were mostly uncultivated. This is where Alfonso decided to settle down. He moved to what was then the small town of Villavicencio, about 45 miles (75 km) southeast of Bogotá in the Departmento del Meta. Even today, this town is also known as La *Puerta al Llano* (Gateway to the Prairie). Located on the banks of the Guatiquia River, Villavicencio today has a population of 380,000. In the 1950s, many people were fleeing from Colombia's civil war to this desolate region, where they could find some safety from the on-going struggle between the National Liberation Army (FLN) and the Revolutionary Armed Forces of Columbia (FARC). This civil war was being waged without remorse and is, in fact, still continuing today. In those years, the economy of Villavicencio and the surrounding region was based on cattle ranching and dry rice farming.

Even though Alfonso had no experience in tropical agriculture, he was convinced that it was his future. He also realized that he would first have to know the lay of the land. So, drawing on the little bit of money he had borrowed from his brother, Alfonso found an inexpensive place to stay and explored the region for weeks in *La Chiva*, a rickety cross-country taxi bus. Squashed in between grunting pigs, squawking chickens, and Indios clutching pitiful burlap sacks, the occupants of the ramshackle bus bumped over dusty and sandy trails and through deep mud holes. This was pure torture for a middle class guy from the big city. But Alfonso patiently endured it all because he was focused on that one goal: to get rich. And rice would be his ticket to the Big Time, if only he could find the right kind of soil in which to grow it. After all, besides potatoes and corn, rice was and *is* Columbia's—even South America's—main staple. As such, supplying rice to a hungry and steadily growing population would be his straightest shot at fame and fortune.

And time would prove Alfonso's strategy right.

Over time, the young man got to know the back country better than almost anyone before him. In the *llanos*, the soil was uneven, hard, and rocky—basically not very well suited for rice agriculture. In fact, in some areas around Villavicencio, the soil was as hard as concrete. The merciless sun and almost total lack of rain had transformed this land into a stone desert. On one of those days, when all you could see was the brown earth and the shimmering waves of heat, when all you want to do was make a dash for the shade and a cool drink, Alfonso noticed a poor farmer trying to work the ground with a beat-up tractor and plow. It was December. 100 degrees (38C) in the shade, and the sun was mercilessly beating down on the field and the farmer. Arduously, the farmer lowered his old-fashioned plow to the ground and started to break up the hard dirt. But the ground was too resistant. As soon as the tractor began to pull, the plow flew apart like a dry piece of wood. This key event, which he would later tell his family over and over again, taught Alfonso that successful farming could not be achieved by conventional means—and not in this particular region either. Rather, the only way to grow rice out here would be to use every last ounce of his intelligence and ingenuity—and change location.

Although countless farmers in the *llanos* made a living growing dry rice, even back then Alfonso knew that he wouldn't get rich doing that. Rather, what he needed was *irrigated* land because the yield of rice in running water is ten-fold over that of dry rice. But building irrigation ditches would cost a lot of money and money was in short supply. So Alfonso kept on looking for the right farming land. Eventually he found the soil he was looking for some 190 miles (300 km) south of Villavicencio. In fact, this soil had never even been used agriculturally. And the best part of all was that the Rio Meta, the river that gave the *departmento* its name, was only a little more than a mile (2 km) away. *This* was what he had been looking for, soil that was softer and much more fertile than the soil around Villavicencio. *This* soil was dark—almost black—and richer in minerals than that depleted dirt he had been stuck with up to now.

It didn't take him long to find the owner of the land. It belonged to a doctor in Bogotá who wasn't the least bit interested in agriculture. Alfonso visited the man and shared with him his dream of growing desperately needed crops for food. In this way, Alfonso was able to lease the land cheaply. He started with twenty-three acres (50 ha) for only one year, paying the lease in advance with a pre-dated check. How to proceed next? He would start with dry rice and install the necessary irrigation once he had made enough money. With the signed contract in hand, Alfonso went to a mutual bank and took out a loan. That was how this business was done. Everybody took out loans, even people who didn't really need to. Next on his list, Alfonso would urgently need farming equipment. He would have to hire people, buy seed, fertilizer, pesticides, and so on. And, miracle of miracles—his plans were starting to work. After much toil and after depleting almost all of the capital he had borrowed, Alfonso managed to plant his rice seedlings. And, lo and behold, they were actually starting to grow. With every day that God provided, the dark soil was turning greener and greener. After only a few days, the little seedlings worked their way through the topsoil and saw the light of day.

After one hundred and fifty long days of waiting and fretting, Alfonso was able to reap his first crop without any major problems. His rice had managed to dodge storms, hail, and pests. In the process, Alfonso had been able to provide dozens of poor farmers with work and he was now the proud owner of many tons of high-grade rice. As was the custom in those days, the crop was sold to a rice mill. So that's what Alfonso did, too. Before long, he was able to use the proceeds from the rice mill to pay off his debt. While he was now by no means wealthy, he *had* learned how to go about this business. But most importantly, Alfonso had acquired the necessary expertise to be a rice farmer.

Once you strike gold at a certain location, you stay put. In fact, you'll probably do your best to mine that location as best you can. Much in the same way, Alfonso clung to his dream. He had ditches dug to irrigate his fields with water from the Meta River. While the irrigation part didn't quite pan out that first year, he *was* able to expand his rice cultivation bit by bit. So Alfonso leased more land, bought heavier equipment, and continued to perfect his irrigation system. His work was prospering. Whatever he set out to do, went well. Consequently, his reputation in the region grew year by year, too. Local politicians and other land owners began to seek his advice; the common people loved him. Holy Masses were said for him in church; children were named after him. Local newspapers started to take an interest in his work and the news of his success started to spread far beyond Villavicencio. After five years of extremely hard work, Alfonso was starting to become affluent. Fame and fortune were knocking on Alfonso's door.

From time to time, Alfonso visited his family in Bogotá. Even there he noticed that his reputation had grown. His father and his siblings were proud of him, parading him around and boasting, "Look at this guy--he's got what it takes." Next door to Alfonso's parents there lived a well-to-do family, the Amayas. They had three extremely attractive daughters who were also starting to take an interest in the successful young man. The *pater familias* of the Amayas came from a wealthy Medellin family. He once was the former Minister of Development during the Government of the late President Mariano Ospina Perez. As far as the common folk were concerned, the Amayas were aristocrats and the three daughters were being raised accordingly, as was the custom in Latin America.

As such, the girls attended a strict Catholic boarding school up to the age of eighteen and were educated in the fine arts. In these circles, practical skills for girls were deemed unnecessary, as it was usually not difficult to find successful young men who would marry them and provide all the luxury the girls were accustomed to. It went without saying that the newlyweds, too, would have servants in the home. And so, young women would move seamlessly from a carefree education to a carefree marriage. Only the households as such changed, with the new husband holding the same position in the family the girl's father had once held. Such was the patriarchal society: The husband was the ruler over all. The wife's main task was to bear children. And the chief duty of the domestic help—the *muchachas de servicio*, as they are known in Latin America—was rearing and educating the children. Wives were not expected to know anything whatsoever about cooking or home economics. Being able to speak English and French was regarded as much more vital.

These were the social circles of Alfonso's father who over time had managed to attain respectability and wealth, despite his modest beginnings. Alfonso's parents were now living in the finest neighborhood of Bogotá, in Soledad, where presidents, admirals, successful attorneys, doctors, and businessmen rubbed shoulders. In this neighborhood people didn't own homes, they owned mansions. In Latin America, image, status, and place in society play a different role than they do in the United States or in Europe. Wealth is to be displayed, and people belonging to this upper crust are expected to be generous, and the privileged class demands recognition and respect. This outward-focused behavior corresponds to an inward-looking attitude: *"I am a part of this high society. I've made it. Whatever happens, my peers won't let me fall."*

Alfonso craved these circles and yearned for the inner peace he thought he could find there. So he was only too happy that the two families, the Valencias and the Amayas, met occasionally—at cozy garden parties or at grand balls. Alfonso quickly fell in love with the prettiest of the Amaya daughters—Fernanda Isabel. She, too, was impressed by Alfonso and returned his love. So it was only natural that they would marry, only a few months after they had met. Mere days after the lavish and luxurious wedding, the young couple moved out to the country, where Alfonso made his money. Those were relatively good times in Colombia. The political landscape was more or less stable and the young couple enjoyed a few beautiful years. Within three years, Fernanda Isabel bore two beautiful children: Maria Fernanda and Diego Alfonso. It was also during those years that Alfonso took his family on extended vacations—to the United States, Europe, and to Mexico. The main purpose for traveling to Mexico was to go deep sea fishing and Alfonso actually caught a huge marlin that he took home with him. The enormous fish was very colorful and the family urged him to have it mounted as a trophy to display in their home. But Alfonso despised the fish, and banished it to the rear of the house.

Alfonso's life revolved around hard, hard work. He continued to buy more land, perfect his irrigation system, and also take out larger and larger loans to pay for these new investments. But one thing led to another… As beneficial as the irrigation was for the rice, it also attracted pests and disease. What really put a strain on production, though, was a fungus that at one point blanketed all his crops. Alfonso first tried to get a grip on the fungus by treating it with expensive insecticides from Europe. But by now his acreage had grown to such an extent that conventional application of pesticides was no longer possible. So Alfonso bought an airplane for the sole purpose of spraying chemicals on his rice seedlings once a week.

The Collapse

Apparently not *everyone* was viewing his success favorably because Alfonso was starting to run into trouble with the local and regional rice mills. They paid him poorly for his product and also communicated in no uncertain terms that he was dependent on their good will. Abusing their relationship with him, the rice mills did not treat him the way a proud, aspiring South American gentleman wishes to be dealt with. His reply was "classic Alfonso" and very simple: "Then I'll just build my own rice mill. That'll teach *you* to cross me!" But since Alfonso was not "your average guy," he also didn't want "your average rice mill." He had often heard about methods of processing rice more gently and thus making it more nutritional than by processing with conventional methods. Today this kind of rice is known the world over as *parboiled rice.*

As such, Alfonso wanted to build the first rice mill in South America able to deliver parboiled rice. As early as 2,000 years ago the ancient Persians discovered a way to produce cooked rice. Then in the 1930s a process was discovered in England which improved this ancient art of rice cooking by applying modern technology. Today this process is used around the world. How does it work? The germ bud and husk of rice grains contain most of the plant's vitamins and minerals but conventional processing and de-husking destroys most of the nutrients. This results in a nutritional deficit for much of the population. Parboiled treatment, however, prevents the loss of nutrients: The rice is soaked in warm water and enriched with the water-soluble nutrients. Pressure washing the rice with this nutrient-rich solution returns the nutrients that had been lost. This yields rice that is almost as white as dehusked rice but contains as many nutrients as brown rice. But there's a catch. Parboiling is complicated and not commercially viable for small amounts of rice, and is thus feasible only for large-scale operations and industrial applications such as those used in the southern United States. For small-scale farmers in Asia, Africa or South America wishing to improve the nutritional value of rice, parboiling is not an economic alternative, even though rice is a key staple in those countries.

Alfonso knew all of this, of course. Therefore his forward-looking idea of building a rice mill to produce healthy rice would only work if he were able to export his rice. To accomplish this, however, he would need the help of the Colombian government. His odds of success were actually quite good because in the 1970s exporting regular white rice was illegal since it was necessary domestically as a staple food. On the other hand, from the government's point of view, a factory able to produce and export parboiled rice would not only be prestigious but also potentially lucrative for Colombia. So Alfonso carefully and stealthily made his plans. What he needed was a lot of capital and excellent contacts with the political class in Bogotá. Using his father-in-law's network, Alfonso contacted the former minister of finance who was looking for a new position at the time. This individual, Luis Carlos Cardenas, was exactly the contact that Alfonso had been looking for, so Alfonso went ahead and hired him. Cardenas was given the task of establishing a commercial relationship between Alfonso's company, "Agro-Socios," and the Colombian government. He would apply for a governmental subsidy of the planned parboiled factory. In addition to all the governmental approvals that Alfonso needed for his factory—which only existed on a drawing board---he needed money, and lots of it.

After some negotiations, Alfonso and his new associate were granted permission from the authorities to build their processing plant. What's more, the government thought his idea was so brilliant that it was going to lend Alfonso $ 11,000,000 USD—interest free. Besides that, he would have five years before he'd have to start paying back the loan in installments, which included large monetary adjustments to make up for the high inflation rate. This opened a new chapter in Alfonso's success story. Suddenly he had all the wealth he had always dreamt of. Alfonso was now entering the world of Big Money.

Alfonso and his associates now spread out their feelers in every direction to try and acquire the expertise necessary for the parboiled rice industry. From Cuban exiles in Miami to American businessmen—all sorts of people were involved. Alfonso hired a number of experienced engineers and started building his factory. But, sadly, the huge amount of resources at his disposal also turned his head. Instead of investing everything in his factory, Alfonso bought several European luxury cars and even an airplane—a Cessna Centurion, complete with its own pilot. He bought the penthouse in Bogotá with this money, plus a life insurance policy for one million dollars benefitting his beloved family. After all, you could never know, he thought. Should he go under or if the government deal should blow up in his face, then at least his family wouldn't suffer. The premiums on his life insurance policy were horrendously expensive, especially since he had a clause inserted guaranteeing the beneficiaries that sum, even in the event of suicide. The only guarantee the insurance company had was a five-year period of restriction. Should Alfonso commit suicide during that period, the insurance policy would be null and void. All of this was in 1975.

The new project devoured millions of dollars. But it didn't work—at least not the way it was supposed to. Over and over again, the factory had to be remodeled, which in turn required reinvestments. Employees who didn't cooperate where fired at the blink of an eye and replaced with new people. Agro-Socios was confronted with a steady stream of problems. And then—it was bound to happen—after almost five years of experiments, setbacks, and despite many rallying calls, the government came calling: It was now time to start paying back the loan, they announced. Alfonso was with his back against the wall. Not only had he used up the loan, but even the profits from his conventional rice business had been spent. This was a crisis of monumental proportions. To whom could he turn for help? The way he saw it, people who ask others for help are just admitting their own weaknesses. And people who admit their own weaknesses can't very well be knights in shining armor. On the contrary, they are vilified and a disgrace.

Alfonso had maneuvered himself into a corner and let only very few associates in on his predicament. He had isolated himself from everyone else—from his friends, acquaintances, and even from his family. Almost no one was aware of the crisis he was in.

In the summer of 1980 the end was in sight. His beautiful and colorful life, a life full of recognition and fulfillment, had reached a dead end—at least as far as he was concerned. Presumably, he had his mind set on putting an end to everything in mid-September, when his last hopes of refinancing were finally dashed.

***

It was 8:30 pm on the night of September 21, 1980. I was at home in Bogotá when the phone rang. Fernanda Isabel was on the line—Alfonso's wife, my sister-in-law. It took me a second to recognize her voice. Somehow she sounded different, confused.

"Arturo, let me talk to my sister, please," she said, sobbing. I handed the phone to Inez Piedad who exchanged a few words with her and then broke down crying. She soon hung up, but it took some time until she had calmed down enough to tell me that Alfonso had committed suicide. Sadly and silently we drove over to the penthouse where he had been found dead a few hours earlier. As is customary in Latin America at important family events like a death, a birth or a wedding, everyone meets in the home of the family. You laugh together and cry together, sharing your joy or grief. We arrived at the same time that my in-laws did. The district attorney, police, medical examiners, and the hearse had already left. By and by, the entire family, which lived all across Bogotá, arrived at Alfonso's home. Some of them were trying to make sense of this tragedy; some were consoling the widow who was shell-shocked as to why her husband had done such a thing. The general feeling was a combination of depression, perplexity, and genuine grief.

By four o'clock the next morning, most of the visitors had retired to the various guest rooms. Sleep was out of the question but everybody did want to *rest* somewhat. I can still remember very clearly how quiet it was that night. You could have heard a pin drop. But suddenly there was a dull thud and then a clatter down the hall where the guest rooms were. Startled, I leapt up. I hadn't been able to sleep anyway and wanted to see what had happened. I switched on the hall light and immediately saw what had happened: The huge marlin trophy had ripped out of the wall, along with the board on which it was mounted, and had crashed onto the parquet flooring. For no apparent reason the entire bracing, complete with dowels and screws, had come loose and was now spread out all over the floor. There was no one around who could have done it, we all agreed. We were stumped as to how this strange, stuffed fish could have torn out of its mounting. I got goose bumps just thinking about it. What was going on here? Was this a sign? Was the place haunted? Of all things… that blasted marlin that Alfonso had despised so much and that had been banished to the rear of his penthouse, lay there, destroyed on the expensive parquet flooring—not even twenty-four hours after Alfonso's death. It would have taken a strong man to rip that thing out of the wall. Before long, other members of the family were milling about around the smashed fish, too, wondering what to make of all this.

On the day of the funeral we family members were once again congregating in the penthouse of the deceased. In a quiet moment Alfonso's younger brother came up to me and asked me to follow him to his brother's bedroom. After we had closed the door behind us, Enrique pulled a few sheets of paper out of a briefcase that was standing on the floor. He showed me the life insurance policy that Alfonso had purchased on August 18, 1975. In the event of the demise of Alfonso Valencia, it read, the sum of $1,000,000 USD was to be paid to his widow, Fernanda Isabel Amaya. "OK," I thought, "So far, so good."

Then he pointed to the line indicating when the contract had been signed: *August 18, 1975.* He also read to me the stipulation that this sum was to be paid even in the event that Alfonso committed suicide, albeit not for the first five years after signing of the contract. Enrique calculated for me that Alfonso had committed suicide exactly five years and 34 days after signing the life insurance policy. Obviously his brother had held out just long enough to be absolutely certain that his family would actually receive the agreed upon amount, he pointed out. "Alfonso had been planning his death, Arturo," Enrique said sorrowfully, looking at me with tears in his eyes. "He gave his life for his family. This man is a hero." That's what I thought, too, at that moment. But years later, we discovered that Alfonso had sacrificed his life for nothing.

Eighteen Years Later

December, 1998. By that time, Ines Piedad and I had been divorced for many years. We had received an Annulment from the Church and I had already returned to Germany. I had since come to terms with the new direction my life had taken and had already begun my pilgrimage work, which was taking me all over Europe. One day my daughter Hannelore visited me in my small apartment in the Taunus, a quaint and hilly region near Frankfurt am Main. When I asked her about the family in Colombia, she told me a story that gave me pause.

"Papa," she said, "Uncle Alfonso has left a message from the grave."

"He what?" I replied.

"Yes, you heard me right. He has left a message from the grave," she repeated. And then she proceeded to tell this story:

"One day a strange lady Aunt Fernanda Isabel didn't know, visited her at home. A black limousine with a chauffeur pulled up where she now lives. As you know, she's not in that expensive penthouse any more. She now lives in a seedy neighborhood in Bogotá. Everything she inherited was lost. So anyway, this elegant lady gets out of the limo, rings the door bell, and goes inside. Señora Botero—that was her name—told her that she is the 21st person to live in Alfonso's penthouse since 1981. Right now she is trying to sell it through a realtor, like every single one of her predecessors. The reason for her visit, however, was totally different: She had a message for the Valencia family."

"What kind of message?" I interrupted impatiently.

"Please let me tell the story!"

"Señora Botero related that she had bought the penthouse about one year earlier. Ever since then, she and her husband, who was still alive at the time, had been molested... by a ghost or some kind of spirit. The penthouse was haunted, Señora Botero said, especially the lower floor, where Alfonso used to live. Vases, pictures, and lamps were always crashing to the floor amid a huge ruckus. These incidents occurred mainly in the private suites, especially in the bedroom and the adjoining bathroom, with things always falling to the floor and breaking. Just imagine, Papa, they were breaking even though there is thick carpeting in that room and things normally would not be able to break there."

"Potted plants were flying horizontally through the room. On top of that, at night you could often hear the pitiful crying of a male voice. No matter how hard you stopped your ears, you couldn't block out that moaning and screaming. After her husband had died of natural causes, Señora Botero moved upstairs, to the guest floor of the penthouse. She couldn't handle the haunted lower floor. One night she had a horrible dream," Hannelore continued. "A tall Mestizo man was standing right in front of her, dressed casually in an English woolen sports coat and a chestnut colored turtleneck sweater. He wore elegant and freshly pressed light brown slacks. His face was well chiseled and his jet-black hair was neatly combed back. She could clearly remember all these details. This man was in trouble, that she could tell immediately. He was asking her for help: 'Señora,' he said, "please notify my family. Have them pray for me and have Holy Masses said for my soul.' "

"And, Hanne, my dear," I asked my daughter, "Are they having Holy Masses said for Uncle Alfonso?"

"No, Daddy, they're not!"

"Hmm...Why not?" I asked.

"I'm afraid because they lost their faith after Alfonso died."

"Hm, little one, that is sad," I replied.

"You know, Daddy, they hate Alfonso because this tragedy consigned them to such a fate and they were so ill prepared for it."

"But that's not true. In fact," I flared up, "he bought the life insurance policy so they could continue to live in the lap of luxury. How in the world can they hate him? And anyway, what happened to all that money that he left them?"

"I don't know, Papa. Shortly after Alfonso died, Aunt Fernanda Isabel went to college and majored in economics. Then things started to go downhill. These days she and her kids are dirt poor. Sometimes they don't even know how they'll make it from one day to the next. On top of it all, they're all very bitter. Can you imagine, they won't let anyone even *mention* the name Alfonso when they're around? And if they can't avoid mentioning him, they just call him 'El' (*him*)."

I was shocked and at first didn't want to believe that that family, to which of course I had once belonged as well, could be so heartless towards their husband and father. For a long time I dwelt on what might be causing this hatred. It didn't seem to make any sense. All I knew was that—even if everybody were refusing to show Alfonso compassion for his tragic life—at least *I* had to show this suffering soul some mercy and compassion. So I decided to pray for him and have Holy Masses said for him as often as I could. This whole thing seemed to be tailor-made for me. After all, I was constantly on pilgrimages anyway and they were almost always attended by clergy. And someone was always having a Holy Mass said.

So at the next opportunity I had the priest mention Alfonso's suffering soul during Holy Mass. I can distinctly recall that first time. It was on a pilgrimage from Lisbon to Paris, in Fatima, about eighty miles (130 km) north of Lisbon. Fatima is one of the most important shrines to the Virgin Mary. I went to the gate to submit prayer requests and Holy Masses and signed in. I wrote down the name *Alfonso Valencia* in the file for souls for whom Holy Masses were to be said and paid the customary 2000 escudos, which was about 10 euros. In Santiago de Compostela I did the same. And in the Cathedral of Saint James in Santiago de Compustela, and in Avila, too, where Saint Teresa of Avila was born. I did the same thing in Segovia as well, where Saint John of the Cross is interred. And in Saragossa, in Maria del Pilar, in Lourdes in the Grotto of the Appearances, and in Lisieux at the Shrine of Saint Teresa of Lisieux. A Holy Mass was said for Alfonso in Nevers, too, where the incorrupt body of Bernadette lies. I had a Mass said in Paris in the Rue de Bac, facing the incorrupt body of Saint Catherine Laboure. And there were many more Holy Masses that I had said for Alfonso. I included him in my daily prayers as well.

Finally I thought of asking the Virgin Mother of Fatima to intervene for the suffering soul of Alfonso. So I prayed my Ave Marias and the Lord's Prayer, like I do every day. Sometimes I prayed the rosary, too. And after every prayer I added the following words in Spanish:

Nuestra Señora de Fatima, porfavor ajuda Alfonso Valencia!"
("Dear Virgin Mary of Fatima, please help Alfonso Valencia!")

Four Years Later

For four years, until 2002, it was my habit to include my deceased friend in my prayers in this way. Just as I always had Holy Masses said for him and included him in prayer requests whenever I was on pilgrimages… But nothing happened. I guess I had secretly been waiting for some kind of sign but nothing came about except for strange dreams that I had, which always involved Alfonso in some way.

I once dreamt that Alfonso was in Paris with his wife. I could see both of them in a hotel room. Everything around them was gray or black and white. This was unusual for me because I normally always dream in brilliant color. As far back as I can remember, I have always dreamt in color. But in this dream I saw everything in black and white. What could that possibly mean? In that dream, everything around Alfonso was still and frozen in time. You could hardly recognize his face. His head was tilted forward a bit but I clearly felt that it was him. In another dream he was on a mammoth farm in the middle of Colombia. Everything around him was huge—even monumental. He and everything around him were the epitome of wealth. And there Alfonso stood—all alone in that big country, with everything bathed in shades of gray.

In another dream I was flying out to his rice farm on a private plane. I did meet him there but, once again, he was completely alone and surrounded in shades of gray. From time to time, these dreams repeated themselves in the same way. But I was never able to talk to him. I came away with an impression from these dreams that Alfonso was still alive but that somehow his life was limited and he was completely isolated. I could never really see his face. I started to think that these dreams might be the signs I had been hoping and waiting for. They encouraged me to keep up what I was doing, to pray for Alfonso, to submit request prayers, and to have Holy Masses said for him. As yet, I kept this to myself. I just had the feeling that I *had* to keep it to myself. Until one day, while traveling, I met a companionable priest from Ecuador who would be able to provide some specific information to help solve my problem.

At the time, I was accompanying a group of Spanish speaking people through France, from Toulouse to Paris. Father Jimenez from Quito, Ecuador, was in this group as well. Right from the start, people were telling me that Father Jorge, as they called him, was extraordinarily well educated. He had studied medicine in the United States and then returned to his Ecuadorian homeland where he met a young lady. They soon decided to marry, but during their engagement he felt called to the priesthood. Changing his mind about the wedding, the young man decided to enter the seminary to become a priest. Every evening he entertained our group, regaling us with his fascinating experiences or sharing some of the many things he had read. We all benefited from these wonderful stories, and so it didn't take long for Father Jorge to become the center of attention in our group. One evening in Lourdes, our entire group got together for some fellowship time and one of the pilgrims told the sad story that her son had committed suicide. And she, as a desperate mother, wished that she could know for sure what would happen to his soul. As you can imagine, this got my attention.

"Can a person who does something like that still go to heaven?" she asked. "Why in the world did he do it? I just don't understand." Her pain cast a deep pall over our group.

Father Jorge replied: "The Bible talks about a number of people who were toying with the idea of killing themselves. For instance, there was Elijah under the broom tree (1 Kings 19:40) or Jonah under the vine (Jonah 4:8). Both men were plagued by severe depression and were contemplating suicide. Samson, a "hero of the faith" as described in Hebrews 11, *did* in fact commit suicide by causing the pillars of a temple to collapse, killing himself and his enemies. Suicide is and remains a form of murder and is thus a sin. But don't forget, it is just one of the *countless* sins for which Jesus died on the cross and which He has forgiven us. There are also multiple examples of murderers whose souls were saved. Anyone familiar with Sacred Scripture knows that a murderer can be saved, and can attain forgiveness even for a sin as grave as murder. Of course that doesn't mean that murder or suicide are trivial matters for which one can be forgiven lightly. But Christ *did* die for the sins of all mankind, including murder and suicide. So people who commit suicide or murder are included in His forgiveness. Christians who kill themselves can still go to heaven. But they *will* have to answer to God when He asks, "Why didn't you choose the best for your life? Why didn't you trust Me to know what is best for you?"

Father Jorge continued: "God says that eternal life is based on our belief in Jesus Christ and that He died on the cross for our sins (Jn 3:17-18), rising again on the third day that we might spend eternity with Him. The sins we commit, such as suicide, disgrace the name of Jesus. But suicide can never be the reason for our damnation—just as the righteous things we do can never be the reason for our *salvation* (Titus 3:5-7). To be sure, people who commit suicide are sinners and poor souls but we are *all* sinners and poor souls, if you think about it. Nevertheless, it is always good to have Holy Masses said for people who commit suicide and to include them in your daily prayers."

We all sat around silently for a while, digesting what we had just heard. Father Jorge's little speech had made a deep impression on me and I asked him whether I might talk to him personally. I wanted to know whether there might be something special one could do for the poor souls who aren't able to find their way, and who are stuck between heaven and hell, souls in "purgatory," as Roman Catholics say.

That very next evening I had an opportunity for a private conversation with Father Jorge. I asked him how one could help free the tortured soul of a person who had committed suicide. He told me, "At the Universidad Pontificia de Salamanca (the University of the Vatican) I had the opportunity to study the issue of souls in purgatory. That is why I maintain that suicides often are a result of *family* issues as well. I know from experience that these poor souls are dependent on their families' help. This is especially important. Simply praying for these tortured *souls* is not enough. The prayer requests and Holy Masses that are said have to include the whole *family*, too."

I had already suspected as much but hadn't been all that certain. Now I knew for sure and realized what was still missing. On the other hand, I wasn't eager for another discussion with Father Jorge. Something kept me from really opening up to him. I still wanted to keep my prayers and Holy Masses for Alfonso a secret for now. So I continued to pray for my late brother-in-law but expanded my ritual to include his family in my daily prayer requests as well:

"Our dear Lady of Fatima, please intervene for Alfonso Valencia, Fernanda Isabel, Maria Fernanda, and Diego Alfonso!"

Now the whole family was included. This is how I said my prayers in the months to follow. About two years went by, during which I continued to have Holy Masses said and prayed daily for the poor soul of my deceased friend. Then something strange happened

A Special Request

In June 2004 I joined a pilgrimage to Rome. A group of believers from Texas had booked a trip with the Swiss travel agency that I do business with and had requested that I should accompany them, something we call a "special request" in travel business lingo. They wanted me to escort them through Rome, so I flew from Frankfurt down to the Italian capital to meet with them.

We introduced ourselves to one another and agreed to get off to an early start the next day. Kicking off the group's visit to Rome, the program featured a city tour with a knowledgeable city guide who came directly to the pilgrims' hotel, as is customary on such trips. The guide was to accompany us on the city tour and comment on the various sights. The actual procedure of these tours is always more or less rigid. You drive along the River Tiber, pass the Piazza Venezia, the Coliseum, the Forum Romanum, and the Circus Maximus. Then you continue on to the Piazza del Populo, the Pantheon, the Piazza Navona, the Vatican, and so on. This standard itinerary hasn't changed in years. It's the classic tour of the city and probably won't change much in the future either. But on this particular day I noticed to my surprise that our itinerary had taken a weird twist. For some reason, one of our stops was at the little church of Sacro Cuore del Suffragio ("The Sacred Heart of Suffrage"), a little-known sanctuary built in the Neo-Gothic style. Located at the Lungotevere Prati near the Palace of Justice, this church does feature an unusual museum, however, The Piccolo Museo delle Anime del Purgatorio ("Small Museum of the Souls in Purgatory").

The city guide accompanying us that day turned to me and asked, "Did someone in your group explicitly request that we visit this church? This has never happened to me. I only know the exterior of this church. Do we really have to go here?"

"I'm at a loss myself," I said to her, thinking that if you only have a short amount of time to spend in Rome, you'd probably want to see Saint Peter's Basilica or one of other large cathedrals, but not a 20th century Neo-Gothic church. So I turned to the group and asked them:

"Who wanted to visit this church?" No one had a clue. Not one person in our group was familiar with the church and nobody had requested to see it. That seemed really odd, so I grabbed my cell phone and called our office in Switzerland where our itinerary had been compiled. Their reply was unsatisfactory.

"A customer requested it. Apparently the customer wants to go there."

"But the tour group is sitting right in front of me and no one knows anything about this church."

"Don't worry about it, Arthur," the young and efficient Swiss colleague on the other end of the line told me. "If it's on the itinerary, then you've got to tour the church," she stated. So I asked my group of Texans once more whether they really wanted to see this church.

"If it's on the itinerary, then for Pete's sakes, let's go inside. Maybe it really *is* interesting," one of them replied.

So that settled it. Our tour guide requested some time off until the afternoon to bone up on the history of this church and museum. And that's how we worked it out. In the early afternoon we entered the Church of the Sacred Heart of Suffrage. What we saw and experienced was nothing less than astonishing. True enough, the church itself was not that special, just one of many Neo-Gothic churches in Rome. But, at least as far as *I* was concerned, the church's *museum* was truly amazing. Located parallel to the nave, but separated from it by doors, the museum houses a unique collection of one hundred and eighteen relics that are one of a kind: "Proof" of the existence of suffering souls in purgatory. You can see the three fingerprints Palmira Rastelli left on Maria Zaganti's prayer book a year after Palmira died. Also, there are the countless fingerprints of other deceased persons on pieces of fabric or articles of clothing. Then there's the night stand on which a deceased man burned a message for his widow, asking her to have Holy Masses said for him. We stood mesmerized in front of many similar finds, mostly from families, from deceased people asking their loved ones to have Holy Masses said for them. Our visit to this church took unusually long. Even though no one had explicitly asked to visit the church museum, everyone found it interesting. And, as you can imagine, this strange museum hit me right between the eyes. It dealt precisely with the situation I had been dealing with and that had been on my heart for years—and for which a partial solution was perhaps in reach. There was no doubt in my mind: This visit was meant for me and for me alone!

As had been my habit the previous few years when visiting churches, I signed my name in the book for deceased souls. I wrote down my name and Alfonso's. I also requested that a Holy Mass be said for him. We then left the church and continued on our city tour.

That day I didn't register much more of Rome. My eyes were focused inward. I was still hanging on to those thoughts. Finally, finally I had received a sign. Actually, even more so. This was a special kind of sign and I interpreted it to mean that I should continue to pray for my deceased friend, Alfonso. I also understood it to mean that, thankfully, I was not the only person in the world worried about a soul in trouble. In fact, as I had clearly seen in that museum, there are many people who submit prayer requests for the deceased, whose souls are in danger. Without a doubt I was being told to carry on, to plow ahead. And that is what I did. I kept on praying for my unhappy friend whenever I could.

Two years later, May, 2006, yet another pilgrimage took me from Lisbon to Lourdes. This time I was with a tour group from Relevant Radio, a Roman Catholic radio station from Green Bay,

Wisconsin. Organized by Mater Dei Tours, the trip was being led by the Franciscan Father John Grigus from the National Shrine of Saint Maximilian Kolbe in Marytown, near Chicago, Illinois. From the moment we met, I felt like we had known each other our whole lives. There was a special bond between us. To this day, Father John Grigus holds a special place in my heart. There are just some people with whom you want to share your whole life, your secrets—the big and little ones—and all the mysteries and complications of our mortal existence. Father Grigus was just such a person. Around him you felt shielded and sheltered. Very soon after we met, I felt a desire to share with him my secret regarding Alfonso. A few days after leaving Fatima, on our way to Alba de Tormes and Avila, Spain, we had an opportunity for a private conversation. On our second evening in Avila I invited him to tour the old town and to have a glass of wine with me. I remember that wonderful evening well. We were both blinded by the beauty of the old town, which was illuminated by floodlights. There was a festive atmosphere all around and a soft, pleasant wind cooled us after a hot day.

"Father, I just wanted to...," were the first words that tumbled out of my mouth as I began to relate my story. And then it all just tumbed forth. Father Grigus listened attentively to what I had to say. We strolled through the streets of Avila as I was recounting the chronicle of Alfonso bit by bit. After about forty-five minutes we sat down at a beautifully decorated *bodega* whose interior was actually built into the ancient city wall. The *bodega* looked very inviting, so we decided to take a break and go inside. We ordered two *carajillos*—black coffee laced with Spanish brandy. By the time we were done with our coffee, I had finished my story. Father Grigus was silent a few minutes before replying.

"Arthur, I had a brother who committed suicide. That was many years before I entered the seminary. His suicide hit me very hard but today I know for a fact that he was saved. The same can come true for Alfonso, too. I've been studying this topic of suffering souls for some time now. That is why I know how incredibly these souls *do* suffer and how painful it is for everyone involved, especially for family members. I will help you and especially Alfonso. From now on – and I can promise this – I will help you."

The next day Segovia was on our itinerary, situated some sixty miles (100km) northwest of Madrid. At the end of the day Father Grigus celebrated a Holy Mass at the Shrine of Saint John of the Cross, right here, where this Saint is buried. Before the service Father Grigus had told me he would be dedicating the Mass to Alfonso. In the meantime he asked me to be praying along with him for Alfonso. During the Mass, he would ask God to break the curse that was not permitting Alfonso's soul to come to rest. The ceremony was built around the normal Eucharistic liturgy and its prayer intention was: "Lord, we ask you to deliver Alfonso's soul from evil!"

Father Grigus and the congregation offered prayers of intercession for Alfonso during the course of the Mass, beseeching God's mercy for the forgiveness of his sins and breaking all of their negative effects upon him and his entire family, living and deceased, through the sacrifice of Jesus Christ manifested on the cross and now made available through the Grace of the Holy Eucharist. This was done particularly through the consecration of the bread and the wine into the Body and Blood of Christ. The power of this type of intercession rests on the fact that it becomes the prayer of Christ Himself, working through his ordained minister, offering His own Body and Blood for the forgiveness of sins and healing its negative effects.

That evening we again talked briefly about what had happened. He recommended that I keep on praying for Alfonso and that under no circumstances should I quit my habit.

"Arthur, I am convinced that something will happen. It's just a matter of time," Father Grigus said. He was to be proven right.

Another few months went by. The summer of 2006 was very warm—outstanding weather for tourism. Germany was in the midst of the soccer World Cup. Everything was going like clockwork. I had a lot of business myself, and was doing well with my pilgrimages and other tours as well. Unfortunately, however, my daily prayers for Alfonso had become routine. The Masses that I had said seemed to have lost that certain focus and intensity. Then in mid August I had an unusual dream. It was about the time I was preparing for a personal Pilgrimage trip, walking the Camino el Santiago de Compastella, Spain.

I dreamt I was sitting in a large kitchen, relaxed and cozy, in that room. I saw people who appeared carefree and were laughing. Everything I saw was colorful, the way my dreams usually are. I was sitting on a kitchen stool and Alfonso was sitting next to me. We were chatting and joking, and were looking at one another from time to time. Suddenly he got up, embraced me tightly, and kissed me on the cheek. I then woke up from my dream, but everything I had just seen and experienced was burned into my brain. I lay on my bed with my eyes open but wasn't able to move. I was as stiff as a board. After many moments I glanced over at the clock and I noticed the date. It was August 18, 2006—thirty-one years *to the day* that Alfonso had purchased that life insurance policy!

Something had changed. At first I didn't understand it. But after a while I realized that something exceptional had happened. For eight years my request for the salvation of Alfonso's soul had been a part of my daily prayers and I had had dozens of Holy Masses said for my friend. And, finally, after all this time the dream I had just had was the first sign that Alfonso's soul might have been saved. This insight took a huge load off my mind. Relieved, I got up.

In February, 2007, I joined a group of American pilgrims traveling to Guadalupe, Mexico—this time not as a tour guide but as one of their group. I wanted to give thanks to the Blessed Mother. I was fascinated by the thought of being able to thank her at the spot where she had first appeared in the Americas. In France, the queen of pilgrimages is Lourdes. In Switzerland, it's Einsiedeln. In Portugal you've got Fatima, and in Poland, it's Czestochowa. Mexico's chief pilgrimage site is Guadalupe. And because Alfonso was a Mestizo and the Mother of God had appeared to a native of the Americas, I thought it wonderfully appropriate to express my gratitude at that glorious shrine in Mexico.

On December 9, 1531, an unknown young girl appeared to a 55-year old Indian named Quauhtlatoatzin in the village of Guadalupe on Tepayac Hill near present-day Mexico City. This appearance took place on the Day of Immaculate Conception of the Blessed Virgin Mary, which was being celebrated that day. The girl called the man, a widower, *Juanito,* and he called her *Mi Niña* ("my little girl").

Even at the first appearance, *La Morenita* ("The Little Brown Girl") said, " ' I am the perfect and perpetual Virgin Mary, Mother of the True God, through whom everything lives, the Lord of all things, who is Master of Heaven and Earth. I ardently desire a shrine to be built for me where I will show and offer all my love, my compassion, my help and my protection to the people. I am your merciful Mother, the Mother of all who live united in this land, and of all mankind, of all those who love me, of those who cry to me, of those who have confidence in me. Here I will hear their weeping and their sorrows, and will remedy and alleviate their sufferings, necessities and misfortunes. Therefore, in order to realize my intentions, go to the house of the Bishop of Mexico and tell him that I sent you and that it is my desire to have a shrine built here—at this level place. Tell him all that you have seen and heard. Be assured that I shall be very grateful and will reward you for doing diligently what I have asked of you. Yes, I will make you happy and give you much happiness."

At the time, this Indio was one of the few persons in the Americas who was baptized. The name he had received at that event was Juan Diego—Spanish for the apostles John and James—and he went to the bishop to report the Virgin Mary's appearance. At first the bishop refused to believe him. However, the next day the bishop agreed that he would recognize the event if he were to receive a sign from the Blessed Mother herself. He was to get his sign. On the last day of the appearances, even though it was winter, beautiful roses started to bloom on the hill where the people had started to congregate. Juan Diego picked some of these roses and placed them into his *tilma* (cape). The Blessed Mother then said:

"These colorful flowers are the unfailing sign that you will bring to the bishop. Tell him from me that he is to recognize my wish, my will, and desire in these flowers. You are my ambassador. I trust you. You will open your *tilma* only in *his* presence. Show him what you are carrying with you. Tell him everything in the greatest detail, how I sent you up onto the hill to pick flowers. Tell him everything you have seen and admired! In this way you will most certainly convince his heart. Then he will do what he is supposed to do and will start building my shrine, as I have commanded."

As requested, Juan Diego went to the bishop. This time he was received much more cordially. The bishop apparently sensed he was about to see the sign of truth. Juan Diego told him everything exactly as it had happened, then spread out his cape before the bishop and his staff, showering the many roses that turned into a sign. An image of the perpetual Virgin appeared on the fabric, at which everyone in the room fell to their knees. With tears flowing down his face, the bishop asked the Blessed Virgin to forgive him for not immediately fulfilling her wish.

Soon afterward the bishop started building a shrine at the place where the Blessed Virgin had appeared. News about the appearance spread fast. From that time on, Guadalupe developed into one of the most important pilgrimage sites of the Roman Catholic Church. In his bestseller *La Morenita: Como la Aparicion de la Virgen Configuro la Historia Universal,* journalist and historian Paul Badde writes: "Immediately after this event, eight million Indios suddenly became Roman Catholics. Yet just ten years earlier they could hardly have imagined anything more delightful than boiling Spaniards—and as such, Catholics—in chocolate and eating them." According to Franciscan Toribio de Benevente 'Motolinea,' the friar who had baptized Juan Diego and his wife, some nine million Aztecs had already been baptized by 1541.

During my stay in Mexico I could not get the story of Alfonso's never-ending death off my mind. Even though I was happy how it had all turned out, I hated to think how Alfonso's family had not participated in Alfonso's salvation at all. I would have loved to go down Colombia to give the Valencias one last opportunity to redeem themselves. Pleased and frustrated at the same time, I reflected on the past eight years, during which I had fought for Alfonso's soul. On the last evening of our pilgrimage I had a conversation with my Mexican colleague, Guillermo. We talked about our professions and shared our experiences. When I asked him what nationality he liked to travel with the most, he answered, quick as a flash:

"Colombians."

"Really?" I said, "That's interesting, I lived in Colombia for a long time."

"Yes, Arturo, many of my regular clients are Colombians. I like working with them. One of them is a priest from Villavicencio.

He lived in Rome for many years and studied at the Gregorian Seminary"

"You don't say…," I blurted out surprised, not quite believing my ears. "Do me a favor and give me his address, will you, Guillermo?" He took out a slip of paper and wrote the following down:

"Padre Nicolas Montoya, phone number, Villavicencio, Meta, Colombia."

I have tried to contact this priest several times because I want to talk to him. But so far I have not been able to reach him. If I ever do, though, I'm going to ask him to contact Alfonso's family and tell them what happened. Maybe it will help them lead happier lives and remember their father and husband in a different light.

* * *

A while back, my Brazilian friend Marilene asked me, "Arturo, why have you been praying for Alfonso for so many years? What was so special about your friend that you sacrificed so much of your time, without ever knowing for sure whether you were really saving his soul?" "Marilene," I replied, glancing over to Niki, her little mutt who was snuggling up to her, "Years ago, when you found Niki on the beach, why did you take him home with you?" "You know very well why," she responded. "He was sick, starving, and one of his front paws was missing. I felt sorry for this poor little creature." "Well, you see," I replied, "That's the way I felt about Alfonso, too."

My longest fourteen days

A few months ago, the four-year old son of a friend of mine was pestering me somewhat, asking me to explain what I do for a living. I wanted to give him an example he would understand. "Well, you see, it's kind of hard to explain…," I said, beating around the bush a bit. "I ride around in a fancy bus with a lot of people. We visit countries where the sun always shines, stay for free at really expensive hotels, get to eat the finest food, and during the day we visit beautiful old churches. Well, that's what I do for a living." "Do they pay you money, too, like my Daddy who gets paid for his work?" After contemplating for a moment, I had to admit that, "Yes, they do pay me, too." Then Kevin proudly exclaimed to his mother, "I sure know what I want to be when I grow up!"

This is pretty much the way conversations go when people ask me what I do for a living.

When I go to work, I don't have to stand around in the mud wearing rubber boots, I don't have to bend over or kneel or do some repetitious task at a conveyor belt. I guess you could say I'm privileged. That is one side of the coin.

But who ever goes to the trouble of flipping the coin over? What's on the other side?

Believe me, where there is light, there is also shadow.

In this book I have certainly highlighted all the bright sides of this profession. But to give you the complete picture, I need to talk about the downside, too. That's why I want to share the story of a pilgrimage in which I almost lost my mind. The only thing that let me hang on was the power and strength of my faith, which kept me humble (I think) and enabled me to survive the "longest fourteen days of my life."

***

It was last summer; I had just arrived in Lisbon, Portugal, the previous evening. It was around noon and I was waiting at the airport to meet a group of pilgrims from Atlanta, Georgia. As is so often the case with flights from overseas, the plane was several hours late, so my new tour group didn't clear Customs until about 4:30 p.m.

We had planned a long journey over the next fourteen days; scheduled to visit famous religious sites such as Fatima, Avila, Santo Domingo de Silos, Burgos, Garabandal, and Lourdes. Our last stop would be Paris, where we were planning to do a bit of regular sightseeing. The travelers in this group were from a charismatic Roman Catholic Church in Georgia.

The chairperson of the congregation was an energetic lady in her mid-sixties, Joyce Miller.[1] Her graying hair was tightly pulled back into a bun. She wore oversized glasses and a classic business suit. She could easily have been a governess around 1900 or an educator or a hospital matron.

Without a doubt, she exuded an air of authority. From the moment I first met Joyce, her "this lady means business" deportment was very obvious. My preconceived notion was confirmed when I shook her hand: "cold as ice," I thought to myself. This impression was even accentuated when looked into her small, ice blue eyes that flashed back and forth, catching every detail around her.

The other members of the tour group made a relaxed and friendly--but basically passive—impression, their southern drawl making it easy to pinpoint their place of origin.

I've noticed for years that it is primarily women who go on these religious tours and dominate the pilgrimage scene. This tour group was no different. More then two thirds of the travelers were female and probably on the wrong side of sixty.

An unusually young priest was accompanying them. It was hard to guess his age. Like many baby-faced people, he seemed to transcend the aging process. He was slim and athletic—even muscular. As usual, I shook hands with every traveler, adding a word of welcome here and there. The end of the line was a bit of a shocker for me, however. This group had not one or two, but *three* travelers in wheelchairs, so ill or invalid that they had to be pushed by airport staff. With three wheelchair users, the rigors of this pilgrimage would be a challenge for all of us.

---

[1] Some names in this story have been changed to protect the not so innocent.

After all the bags and the wheelchairs were stowed aboard the bus, we headed out to Santarém, the traditional first stop for such a trip. We had originally planned to celebrate a Thanksgiving Mass there at 4 p.m. But by the time we were finally pulling out of the airport, it was already 5:15 p.m. Visiting Santarém that evening would obviously be out of the question, all the more so since the local church would be closing at 6 p.m. And in addition, our fully loaded bus would need at least an hour to get there.

Santarém's bus parking lot is located outside of town and it takes about fifteen minutes just to walk from there to the church. A group with three wheelchairs would, of course, need even more time to get to the sanctuary.

As we were leaving Lisbon, I informed Chairperson Joyce Miller about the situation, assuming she and I would discuss how best to proceed. She listened to my problem and then resolutely and unilaterally decided that the church's sacristan would simply have to wait up for us.

Joyce requested I call the sacristan and give her this information. Several times I valiantly tried to explain to "Miss Miller," as she was called, that this simply wouldn't do. But my feeble attempts to get her to change her mind rolled off her like water off a duck's back. Pointing out that the sacristan had certain office hours and was a volunteer to boot, I tried to reason with her that we couldn't very well expect the sacristan to work overtime just because of us. Joyce's reply—I would even say her *order*—shot out of her mouth like a burst of bullets: "She'll simply have to wait. After all, we had an appointment."

Well, it turned out I was in luck. The sacristan *was*, in fact, very accommodating and *did* wait for us. We were able to celebrate Mass anyway and view the relics of the Eucharistic Miracle behind the altar of the Church of Saint Stephen. But at what price?

"I sure hope this bumpy start isn't a sign of things to come...," I mused.

The Last of the Autocrats

Almost everyone dozed off on the ride between Santarém and Fatima. I figured my best course of action for this pilgrimage would just be to try and avoid any future mistakes and run-ins with this intransigent woman.

Fortunately, the next few days at Fatima we were able to check off all the items on our itinerary.

We celebrated several Masses, visited the Chapel of Apparitions, viewed the graves of the children seers in the basilica, toured Valinhos and Ajustrel, but, strangely enough, did not once step *inside* one of the churches. This is usually a top priority for pilgrims. The reason was as obvious as the nose on your face: Joyce Miller.

Evidently Miss Miller regarded my carefully worked out program as *optional*, preferring instead to dream up her own *impromptu* activities. For instance, she impetuously decided she wanted the group to celebrate Mass in English in the Chapel of Apparitions. Or she wanted the group to watch the Fatima documentary without prior reservation in a room reserved solely for our group.

Her *modus operandi* was to ignore any item scheduled in our itinerary and, instead, to generate activities that were totally unprepared (and which often made no sense whatsoever) and which had to be implemented immediately.

All of this created a situation that was becoming untenable for me as a tour guide. Not only was this Joyce Miller pushing me aside, she was making me the "accomplice" for her spontaneous, half-baked ideas.

Just imagine you've booked a pricey trip, one that has been planned to a "T," has been repeatedly tested and endorsed, conforms to the doctrine of the Roman Catholic church, and which an experienced tour guide wants to implement, but *can't* because one of your travelers has usurped his position. Instead, this traveler wants to run the show without the faintest knowledge of the country, the people, language or customs.

Such a procedure is a recipe for disaster--there's no other way to put it.

On this trip I was being treated like a pesky servant whose services are sometimes needed but who doesn't have a say in anything. Another issue I had was that Joyce Miller didn't communicate any wishes or ideas that she and I could have talked about or worked out. Instead she just uttered commands—short, barbed orders that she actually expected I would carry out on the spot. As far as I was concerned, this woman was one of the last autocrats on the planet, a person who evidently had no regard for team work, meetings or collaboration. She never had any doubts or—to be honest—a lick of sense. In *her* world, these things simply didn't exist.

I realize I'm whining somewhat, but I struggled with the fact that the people in Joyce Miller's world were nothing but hirelings for her harebrained ideas. And no one seemed to have the guts to rain on this female bully's parade either. Should that have been my role?

For about half a day, I seriously deliberated jamming a stick in the spokes of her wheels. In prayer I sought counsel and consolation from the Lord.

But finally, I decided that as a practicing Christian, I would just have to ride out this pilgrimage in humility and harmony. So I accepted this journey as a challenge, yes, even as a trial.

The key point, however, was: If this woman *was* a trial for me, how well would I be able to deal with it?

So, toeing Miss Miller's line as well as I could, every morning I tried to read her mind and see how I could be of service to her that particular day. No matter how difficult it was to implement her contrary ideas, I tried to make them a reality. Quite frequently I was successful, but not every single time. When I *did* fail, she seemed greatly irritated. Evidently there was no room for failure in *her* game plan. This woman was used to having her orders obeyed—and carried out successfully.

On the second evening of our pilgrimage—right before the Procession of Lights in Fatima—she and the young priest came up to me and asked if they could have a word with me. They wanted to talk about Kathy, Joyce's 26-year old great-niece. Kathy was tall and slender, had long blond hair, and a pretty face—a young woman who was friendly, lovable, and truly charming.

Kathy was a journalist, but hadn't worked in her profession for some time because she was suffering from a liver disease, which was not obvious at first glance. Joyce and the priest informed me that some two years before, Kathy had had a liver implant.

But Kathy was tough, a "doer," and absolutely determined to master her fate. As such, her lifestyle was very structured and healthy, and she was very conscientious about her nutrition.

But Kathy had also noticed that her health was imposing limits on her. Thus, she had to protect herself from infections, had to have her liver implant checked regularly, and had to take a plethora of medications to prevent the new liver from being rejected. All of this must have been very frustrating.

Understandably, her great-aunt was very worried about Kathy's nutrition. Fair enough. But here was the rub: Kathy ate very little, as it was, but apparently had hardly eaten *anything* since the group had left the U.S. In fact, Miss Miller informed me that Kathy hadn't had a single bite since they had arrived in Portugal.

I sympathized with Joyce's concerns. She asked me—for once, very pleasantly—whether I could make sure that room service would always be available for Kathy, so food could be brought up to her room.

Immediately after our little talk, I called up Kathy from the front desk and asked her how she was doing. She replied that she was doing fine and that there was no cause for concern. When I asked her whether I should have any food brought up to her room, she modestly declined. She wasn't hungry, she replied. I asked her whether she was in pain. No, not really, she answered. I stuck to my guns and told her that her great-aunt had shared with me about her liver disease. Would she like room service to bring up a little snack? How about a steak with French fries and a salad?

I guess this approach worked because she changed her mind and said she'd enjoy that. "A medium cooked steak and a salad. Yes, that would be wonderful," she replied. I was honestly re-lieved and told her I would take care of her order pronto. On my way to the kitchen, I thought about Kathy. She certainly *was* very slim--almost thin. I felt sorry for her and resolved to keep an eye on her during our journey.

From then on, I tried to provide for Kathy's daily welfare. Every evening I asked her how she was doing and whether I should have room service bring anything up. Needless to say, I never visited her in her room--I just called her up on the phone. For tour guides in particular, keeping one's distance and treating customers with the greatest respect are a must. These simple facts of life are obvious. Nevertheless, it was unavoidable that Kathy and I would become closer. After all, we talked a lot and I took care of her. And that had been her great-aunt's and the priest's explicit wish. So Kathy and I became friends—in a strictly Platonic way. Anything else was completely out of the question.

Porter Services Canceled

We had just concluded our pilgrimage to Fatima and were preparing for the next leg of our journey. That evening I posted the next day's itinerary on the bulletin board next to the elevators in the lobby, as usual. The next morning after breakfast, I indicated to the head porter that we were ready to have our suitcases brought down and stowed in the motor coach. However, a few minutes later he informed me that there *were* no suitcases sitting out in the hallway in front of the rooms. Not one single person in our group had wanted to use the hotel's porter services. I was thrown off guard. In all my years as a tour guide, this had *never* happened before.

I was standing at the front desk trying to figure out what was going on, when the young priest approached me, somewhat unsure of himself. Somewhat awkwardly, he explained that no one wanted to use the porter services because they were afraid their bags might be stolen. This took me aback. In a four-star hotel, who in the world would steal suitcases within minutes? If you wanted to do that, you would need several accomplices and a hiding place as well. To the best of my knowledge, a theft of this kind had never occurred in Fatima.

But I bowed to the wish of my client, albeit reminding him that we would have to avail ourselves of porter services at *some* point on the long journey. I pointed out that we had wheelchair users in our group to consider. Besides, in some towns such as Avila, we would have to park our motor coach outside the old city walls and walk almost half a mile until we reached the hotel. There was *no way* we could do that without porter services.

The priest hemmed and hawed and then the whole truth came tumbling out. He wanted to cancel the porter services for the *entire trip*. Every traveler would be responsible for getting his or her suitcase into the hotel, he explained. He concluded his little speech with, "Do I make myself clear?"

"Orders are orders," I thought to myself. So I picked up my cell phone and canceled the group's porter services on the spot, even if unwillingly. On our way to the breakfast I ran into Miss Miller. She was looking somewhat disheveled, not as prim as she usually was. Maybe she had had a restless night.

I didn't have to wait long for the day's first run-in with her. Without even a good morning or a greeting, she immediately launched into a tirade, buttonholing me as to why there weren't any porter services. After all, she explained, it was almost time to go and *somebody* would have to stow all the heavy suitcases. I almost fell out of my shoes because I had assumed that the order to cancel the porter services had been *her* idea. When I replied that the priest had requested that porter services be canceled, she blurted out, "Why would he do that?"

When I relayed to her what the priest had told me, she almost blew her stack. "No porter services on the entire trip? How are we supposed to get to Avila?" When the consequences of canceling porter services for the entire trip sank in, she started to get personal. "Now you listen to me, you "tour guide" you, the only one giving orders around here is *me*. If you want to stay employed by this group for the rest of this trip, don't you ever do that again." Then she turned around on her heels and stomped off, even though I was still talking.

Altercations of this sort were to become a standard feature of this pilgrimage. It got especially dicey on our drive to Avila. Whenever I tried to explain something noteworthy about the country, the population, culture or history of the region on the PA system, Joyce tossed mean-spirited little one-liners and zingers in my direction. No matter what I said, she managed to find some fault with it, disseminating her views around the bus in an acrid voice. After a while I finally had enough and just silently handed over the microphone. She disdainfully ignored this gesture as well.

I was starting to realize that Miss Joyce Miller was out to get me. But what *could* I, what *should* I do? I silently prayed to our Savior to give me the strength to remain humble. But even though I was more or less able to keep my spiritual equilibrium with

181

these devotional exercises, my body was beginning to signal the first signs of stress—and this was tormenting me. I started to get heartburn, my pulse was beginning to race, my blood pressure was rising, I was constantly uneasy, and I couldn't fall asleep. In short, I simply felt lousy.

Once again, I was uncertain how I should react. Should I bring up my problems openly and discuss them with her? That seemed to be a hopeless approach—and somehow inappropriate as well. So I pulled myself together and tried to make up for the blows being dealt to my psyche by turning to my Creator all the more intensely.

By the time we had arrived in Avila that afternoon, I felt like I had just run a marathon race. I was exhausted. I felt empty, full of apathy, and had to force myself to complete my daily schedule. And my trials continued.

Our bus parked outside of the historic city wall and the driver immediately started unloading the many suitcases, bags, and the three wheelchairs. Standing around on the street, we looked at one another quizzingly, as if to say, "Now what?" Most of the travelers simply grabbed their suitcases, but since a lot of them also had carry-on bags and thus had both hands full, we were posed with a problem: Who was going to push the wheelchairs?

Joyce Miller took the initiative and plopped one of the wheelchairs right at to my feet. In it sat Louise, seventy years old. Joyce then started blazing the trail toward the hotel—albeit without knowing the way. Some of the travelers were already following her, but there were still dozens of suitcases standing around. "How is this supposed to work?" I called out to her. Without even turning around, she barked back, "That's *your* problem!"

Meanwhile, "General Miller" kept on walking—without a suitcase—up the steep hill toward the Old Town. I stood there, feeling like I had just been run over by an eighteen-wheeler. This woman's aggressive behavior was neither understandable nor acceptable. When the young priest tried to show me what a tough guy he was by lugging a suitcase in one hand and pushing a wheelchair with the other, I figured I might as well give it a try. But my suitcases have always weighed a ton. I'm invariably dragging around a lot of high-tech equipment like my camcorder, a camera, a laptop, and a cell phone—not to mention clothes for a two-week trip. I tried lifting my own suitcase but had to drop it in an instant. It was simply too heavy for me to handle.

For a moment I stood there at the city gate of Avila, totally flummoxed and trying to figure out what to do. Then I flipped my cell phone open and called up our hotel, asking them to please send down their porter. He wasn't available at the moment, they told me, but they said he would be down in about an hour. Since the bus driver was not thrilled about putting in another hour of work, I pushed one of the wheelchairs up the hill and walked into the hotel. At least our travelers had gotten to the hotel safely and had received their room keys.

Most of the pilgrims were already in their rooms—bereft of suitcases because they weren't scheduled to arrive for another hour or so. I stayed downstairs near the lobby, with my head on the block, so to speak, anticipating the clang of the guillotine blade. I didn't have to wait long. After about thirty minutes, Miss Miller blew into the lobby, spotted me, and barked, "Where's that damned baggage?"

The concierge happened to be standing next to me. We had just been talking about the delivery of the suitcases, when Joyce Miller stomped over to us.

"You'd better hurry up and get those bags," she threatened.

Now the concierge was incurring Miss Miller's wrath as well. Again, a tug of war was going on inside of me.

Should I let her drag me into a showdown? Could I count on the concierge as an ally?

But I stuck to my principles, trying to swallow my anger as best I could. I attempted to explain the situation to her, but she cut me off: "You're obviously new in this business…Well, you can't teach an old dog new tricks…Perhaps you should think about retiring?" Et cetera, et cetera, et cetera.

"Lord, give me patience and stand by me!" I silently prayed, wrapping my thoughts around the Lord. Prayer was the only way I was able to survive this humiliation. Two minutes later, the hotel bus arrived, delivering the remaining suitcases. After a few minutes, they were all distributed.

In contrast to our inglorious arrival, our first dinner in Avila was magnificent. The kitchen—no, the entire staff—outdid itself.

Everyone in our group was supremely content and chatting away happily. As is my custom, I went from table to table—not only to take pictures, but also to make sure everyone was happy. By doing this, I automatically create a digital diary of each of my trips. Upon departure, I give the group representative a CD with the photographs. I've been doing this for many years and, by now; my digital photo archive is quite substantial. But this habit also has an added benefit: I am able to credibly document any complaints and add them to the official report of the tour.

After making sure that Kathy was well provided for, I retired to my room for the rest of the evening, yearning for a time of repose and prayer. Those evening mini-retreats were the only way I was able to handle that trip.

Moodiness and Spitefulness

The next morning, the High Plains of Castille blessed us with the finest weather possible: a deep blue sky above and a pleasant breeze. The air was so pure, you could see for miles and miles. I felt really great, perhaps also because it was my birthday. But no one knew that. In fact, I did everything I could to keep it a secret. There was nothing to celebrate on this trip anyway, as I was soon to discover.

That morning we visited the birthplace of Saint Teresa of Avila and the Convent of the Incarnation where St. Teresa had lived and worked for many years. We celebrated Mass—but, you guessed it, not at the scheduled place. Rather, it was where Miss Miller deemed preferable, namely in the monastery right next to the former convent cell of Saint Teresa's. In order to make this switch possible, I had to draw on all the persuasiveness and charm at my disposal. Thankfully, the nuns in charge turned out to be extremely cooperative.

By then it was already 1 p.m. and time for our noonday meal. People were already asking me what was for lunch and—ZAP!—our "glorious leader" once again hurled one of her lightning bolts at me. *Now* was the time to visit the convent museum, she stated. Some of the travelers grumbled, but Joyce instantly squashed their feeble attempts at dissent.

And so our tired and hungry pilgrims dragged themselves through the museum because this was the wish of Miss Miller. I let them do their thing, preferring to wait outside in the fresh air.

This museum has an inner courtyard that has fascinated me for years. Whenever I am there, I cannot help but take a look around. There is a symbolic model of the "Interior Castle," the mystical teaching of St. Teresa. In the center is a cross, symbolizing God, which is surrounded by seven concentric circles, each one larger than the previous one. These seven circles represent the seven "mansions" of the "Interior Castle," which one must enter and pass through to reach God. I sat on the ground, at the foot of the cross, praying, my eyes raised up toward heaven. My soul was resting in deep meditation when, suddenly, a voice jerked me out of the depths of prayer.

"I guess Joyce Miller has already lifted you up to the seventh mansion of the Lord, you lucky duck," said a familiar voice. I turned around, blinking in the sunlight, and saw Carol Robinson, one of our travelers.

"Yes, I guess so, Carol. Is the tour over yet? It looks like the first people are coming out."

Hinting at the struggles I had been going through, Carol encouraged me to be patient. "I can well imagine how tough this must be for you. I'm praying for you, Arthur." Then she asked me to take a picture of her and the two of us joked around for a while. It was a wonderful moment of reprieve and it felt so good to finally have someone who was feeling for me; an ally.

We couldn't talk too long because we still had to get to Santo Domingo de Silos that afternoon, some one-hundred and ninety miles (300 km) away. Including breaks, you need a good four hours to get to the little town in the north Spanish province of Burgos. Our itinerary wouldn't allow for any more delays.

Our plans were to visit the abbey of Santo Domingo de Silos at the monastery of the same name before dinner and hear the monks and their Gregorian chants in the monastery church. Having released several CDs with sacred music in 1994, these Benedictine monks launched from oblivion to stardom. Some of this popularity has rubbed off on the abbey as well and, ever since the mid-1990s, pilgrims have been visiting the monastery to listen to the famous monks of Santo Domingo de Silos "unplugged."

After a quiet and, thankfully, uneventful drive, we actually got to the province of Burgos on time for the Gregorian vespers in the monastery church. The monks' festive chanting was indescribably beautiful—even more impressive than anyone had imagined. Afterwards we enjoyed a bit of private time until dinner, which in Spain customarily does not begin until 9 p.m.

For senior citizens—at least American ones—these late meal times are a strain. We had three hours to kill and our travelers had no other choice than to retire for some private time—most of them probably going up to their rooms at the hotel where we would be spending the night. I chose to patronize a cozy tavern that I knew from previous trips. I was hoping to be alone for a few hours, to recharge my battery, as it were, to enjoy a glass of wine, and to reflect on my mother and my birthday.

I was sitting alone at the bar and the barkeeper was just about to serve my wine. All of a sudden, Kathy Miller—accompanied by Esther and her son—stepped into the tavern. The latter two provided musical accompaniment during our Masses, with Esther playing the guitar and her son singing. While the two of them were sitting at a table of their own, Kathy joined me at the bar. Noticing my glass of red wine, Kathy said, "Arthur, my health being what it is, you can imagine that I hardly drink any alcohol at all. But once or twice a year I *do* allow myself a glass--usually at New Year's or on my birthday. I need a reason to celebrate, a kind of inner feeling, before I'll have a glass of wine. You know what I mean, Arthur?"

I nodded and took a sip, not in the mood for chit-chat.

"Today *is* such a day. I don't know why."

"May I buy you a drink?" I didn't want to tell her that I was sitting here all by myself to celebrate my birthday. "What would you like?"

"Actually, I wouldn't mind a Riesling, but I guess they wouldn't have that here."

I asked the barkeeper and, as Kathy had expected, he shook his head. All they had here was Spanish red wine and Spanish beer, he said (in Spanish), which Kathy was able to interpret. I guess that was about all you could expect in a village with a population of about five hundred.

"Well, then I guess not. You know, Arthur, I'll just wait until we get to Paris and then I'll allow myself a glass of champagne."

"As you wish, Kathy," I said, raising my glass and drinking to her health. She joined Esther and Patrick and I heard her order a Coke. While I was talking to Kathy, Esther and her son had been feeding a slot machine hanging on the wall. Both of them had been eavesdropping on our conversation, as I was to soon find out.

Around 9 p.m., we all regrouped in the dining room of our locally-owned hotel. The room was richly appointed with dark oak furniture in the colonial style and the owner had decorated everything with great attention to detail. The staff had also prepared a separate table for the driver and me, over in a corner. While two young girls were serving our *hors d'oevres*, I could see from a distance that Esther was talking to Joyce. Both of them were whispering excitedly. The driver and I were discussing our plans for the next day, when Joyce suddenly appeared at our table, hands on her hips, and proceeded to give me a tongue-lashing.

"How *dare* you hit on Kathy and even tempt her with alcohol? Arthur, you are a dirty old man. Kathy could die if she drank alcohol. I will not tolerate this any longer. Who do you think you are? I demand an explanation this very instant!"

Feeling my blood beginning to boil, I waited for a moment to reply. Every fiber in my body was about to explode, ready for that showdown. *Finally* it was payback time. I was mentally preparing an inflammatory speech, when an inner voice told me to "Cool it." All of a sudden, I was able to contain myself and I heard these words pouring of my mouth:

"I did *what*? Come on now, you don't believe that yourself. Who told you that? I would suggest you ask Kathy herself. I'm sure she'll be able to explain what happened."

I got up abruptly and left the restaurant. I couldn't stand it in there one more second. Deeply hurt and feeling absolutely horrible, I went to the front desk and called up Kathy to see if she would like a little snack. I had to work hard to get her to at least order an onion soup. The tone of my voice probably gave away that something was on my mind. She asked me whether I was alright.

I had not wanted to tell her about the incident in the dining room, but I just couldn't keep it to myself.

"Your great-aunt is claiming I was hitting on you and was trying to get you to drink alcohol. She even called me a 'dirty old man'."

"Oh, Arthur, please don't crack these jokes. I'm not feeling well this evening."

"Kathy, I swear…I'm not joking."

"I don't believe it."

"Kathy, I am very sad and very hurt by this accusation. How can your aunt do this to me?"

"I'm so sorry, Arthur. I don't understand it myself. I'll talk to her about it this very evening. She shouldn't be saying things like this."

I was somewhat encouraged when I heard Kathy's voice and her willingness to stand by me. "OK, I'll have them bring some soup up to your room then. Good night, Kathy."

I went to my room, took a hot shower, and dropped into bed, feeling depressed. I tried to sleep, but it was impossible.

Suddenly my cell phone rang. I had forgotten to turn it off. I just let the voicemail take care of it. I wasn't able to talk about this situation with anyone, not even with my poor mother who was probably calling to wish me Happy Birthday. I assumed that anyone calling would be able to tell from my voice that I was up to my ears in a crisis. But I wanted to keep it to myself. I would have to deal with this mess on my own.

I couldn't keep my brain from churning. Crazy, uncontrolled thoughts were chasing around in my head. I wanted to pray, but couldn't even do that. Could there be any deeper meaning to the fact that this was happening on my sixtieth birthday? I kept on brooding, and then perked up my ears. Right in front of my door I could clearly hear a discussion going on between Joyce and our priest. Evidently their rooms were very close to mine and they were talking in the hall for a while before turning in for the night. Well, there was nothing wrong with that.

What I was about to hear was the icing on the cake, the finishing touches to an absolutely catastrophic evening:

Joyce Miller: "What that guy did today is the absolute pits. What do *you* think?"

Priest: "Absolutely. I can't believe he had the gall to hit on Kathy like that. If we were in the States, we could have him arrested on the spot. We could also have him replaced by another tour guide. But we're in Europe. They don't give a hoot about such things over here."

Joyce Miller: "I'm going to call back home tomorrow. I couldn't get anyone this afternoon. Maybe we'll have more luck tomorrow. I'm going to tell Bob in Texas all about this. I'm sure he'll switch that guy out."

Priest: "It's such a pity that we have to travel with a person like this. Let's hope we'll be able to work something out tomorrow."

Joyce Miller: "But keep your cool, nonetheless. Good night, Father."

I couldn't help from overhearing that conversation. Now I felt I was going to die of shame. "God help me," I kept thinking over and over. As far as this priest and woman were concerned, I was already a convicted sex offender. I started shaking all over and felt a rage boiling up in me like I have never experienced in my whole life. I slammed the side of the bed with my hand, threw my pillow across the room, leaped up, and paced back and forth, like a tiger in a cage. "I can't take this any longer. This has got to stop. How is this going to end?"

I was almost about to "lose it." But after a while, I noticed that the huge wave of anxiety that threatened to consume me was starting to subside. I was gradually calming down. I breathed deeply a few times. After a while, my heartbeat slowed to a regular pace and I contemplated what my prayers should be that evening.

What prayer would be strong enough to address the tribulations I was experiencing that day—my sixtieth birthday? Almost every day I direct my prayers to God the Father, God the Son, and God the Holy Spirit. I regularly focus my innermost thoughts on the triune God, asking the Holy Spirit to enlighten me, especially when I am in great need.

As my reliable intercessor, the Virgin Mary also stands by me. As far as I am concerned, the Holy Family is the center of my spiritual life. In fact, I can't imagine the Holy Family without Mary and the communion of saints.

It is to the triune God and the Virgin Mary that I normally direct my prayers and prayer requests. But on this memorable day my trials were so great that I wasn't able to express such a prayer. I was neither able to pray to our triune God nor to Mary.

Suddenly, I recalled a largely forgotten saint, St. Conrad of Parzham, born and raised in Bavaria and still remembered there, especially at Altötting, Germany's oldest pilgrimage site and also the place of his birth. A Cappucine monk who lived at the Monastery of St. Anne in that town and who was the doorman at the monastery for decades, Brother Conrad, as he was known, was canonized by Pope Pius XI in 1934. People in Bavaria, where I grew up, pray to him when they are in great need. At that moment I recalled that years ago I had picked up a little picture of him, which I always carry around with me. On the back is a little prayer that has helped me several times in the past. I use it here and there and hope that it might be useful to you as well, dear reader. The prayer goes like this:

Holy Brother Conrad, lover of the poor and the oppressed. Poor pilgrim on this earth that I am, I humbly greet you in love! I trust greatly in you because even when you were on this earth, you helped and consoled the poor and those with afflicted hearts every day. But your love for the poor has grown even more since you ascended to heaven. So I now approach you full of hope. I stand before you and cry out to you in my misery and suffering. Poor human that I am, I know that I am not worthy of your love. Do not look at my wretched state, but rather remember your great loving-kindness and hear me! Amen.

After I had completed my prayer, I felt a certain amount of relief. But it didn't last. I still kept on tossing and turning in bed. I finally thought of calling my employer and having him release me from this awful trip. But I soon discarded that idea. After all, if I fled, it would look like an admission of guilt. No, I would have to meet this challenge, this trial, head on.

Finally, many hours later, this night—the worst in my whole life—was over.

When the first rays of sunlight streamed into my room, I got up and took a walk in the fresh morning air, which did me good. Then I went to breakfast. I did not want to hide.

According to our itinerary, we were scheduled to celebrate morning Mass in Santo Domingo de Silos, but on this pilgrimage *everything* was different. As I was having my second cup of coffee, trying to shake off the weariness in my bones, our priest came up to my table.

"They" had decided that they did not want to celebrate morning Mass here in Santo Domingo, but wanted to go to the Cathedral of Burgos instead. "Hmm, the Cathedral of Burgos? " I thought with a smirk, "Why not go all the way and have it in the Notre Dame?"

"That's where we want to do a stopover," the priest said.

I pointed out to him that no preparations had been made for this and that the world famous Cathedral of Burgos would be jam-packed. I also explained that it would probably be impossible to find a chapel for Mass on the spur of the moment. But he wouldn't budge. So all I could do was to nod silently, acknowledge my agreement, and try to accommodate their wishes. So we packed our things in a hurry and drove off toward Burgos.

Practicing Humility

Even at breakfast I had noticed a certain calm around me—like right before a storm? "They" were letting me eat my breakfast in peace, too. Something was going on here. On our drive to Burgos that same hush and strange atmosphere hung in the air. The only way I could explain it was that everyone on the bus had probably heard what had happened and what they were accusing me of. Even Joyce Miller sat in her seat—frozen like a statue. Not a single word came across her lips.

Then, all of a sudden, Carol Robinson got up and walked to the front of the bus, where I was sitting. "Could I please have the mike?" she asked. Somewhat puzzled, I handed it to her. She sat down next to me and began to speak:

"Last year I went on a retreat at a monastery for a few days. During that time, I finally understood something that had been bothering me for many years. I had always been very quick to jump to conclusions about other people, adopting prejudices and opinions of others without bothering to check what was really going on. I had picked up the habit of adopting preconceived notions from others and passing those prejudices on, and thus multiplying them.

I wanted to know why *I* was so susceptible to this sin. So I examined my conscience, confessed all my sins, and was determined to no longer fall into the trap of prejudice. The Gospel of Matthew helped me do this. Chapter 7:1-2, reads:

"Do not judge, or you too will be judged. For in the same way you judge others, you will be judged, and with the measure you use, it will be measured to you."

From personal experience I knew how quickly prejudice can turn into injustice. I would like to share two examples with you. Once, when I was out of town, my husband was invited out to eat by friends of ours. After dinner, the three of them visited for a while and, at one point, Tim—the host—went to the restroom. At that very moment an acquaintance of ours walked into the restaurant and saw my husband sitting at a table with "a strange woman," engaged in conversation. About two weeks later I heard through the grapevine that my husband was apparently seeing someone—which of course was totally wrong. Thank God, there were no repercussions from this incident.

Here's another example: A few years ago I was on a pilgrimage. One evening in our hotel, I happened to see a well-dressed man leaving the room of a single woman. I immediately started to pass judgment on the situation, basing all my prejudices on appearances. Later I found out that it was only the hotel manager, personally tending to some technical problem the lady had had in her room. That was the extent of it.

Things like this have happened a lot in my life and I bet they have in yours as well. God invites us to think only the best about people and to let us be compassionate in our thoughts and words. It is not up to us to judge other people. Rather, God invites us to speak the truth, to love our neighbors and—if necessary—to pray for him or her.

I would ask all of you to point out to me if *I* should become unfaithful to these standards on this pilgrimage.

Please do me another favor: I would ask you to join me in prayer that neither I nor anyone else would cause trouble for others because of the evils of prejudice.

She paused, collected her thoughts, and folded her hands. Then she began to pray:

"Dear Lord, please preserve me from preconceived notions and prejudice toward all people. Please give me the serenity and the peace of mind to, with Your divine help, recognize difficult situations and to deal with them in a dignified manner. Do not let me become a tool of evil. Let me understand the consequences of my deeds and help me to always make decisions with the best intent. Also, please give me the humility to ask for forgiveness when I have made mistakes, and do not let me pass judgment when I am not in a position to judge."

When Carol had finished, there was a numbing silence on the bus. I was speechless, too, and very touched. In fact, I have to admit that I was close to tears. The calamities of the past twelve hours had hurt me so profoundly that, deep down inside, I was crying tears of relief and joy at Carol's little speech. But I didn't want to cause a fuss about myself—all I wanted to do was get this trip over with as fast as possible.

As we continued our drive to Burgos, it was as still as a graveyard on the motor coach. Everyone was just glued to their seats, lost in thought, letting the landscape glide by.

And, once again, I was in luck. Even without any reservations, I was able to secure the side chapel of the huge Burgos cathedral for our service. The short Mass was very beautiful and afterwards we took a short tour of this monumental sanctuary.

As we were walking toward the exit, our priest came up to me. He took me aside and apologized for what had happened. He admitted that he had suspected me unfairly. When I asked him why he had changed his mind, he said that Kathy had confirmed my version of the story. I accepted his apology, but did add that Miss Miller would *not* be able to get off the hook as easily as he had. I told him I was expecting her to take back that comment about me being a "dirty old man." He promised me that he would talk to her about it.

After that little conversation I gave all the travelers about an hour to purchase souvenirs. The people who didn't want to buy anything were already starting to file back to the bus and I joined them. As I was ambling along, I noticed Joyce Miller was coming up right behind me.

"Arthur," she said haltingly, "I'd like to have a word with you about last night. You know that in America we shake hands when we make up." She stuck out her right hand.

I was taken aback and replied, "I'm always ready for reconciliation. After all, we are practicing Christians and should set good examples for others," I exclaimed. But I didn't shake her hand. "Before we make up, you'll need to take back that horrible and unfair remark. You know which one I mean…" She retracted her hand and got that pouty and arrogant expression—the expression I had already become quite familiar with. "You need to understand *me*, too," she rebutted. "I was just concerned about my sick niece. Please understand me!" For a few seconds we faced one another—irreconcilably, until I said, "Joyce, are you going to take back what you said or not?" Then she turned on her heels, climbed onto the bus, and left me standing there.

Evidently she did not have the grace to take back her unfair accusation. But as far as I was concerned, I nevertheless wanted to put an end to this whole affair and move on. After all, I had a job to do and we still had to travel almost 200 miles (300 km) until we reached San Sebastian de Garabandal.

The Event at Garabandal

Garabandal, as the Spaniards call it for short, is a little mountain village in the north of Spain, about fifty miles (85 km) southwest of Santander. Between 1961 and 1965, the Virgin Mary is said to have appeared to four young girls at this place. Up to the present day, the curia in Rome has yet to issue a definitive ruling on the reported appearances. Our drive to Garabandal went straight through the mountains and was a real challenge for our driver—negotiating that mountain pass along deep gorges and steep cliffs. As you work your way up the ridge, at one point the blacktop starts to disappear and the road deteriorates to a dusty and narrow trail, which forces every vehicle to a crawl. As we continued our ascent, some of our pilgrims kept on switching back and forth, from one side of the bus to the other, so they wouldn't have to stare out the window into the void below. At the end of the trail you reach Garabandal—a little outpost of humanity with a population of about one hundred.

Up here you really couldn't help thinking you had arrived at the end of the world. And anyone wanting to avoid the gut-wrenching pass on the way down would have to ride on the back of a donkey—or walk.

In all my years of leading pilgrimages, I've visited this wilderness several times, although usually only for a few hours at a time. A *day* trip is standard fare for anyone wishing to visit Garabandal because the average tourist—or pilgrim for that matter—wants to flee as soon as possible from this rough and barren place that offers so few amenities.

Once they leave Garabandal, travelers normally spend that same night in Santander, and then continue on their way. But Miss Miller wasn't your average pilgrim. And she made darn sure her minions—that included me--wouldn't remain average pilgrims either.

That is why she decided that the whole group should spend *three full days* up on that mountain. She had even managed to find a modest *posada* (auberge) where we could stay. As we were unloading the luggage, Nono, our driver, asked me what we'd be doing for such a long time up there. I hadn't the slightest idea. The best I could do was to offer a sarcastic one-liner—sarcasm being one of my areas of refuge on that trip: "But I'm sure *Joyce Miller* will find something for us to do..."

The owner of the auberge, Miguel Gonzalez, was from Garabandal and even knew the four girls who had witnessed the appearances back in the Sixties. At the age of twenty, he had worked in the United States as a waiter. Years later he married a Spanish woman and returned to his native Spain with her. The auberge that he operated was his boyhood home, which he had later remodeled.

The auberge had neither a lobby nor a front desk. You just walked into the house and went right up to the rooms, which were simple and clean, but lacked any luxury whatsoever—no telephone, no TV, and most certainly no Internet or email services.

Each floor had a community bathroom with a few sinks and one separate toilet. The only telephone in the entire building was in Miguel's home, but phone service up here was often spotty, which was why he was often unreachable for days at a time.

My first thought when I saw this place was, "I hope we don't have any medical emergencies up here." After all, several of the travelers in our group were well advanced in years. And of course, we even had some invalids in our group. "Well, at least we've got our cell phones," I thought.

Just to be on the safe side, after looking around upstairs, I went downstairs to Miguel's and asked him how far it was to the next doctor or to the next hospital. You learn from your experiences...

As I was walking upstairs, I heard somewhat cry out, "Quick, quick, we need a doctor! Fiona fainted!" Fiona was one of our three wheelchair users, all of whom had dispensed with their vehicles for the rest of the trip because it was too much of a hassle for everyone to be lugging those wheelchairs around.

What *I* didn't know at the time, was that Fiona was suffering from diabetes and needed certain medication on a regular basis. For some reason, her meds weren't working that day and she had fallen into an insulin coma.

Unfortunately, the nurse traveling with us and who would have known what to do in such situations was in the village with Joyce and a few others. The only means of communication I had at my disposal was my cell phone. I quickly dialed the emergency number they use in Spain—and actually got someone on the other end of the line.

It was a lady doctor and I explained our situation to her. She gave me a few practical tips on what to do, telling me to give Fiona sugar water and to try to wake her up by gently shaking her. If that didn't work, she said, we should attempt mouth-to-mouth resuscitation. The doctor asked me whether I could still feel a pulse. "Yes," I replied. She said she'd be there in about twenty minutes and urged me to "Hang on!" Then the line went "click."

As Miguel was running down to the kitchen to get some sugar water, I shook Fiona and tried to wake her from her coma. Unfortunately, my attempts were not showing any effect. In the meantime, the nurse had returned and had now taken over with resuscitation efforts. All of a sudden she called out, "There's no pulse!"

She looked up at all of us—her face clouded by helplessness and despair. It was at this point that our priest started to make his way through the throng of people crowded around the gravely ill woman. He had put on his purple stole and was starting to give Fiona the Anointing of the Sick, praying for the forgiveness of her sins and blessing her. Fiona was lying on her bed, her mouth wide open. No one knew whether she was still alive or not.

In the distance we could now hear an ambulance siren. It took a few moments for them to find us, but then in rushed a young female doctor, carrying a doctor's bag, and a medic. The first thing they did was to shoo all the onlookers out of the room. My services as an interpreter were required, so I was asked to stay. Besides the three of us, Miguel's wife and, of course, Joyce Miller, and the priest (??) were present. Before long, the doctor and medic were able to rouse Fiona from her coma. We all breathed a sigh of relief.

The worst case scenario having been avoided, Fiona would need to get to a hospital immediately, the doctor said, so they could examine her and see what the matter was. But before the doctor could even finish speaking, Joyce cut her off:

"Nonsense. She doesn't need to go to the hospital. Before we left, her doctor prescribed all the right medication. And she takes her meds regularly. I know that for a fact. She just swooned a little. That's all. She'll be fine."

Then Joyce turned directly to Fiona who was lying there and who had followed the conversation. "You're OK that we're not going to take you to the hospital, right, Fiona?" Fiona nodded ever so slightly, which Joyce evidently took for a "Yes."

"You see, Señora Doctora… She doesn't want to go to the hospital." The doctor stood there dumbfounded, just shaking her head. What could she say? So Señora Doctora packed up her stuff, attended to the necessary paperwork, and drove off with her young driver.

For the next few days, it appeared that Joyce had made the right decision. Fiona had, in fact, bounced back and once again looked normal. However, at the time we had no way of knowing that only three days later, in Lourdes, we'd have to deal with that same emergency...

The events that occurred at Garabandal between 1961 and 1965 are quite remarkable. During that period of time, those four girls between the ages of eleven and twelve, Conchita, Marie-Cruz, Jacinta, and Marie-Lori, were supposedly visited by the archangel Gabriel a total of eight times, announcing that the Mother of God would appear. During these appearances, the girls fell into a trance of ecstasy—staring skyward with their eyes wide open, their heads twisted at odd angles, wearing transformed expressions on their blanched faces.

The appearances lasted from a few minutes to several hours, during which the children fell to their knees even on stone floors, walked around in the snow in winter without shoes, or spasmodically knocked their heads on hard stone floors. All of this happened without them injuring themselves or showing any signs of exhaustion.

In these ecstatic processions, the children sometimes ran forwards or backwards at lightning speed—so fast that the human eye was hardly able to follow them. Many photographs were taken of these events and they can even be viewed on the Internet.

During one of the events, one witness even made a movie that is sometimes shown on educational TV. In this documentary, a white communion wafer—that seems to appear from nowhere—appears on Conchita's tongue. Afterwards, Conchita said that the angel had given her Holy Communion and had placed the host on her tongue. To this very day, this whole event is quite mysterious. The details of the appearance and everything surrounding it are unexplainable, even though it occurred in front of tens of thousands of spectators. Witnesses' say that the Blessed Virgin appeared wearing a wide light-blue cloak and a white dress, with a diadem of stars in her hair. She was holding Baby Jesus in her left arm and had a brown scapular on her right arm.

According to the girls, the message of the Mother of God was that terrible judgment would come upon humankind if we did not find our way back to virtue, atone for our sins, and start discerning our actions.

Even today, more than forty years later, the prophecy given to the four children has not yet been fulfilled. The Roman Catholic Church has yet to legitimize the appearances of Garabandal, a stance that has led to serious controversy in many circles. In my opinion, until Rome recognizes these events, we should exercise restraint and wait to see what further events might develop at Garabandal.

However, evidently Joyce Miller and her priest were of a very different opinion, attributing much more importance to the apparitions of Garabandal than the Roman Catholic Church does.

Reflecting on the past few days, it was interesting to note how superficially, even listlessly, our "Dynamic Duo" had taken note of the sites and events of Fatima, which have been officially recognized by a number of popes for decades.

On the other hand, Joyce and our priest were enthusiastic about anything even remotely connected with Garabandal. I wonder why the two of them preferred the "unofficial" events at Garabandal to the officially recognized miracles of Fatima.

Be that as it may, for three days Miss Miller chased us around that desolate hamlet that is visited by very few people. In fact, people who visit Garabandal seem to do so more out of curiosity than out of devotion.

One time, Joyce marched us up and down the hill, just to sit for hours on end in the grass where the angel had supposedly appeared to the children. Then we assembled at the house of Conchita's aunt, so we could all kiss the rosary that the Blessed Mother had supposedly also kissed and could worship everything that had belonged to Conchita during her lifetime. Joyce was revering Conchita as if she had already been canonized by the Roman Catholic Church, which is not the case.

But even the "best" things in life must end, as did our visit at Garabandal, which was quite strenuous for our pilgrims. After three days of sitting on pastures and kissing unofficial relics, we packed and girded ourselves for the remaining three hundred and fifty mile (550 km) trip to Lourdes. On our drive there, our itinerary called for a quick stop at Azpeitia in the Basque country, where the Basilica of Ignatius of Loyola is located.

Not surprisingly, Joyce changed our itinerary once again, scratching the morning church service at Garabandal and, instead, ordering me to arrange a spontaneous Mass at the Basilica of St. Ignatius. Joyce acted as if all this chaotic reshuffling of our itinerary were simply a piece of cake and she continued to demand that I perform one "miracle" after another. Par for the course, she and her "stooge" rudely, tactlessly and ungratefully turned practically everything on this pilgrimage on its head, completely ignoring all the bonus events I had planned. These two amateurs were constantly demanding extras that weren't on any itinerary—and which weren't being remunerated either, by the way.

Perhaps fueled after our botched attempt at reconciliation, Joyce Miller treated me like a doormat even more. And whenever I was not able to "perform," my status, which was already comparable to that of a garden gnome, was knocked down another peg.

So I came to the following conclusion: if I wanted those remaining days to be even halfway bearable, I would have to be at Joyce's (and the priest's) beck and call. For better or for worse, it was my fate to carry out to the very best of my ability whatever they wanted me to do.

After a tortuous bus ride, we finally reached Azpeitia by noon and headed straight for the Jesuit monastery. The young lady at the cash register immediately recognized me and commented cheerfully that I had just been there recently. After she had counted the people in our group and had handed out our tickets, I asked her whether it might be possible to celebrate a mid-day Mass—without reservations—around 1 p.m.

Again, the Lord was blessing my efforts. The cashier told me that, as yet, no one had signed up for Mass for that time slot. "Thank you, Lord…" Once again, I had just barely escaped the hangman's noose. As we were walking into the monastery, the lady reminded me that they would soon be closing for their three-hour afternoon siesta. "Yes, I know," I replied.

Ignatius of Loyola, who with some associates founded the Society of Jesus (a.k.a., "Jesuits"), was born in Azpeitia on December 24, 1492. Belonging to the landed gentry class, Ignatius was a professional soldier until the age of thirty. He was severely injured at the Siege of Pamplona and discharged from the military. Returning to his parents' castle in the province of Guipúzcoa, Ignatius had a deeply religious experience that he would never forget. Today, the room in which this experience occurred is a sacred chapel, the Capilla y Camarin de San Ignacio. And—you guessed it—it was here that Joyce Miller wanted us to celebrate Mass.

Another slight problem we had to work around regarding the new location for our Mass was that the chapel was on the fourth floor—and the last time that building had been remodeled was in the 17ᵗʰ century. Consequently, there was no elevator—a slight problem for our disabled pilgrims who *did* use their wheelchairs on occasion.

Luckily, there *was* one—albeit very awkward—way to get our physically challenged pilgrims up to the chapel: by means of an elevator in a remotely removed wing of the building. But to make it over there, you had to take a huge detour through the basilica, from where you could reach the west wing. A great deal of patience was required to get our disabled pilgrims over there because the monks carefully guarded the key required for the entrance to the west wing. And it wasn't easy to find the right monk. In fact, the only way you could identify him was by his long metal key chain.

Needless to say, *I* was chosen to hustle the aging and fragile travelers over to that distant side entrance, which was just barely located on the Iberian Peninsula, it seemed to me. Finally, after more than half an hour, I succeeded in maneuvering everybody up there.

The rest of the group was still waiting in the chapel, impatiently. I was nervous myself, perspiring as if I had *carried* those disabled people up four flights of stairs. I knew the axes would be flying as soon as I stepped into the chapel, if I dared disappoint Miss Miller again.

But somehow I was able to pull it off halfway and "they" didn't axe me, even though Joyce later whined somewhat about that "wheelchair thing."

The Mass went well and our priest seemed to be in a good mood as he climbed back onto the bus. He was tickled pink because he had bought a beret for himself, "just like the one the Holy Father used to wear when he was still a cardinal." For once, he was in a good mood. Unfortunately, probably unbeknownst to him, his coal black beret made his pale face look like death warmed over—actually quite fitting, as I contemplated his role as the Wicked Queen's "henchman."

The Nadir: Lourdes

We continued our journey eastward along the Atlantic Coast, past San Sebastian, all the way up to the French border. Early that evening we reached Lourdes. With our itinerary all fouled up after Garabandal, we of course couldn't stay at the hotel that had originally been reserved for us. Oddly enough, an international military conference convening that weekend had the whole town booked solid. Even from the bus, we could make out an "army" of uniformed people running around. But I had known in advance about this conference, so I had already booked rooms at a hotel in Tarbes, about six miles (10 km) away from Lourdes. It wasn't ideal to always have to drive back and forth to Lourdes, but, fortunately, for most of our travelers it was "no problem."

Everyone was looking forward to Lourdes. As far as they were concerned, this was going to be the highlight of the trip. I assume Joyce Miller was of the same opinion because she was zipping around like "The Tasmanian Devil" cartoon character, which of course made my life extremely difficult. She got off to a "great" start by unilaterally and, as always, at the last moment, canceling our city tour, with which I had planned to introduce the sites of St. Bernadette to the pilgrims. I had hired a highly professional city guide who was to give us some background information on St. Bernadette. Joyce simply sent this lady home.

Joyce's excuse for usurping the status quo was actually pretty clever: She claimed it would be more important for the group to take a "healing bath" than to run around town.

In reality, though, Miss Miller was creating a false dichotomy. We could easily have done *both* things. But I couldn't help chuckling because Joyce had apparently met her match in this city guide. Miss Miller had underestimated this lady's backbone who insisted that she be paid the honorarium promised her—even though the city tour had been canceled. "You reserved it, you bought it," was her *modus operandi*.

The city guide had a point—and I was only able to settle the dispute triggered by Joyce when I gave her my word of honor that she would receive her honorarium.

I guess most every traveler to Lourdes has his or her own personal trials and tribulations to deal with. Some people are wheelchair-bound, some are on crutches, and others suffer from hundreds of other ailments from which they are hoping to be miraculously cured.

The location where these miracles occasionally occur is Massabielle Grotto, famous for its healing waters. The main reason most pilgrims come here is that they hope some ailment will be cured. But, similar to the crippled man in Chapter 5 in the Gospel of John, some disabled people aren't even able to reach the waters of the grotto by themselves, so their relatives have to carry them to the waters on stretchers.

When we arrived at the baths in Lourdes, there was a strangely rushed and hectic atmosphere—more than is usually the case. Everyone was squirrelly and jumpy, with people calling out to one another or cursing in a dozen languages. They were pushing and shoving, with long lines everywhere—in the baths and even waiting for the blessing. That particular day, the lines in the ladies' baths were exceptionally winding. It took several hours to be able to step into the holy waters. Of course, our group had to endure these long lines as well.

And so we spent that whole first morning just waiting. While some of our travelers were standing in line, others utilized the time to attend one of the many devotions at the Sanctuary of Our Lady of Lourdes. In the early afternoon we all met at the Chapel of St. Michael to celebrate Mass. I enjoy visiting this chapel, which is located to the right of the crypt up on the hill above the Rosary Basilica and which is perfectly suited for smaller groups. I had already made sure beforehand that the altar and chapel itself had been prepared for Mass. And so I waited up there for my little flock of pilgrims to show up. Once again, they were late. "What happened *now*? " I wondered.

The first thing I noticed was a wheelchair being pushed uphill by Joyce Miller. In it sat—or, more accurately, was slouched over— Fiona, our diabetic. Her head had dropped forward onto her chest and her mouth was once again wide open. She was obviously in a coma. You could tell from the expression on Joyce's face that *this* time she was more concerned about poor Fiona's health than she had been a few days ago at Garabandal—especially since Fiona was not reacting to anything. But once again, Joyce was adamant that Fiona not receive any medical attention. "It'll all work out," she said flippantly. "This happens all the time. *I'll* take care of it. By the way, what's with our Mass?"

And it was then, after some twelve days of traveling with this woman, that I finally lost my composure.

I'm a good-natured guy and I would prefer to avoid a one-on-one conflict, but this was just too much.

I blocked Joyce's path and started raving, "Miss Miller, this is the second time in four days that Fiona has fallen into a coma! How long do you want to wait until you let a doctor examine her? I am warning you! If something happens to Fiona, I'm not going to let this matter rest. You can count on that. And besides, today I am going to inform our travel agency in America and in Switzerland about your *impossible* behavior. I've had it up to *here* and am no longer willing to take responsibility for this!"

With a sneer Joyce replied, "What in the world are *you* going to do?"

"I'm going to take Fiona to a hospital, *that's* what I'm going to do. This woman urgently needs medical attention. And you had better not try and stop me!" I grabbed my cell phone and called a taxi, which arrived within one minute. The priest and I lifted the seemingly lifeless woman out of her wheelchair as fast as we could and laid her in the cab. I got in the backseat, so I could hold onto her.

Fortunately, the hospital staff was quickly able to revive Fiona from her coma.

"You did the right thing by bringing her here," said the attending physician at the hospital. "Without the proper medical attention, you would have been running a great risk—in fact, a worst case scenario would have been quite possible."

Upon leaving, I thanked the hospital staff and Fiona and I took a cab back to the hotel.

In the taxi, Fiona told me that she was not a "normal" diabetic who would have been able to lead a normal life with the proper medication. Rather, she was suffering from a severe form of diabetes, which everybody in the *group* knew about, but which no one had bothered to tell me. Back home, Fiona even had an "insulin dog," she explained, specially trained to recognize an approaching insulin shock and trained to alert someone. These coma spells had happened more than once, she said.

Amazingly, Fiona didn't really find these attacks all that dramatic. The "only" reason she was having them, she said, was because she was using up much more insulin than normal due to the rigors of the trip. Her general practitioner back home, who had prescribed the correct amount of insulin for *everyday* activities, didn't know anything about her trip to Europe, she admitted.

Fortunately, the doctors at the hospital had been to recalibrate her medication very quickly, so that she should be able to complete the journey without any further complications—or so they claimed.

On the ride back to the group, I thanked my Creator that he had given me the strength to mutiny against "Captain Bligh." Not surprisingly, the price I had to pay when I got back was stiff. From that day on, Miss Miller penalized me with the fullest load of loathing she could muster. As far as she was concerned, I had ceased to exist. But by now I no longer cared. I had helped a person in need. That alone made everything worthwhile.

"Never look back," especially if yesterday was bad. "Just keep on looking ahead," that's my motto. "Be optimistic, believe in goodness and help it break forth."

From that perspective, the next day at Lourdes could only be better, I told myself. I was up bright and early as we had scheduled a Holy Mass in English at 7:30 a.m. at the Shrine of the Grotto, where the Virgin had appeared to Marie Bernadette several times.

Of all the shrines in France, this one is probably the most popular. Day after day, up to twelve Masses are celebrated here. To be able to officiate a Mass here is the lifelong dream of probably every Catholic priest in the world. As a matter of fact, I know of bishops who have not yet had this honor.

As I was hurrying up with my breakfast, I saw our priest walk into the hotel dining room. He spotted me and came over.

"I want to cancel this morning's Mass." I was dumbfounded

and asked him why he would want to do such a thing. He mumbled something unintelligible, which ended with "Miss Miller." Of course... I should have known.

What a pitiful anticlimax: Pilgrims come all the way from the United States, go on a strenuous bus trip, are finally able to experience Lourdes—a center of the living Roman Catholic faith—and then their Mass at the Shrine of the Grotto is simply canceled. I just didn't get it.

"What *is* with this woman?" I thought to myself. As I was pondering this enigma, I heard her nerve-jangling voice—like fingernails screeching across a blackboard.

"Where is that *German* man?" I turned around and saw her charging toward me with giant steps. My mind was flashing, *"Red alert!"*

"The German man is over *here*," I replied, slightly irritated.

Without greeting me in any way, she launched her first salvo.

"Kathy is not doing well. She's got problems with her liver. I want you to go with her to the hospital right now!"

Yet another bitter pill for me to swallow, dealing with her frosty imperatives.

"Are you sure?" I asked. "With Fiona you wanted to do the exact opposite. "

Salvo number two: "That's none of your business. Do what I tell you!"

"And who is supposed to take care of the group?"

"Uh...," she just grunted, rolling her eyes. "You leave that to me! Take a taxi and get Kathy to the hospital. You're the only one around here who speaks French."

"As you wish. Where can I find Kathy?"

"She'll be right down. Hurry, call a taxi!"

The taxi was just pulling up as Kathy crept down the stairs— white as a sheet and bent over, apparently racked with pain. It took us only a few minutes to get to the hospital in Tarbes, where they admitted us very sympathetically and immediately began treating Kathy. Nonetheless, the medical examination took several hours. That whole time, I say out in the hall, waiting. Around noon, a very cordial ward physician came out. She explained her diagnosis to me.

Kathy had contracted a bad intestinal virus, she said, extremely painful and unpleasant—but, fortunately, not a cause for alarm. The patient would have to spend another day in the hospital for observation, the physician recommended, because the department head, a doctor of internal medicine, was not in that day, it being Sunday.

Our group was scheduled to take the TGV bullet train back to Paris the next day. This stomach virus was throwing a monkey wrench into our plans. What to do?

I would have to reschedule her TGV ticket, if we didn't want to forfeit the purchase price. But, as always on this trip, the buck stopped with *Miss Miller*—not with me. I had taken so many knocks over this issue that I had learned my lesson well. I called Nono, our driver, and asked him to find Miss Miller. He said he would have her call back as soon as he found her.

After about ten minutes, Nono called back, and put her on the line. I asked what she wanted me to do.

I should have known…

Without skipping a beat, Joyce decided that Kathy *would* be joining the group the next day on the train ride to Paris. "She's had these infections before," Joyce said. I pointed out that *she,* Joyce, could not make that decision, it was up to Kathy. And besides, Kathy would have to sign an agreement of consent, if she wanted to be released against the advice of the physicians. "Kathy will sign it," Joyce barked.

At that point I handed the cell phone to Kathy and left the room, disgusted. I was standing out in the hall when, a moment later, Kathy called me and asked me to get the doctor. It didn't take me long to find her and we walked back to Kathy's room together. Once again, I waited out in the hall. A few moments later, the doctor left the room, avoiding eye contact with me. After about a minute, Kathy stepped into the hall—fully dressed.

"Come on, Arthur. Let's go. I need to find a pharmacy for my medicine. I need you as an interpreter."

"Are you going to be traveling with us to Paris tomorrow? Do you think you can handle it?"

"I'll manage somehow," she whispered with a pained expression on her face." It was obvious that she wasn't feeling well at all. "I sure hope this works," I thought to myself, as we walked to the taxi. The cabbie knew immediately which pharmacy was open that day because several other pilgrims in our group had already hired him to take them there earlier in the day.

He warned us that the pharmacy would be "hopping" because Lourdes was terribly overcrowded that weekend. And, sure enough, as we approached the pharmacy, we saw a depressingly long line. We got out and queued up. It took over an hour until it was finally our turn. When Kathy handed the pharmacist her prescription for a certain antibiotic, the pharmacist told us she was out of it. All day long, dozens of patients with similar infections had been asking for that same medication and the pharmacy was now sold out. And, being a Sunday, the pharmacy wouldn't be able to restock until the next day. "I'm sorry, but what can I do?" she offered.

Already eyeing the long line behind us, the pharmacist was about to send us away empty-handed, when Kathy suddenly exploded, "I'm not leaving here without that medicine! *You* figure out where to get it. I'm sick and I *need* that medicine!"

I remember that moment well. I felt like the proverbial camel on which that last straw had just been placed. Everything around me was starting to spin. I just stood there helplessly, not able to utter a single word. My heart was beating like a hammer. *"No, please don't...No, there must be... I can't ... What if..."* My thoughts were spinning around my head, cold sweat beading up on my forehead. I wanted to scream, but couldn't. I wasn't even able to open my mouth. At any moment I thought I would shatter like a pane of glass. Clutching my forehead, I staggered out of the pharmacy, breathing heavily. Once outside, I grabbed the wall of the building and started to take deep breaths—in and out, in and out. I silently mumbled a prayer, "Lord, give me the strength...", but that was as far as I got.

Kathy followed me out, taking hold of my arm in an understanding way, and led me back to our taxi, which was still waiting. Apparently our cabbie had been hoping to catch another customer from the steady stream of people leaving the pharmacy.

We drove back to the hospital, hoping that they might have that antibiotic there. The female doctor who had treated Kathy had already gone home. Now a young male doctor attended to Kathy. I explained our dilemma and he wrote up a different prescription. We then returned to the pharmacy and finally double backed to the hotel.

Joyce and the entire group were waiting for us. "Well, *finally*..." That was about as much sympathy as Miss Miller was able to drum up for her sick niece.

By now I was wiped out—not only physically, but especially emotionally. This kind of stress was simply too much for me. I retired to my room, stretched out, and immediately fell asleep.

I don't know how long I had been sleeping, but it was still daylight when the phone rang. It was Bob from *Catholic Travels* in Texas, a friend of Joyce Miller's and the agent through whom she booked the pilgrimage—and also the same man I had overheard her talking about with the priest that night in the hall.

Bob asked me how the pilgrimage was going. At first I had decided not to divulge any details about the trip, but I just wasn't able to contain myself. It all came tumbling out and I told him how this pilgrimage was just one continuous cascade of bad news. He listened to my story, interjecting a "Hmm," or "Uhuh" here or there. That was all... No consolation, no words of encouragement, no explanations, no compassion. I was deeply disappointed. Apparently, Joyce had already reached Bob and "brainwashed" him. That was all I needed...

I finished that most depressing phone call abruptly and went back to sleep. Sometime later I woke up, went to dinner, and had Kathy sign a disclaimer I had quickly drawn up. I didn't want to be held responsible if something were to happen to her.

Later on, Kathy told me that this whole thing was just a matter of money. Apparently, Joyce didn't want to pay for Kathy's hospital stay (or for Fiona's, for that matter) or for any other additional expenses that would have ensued from Kathy spending two days in the hospital, such as her having to travel up to Paris by herself.

But I've got to hand it to her: Joyce had certainly done a clever job of concealing her true intentions when she stymied Kathy's hospital stay.

Next morning, we took the TGV bullet train to Paris as planned, arriving at the Gare de Lyon around noon. A rented motor coach was waiting to take us to the Rue de Bac and the Vincentian Service Corps, a women's order founded in 1633 by St. Louise de Marillac, building on the tradition of St. Vincent de Paul. The nuns of this order call themselves the Daughters of Charity. St. Louise's incorrupt body is interred in the convent chapel in a glass coffin and is open for public viewing, as is the incorrupt body of St. Catharine Labouré, another nun of the same order. St. Catherine is remembered by many Roman Catholics because the Virgin Mary appeared to her in 1830 at the very spot where she is now interred. The Mother of our Lord had asked her to create a "Miraculous Medal" with the inscription:

"O Mary, conceived without sin, pray for us who have recourse to thee."

I know many believers who wear a medal with that inscription, appealing to the promise of the mother of Christ who gave her message to every person through St. Catharine, promising that

"I will have mercy on all people who ask for it in faith."

The rooms in the Vincentian Center are cramped, especially with all the pilgrims who visit there every day. Unfortunately, it was not possible to celebrate Mass at the main altar, which every visitor secretly hopes to be able to do. Instead, we were led to a side altar, which is up one floor and located to the right of the main altar. Once again, we had to push our wheelchair users down dark hallways and somehow get them upstairs on rickety elevators. After the tour, everyone had the opportunity to view the incorrupt bodies of the two saints. That took a while, however, because another Mass was being held down at the main altar, where the saints are interred.

In the meantime, our French driver was urging us to hurry up because we had only booked his services for a few hours and he had to move on to another engagement.

"Here we go again: stress and confrontation," I thought, trying to figure out how we might be able to work our way out of this latest predicament.

That's when Jim came to mind--Carol's husband who had joined us at Lourdes. He was built like a quarterback and was extremely assertive. I entrusted him with the delicate mission of informing our priest and Joyce that we would soon have to go.

Jim was glad to do me the favor. I wiped the perspiration off my brow with a "Whew!"

In retrospect, I was probably counting my chickens before they had hatched because two minutes later our dear priest was standing next to me—seething.

"Arthur, now you listen to me! *Joyce and I* are the bosses around here. Not Jim. We have yet to see the saints or anything else in Paris. So stop pestering us with all of your blasted scheduling!"

"I'm terribly sorry, Father, but we've only reserved that driver for a certain amount of time. He has to pick up a tour group from the airport very shortly and is threatening to dump our bags on the sidewalk."

"That's just too bad. We are going to take our own sweet time and look at everything around here. *You* figure out the problem with the driver."

He turned around on his heels and was gone. Slightly out of breath after another run-in with Joyce's "frocked flunky," I walked outside to our French driver who *was* actually starting to unload our bags. I asked him for the phone number of his boss, called him, and managed to squeeze in another hour. Grumbling, the driver began loading the bags back onto the bus.

That evening in the hotel, after everybody had calmed down after a good dinner, our young priest came to me and apologized for his rude—actually, aggressive—behavior. He was embarrassed that he had lost his temper— in a church, too! We shook hands and put the whole thing to rest. Before he turned to leave, I suggested that we might take a walk through Paris by night. "Why don't you ask the group whether anyone would like to join us?"

With great enthusiasm, he took me up on my suggestion and almost everyone joined us. We took the Metro from Station Opera to Hotel de Ville, crossed the Seine, and admired the exterior of France's most famous church, the Notre Dame.

Notre Dame is situated on a small island of the river Seine, the Ile de la Cité, toward which we headed on foot. The cathedral was illuminated from every side and many other tourists were marveling at the gorgeous sight of the twin-towered gothic cathedral, in which many emperors were crowned. To the right of the entrance is the impressive statue of Charlemagne astride his horse, a ruler whom two countries, France *and* Germany, claim. Not surprisingly, our digital cameras were firing away, but after a few hours I had to urge the group on because it was getting late. We all walked back to the hotel and everybody seemed very content—even Joyce, wearing a pinched smile on her wrinkled face.

A good night's sleep worked wonders and everybody was in high spirits the next morning. We enjoyed an extensive breakfast and then drove out to Nevers, a good two hours south of Paris. Experienced pilgrims know what is special about this place: This is where the nuns' convent of St. Gildard is located—famous because St. Bernadette of Lourdes is interred there. She left her hometown in 1866 and joined the Sisters of Charity in Nevers. One year later she took a vow of silence, receiving the monastic name Marie Bernard. She died twelve years later, in 1879, at the age of thirty-five, her incorrupt body interred in the right side altar of the convent chapel, looking as if she had just died yesterday.

After the service we met for prayer around St. Bernadette's tomb, kneeling and meditating for a moment. Afterwards we had lunch, prepared for us by the convent kitchen. The driver and I didn't get anything to eat because they had simply "forgotten" to reserve a table for us. But very often, I have noticed, there is a pattern to coincidences.

Throughout the whole trip, it had been pretty obvious that Miss Miller had striven to keep the tour group at a distance from the "servants." Wherever possible, she had tried to implement this elitist attitude. Normally, I wouldn't mind such a situation, but here in Nevers—where we were sitting at long tables—her covert strategy was exposed because it would have been so easy to make room for two more plates.

So I took the driver by the arm and the two of us marched out of the dining hall. We found a Turkish snack bar across the street, serving outstanding *döner* sandwiches. I treated the driver to a Coke and a *döner*, and the two of us had a great time—liberated from the stiff atmosphere surrounding Miss Miller.

The drive back was uneventful, everyone being simply tuckered out. It was time for this pilgrimage to come to an end.

That last night we had a joint dinner, with everybody in a great mood and looking forward to going home. After dinner, most everyone unpacked the religious souvenirs they had purchased and which they wanted the priest to bless. But our fellowship time didn't last. The travelers soon retired to their rooms to pack and get a good night's rest before the long flight home.

We all met early the next morning, had our last meal together, and then drove out to Charles de Gaulle airport in thick morning traffic, arriving there on time. While the driver was handing everybody their bags, Joyce Miller stepped up to me. A turnaround at the last moment?

Without saying a word, Joyce gave me a sealed envelope with the gratuity the group had collected for me—holding it by the tips of her fingers, as if she were handling a squirming insect. She didn't even bother to look me in the eye. Shame? Naughtiness? Who am I to say?

Turning on her heel, she walked away.

"Goodbye, Miss Miller," I called after her. She didn't bother to reply.

The driver handed me my suitcase and we all pulled our luggage over to Departures to check in. This was the moment of farewell. Everyone in our group came over to me to say goodbye. With Joyce already standing at the check-in counter, demonstrably turned away with an aloof expression on her face, the priest came up and clasped my hands with both of his. He bade me goodbye with a wink, saying, "Thank you, Arthur. I'll be praying for you. I hope you will for me too, on occasion."

"You got it, Father. You guys get home safely."

I wheeled about and walked away from that group for the last time, breathing a sigh of relief. I strolled towards my gate for the flight to Frankfurt, which was already boarding.

As our jet was rolling down the runway, I said a silent prayer of thanks. "Thank you, Lord, for helping me survive these longest fourteen days of my life."

In the following few weeks I had a lot to do and thus had little time to process this strange trip. Over time, I more or less forgot about the "pilgrimage from hell" that had almost caused me to lose my mind. Months later, however, when I was relating the horrors of this pilgrimage to my old mother, I happened to mention Joyce

Miller, dumping most of the reproaches and complaints that had burdened me ever since, on her.

Mom listened to my whining for a while and then remarked, "Remember what you told me about fifteen years ago? You probably don't remember. It was about the time you were deliberating whether you wanted to make a living with pilgrimages."

I reflected a moment and said, "Yes, I remember that conversation..."

"Well, then you probably also remember what I told you back then." I pondered and pondered, trying to recall what she could be driving at. But somehow it wasn't clicking.

"That's what I thought," said my mother with a chuckle. "I asked you whether you thought you'd be able to practice true Christian humility. Because that's one of your growth areas, Arthur. That's what I told you back then.

I've been watching you over the years, my boy, and I've noticed that you really struggle with being humble."

She paused and reached over to a book lying on the coffee table. She opened it up to a certain page and said, "This book is a collection of wisdom. Here is something that caught my eye, a very fitting medieval definition of wisdom. 'Without humility, every virtue is a sin.'

You see, Arthur, humility is different from all the other virtues. It is something very special; it is the window to your soul. Humility opens God's heart, it opens my heart. Yes, it opens every heart."

Warm-hearted soul that my Mother is, she added with a twinkle in her eye, "Well, almost every heart. That's why I would suggest you to regard these *longest* fourteen days of your life as a useful time of apprenticeship. Chalk that time up to experience. That pilgrimage was the best thing that could ever have happened to you. What you got is a free lesson in Christian humility. Maybe God just used this Miss Miller to teach you this lesson. So be grateful!"

Hmm, I had never looked at it that way. But the more I thought about it, the more I came to agree with her wise assessment.

Today, I guess I'd sum up this entire experience like this: "Sometimes you've got to be on your back before you can look up."

A Walk down Memory Lane

Where is "home?" Where you were born, grew up, and went to school? Or where you happen to be living right now? Or where you had the most life-changing experiences? Well, I guess we all need to figure that out for ourselves. For me personally, however, there's a straightforward answer to that question.

We Germans have a wonderful phrase that is hard to translate: Heimat [pronounced sort of like "high mott"]—*which means "native home" or the "area where you grew up." Well,* <u>my</u> Heimat *is in the Spessart region of Franconia, Germany—not far from Würzburg, the town of my birth.*

And here is the "epicenter" of my Heimat: *Leaving Würzburg in a northwesterly direction, take one of the two roads on either side of the Main River, pass Karlstadt, and go all the way to the town of Lohr. At Lohr, head southeast, following a very plain looking sign pointing into the forest. Before long you'll see a little chapel built out of reddish sandstone [so-called* Buntsandstein]— *a typical building material in this region.*

In this narrow and still somewhat untamed valley with a thick blanket of beech trees, it looks like it probably did some several hundred years ago.

All I have to do is close my eyes, and take a walk down "memory lane." I can see that idyllic trio of forest, valley, and chapel. Without a doubt, that trio is part of my soul, childhood, and family history.

In my mind's eye, I amble into the valley from the edge of the forest and once again hear the steps of my parents—the stern voice of my father and the soft soprano of my mother. Many a Sunday we came to this particular place—Mariabuchen ["Mary's birch trees"], as this idyllic spot is also known.

Mariabuchen is one of the countless Marian pilgrimage sites of my Franconian Heimat—*sites that we locals cherish dearly. Legend has it that around 1400—almost a hundred years before Columbus discovered America—a shepherd carved a figure of the Virgin and Child and placed this piece of art in the knot-hole of a birch tree. Over the years, the wooden statue was overgrown by the tree and became the site of many miracles.*

Before long, this "forest sanctuary" was renowned, and only one generation later the first Marian pilgrimage to Mariabuchen took place. As early as 1430, the first chapel was built in that forest. For several centuries, Catholics far and wide held to the tradition of Mariabuchen. Finally, in 1701, the pilgrimage chapel that was to become so familiar to me was consecrated. And the day after Pentecost in 1726, the first Capuchin monks arrived, founding the cloister that still exists today.

***

It was late summer, 1997, I was on my way from Frankfurt to Würzburg to visit my mother. As I often did, I took a detour and visited *Mariabuchen* before heading directly for my hometown. It was a Saturday afternoon, the shadows were already lengthening,and the first fallen leaves were blowing across the narrow path leading down to the chapel.

But this time I was not alone in that little sanctuary.

A few people in festive clothing quickly walked past me. As I stepped into the sanctuary, a wedding ceremony was about to begin. The chapel, which seats about a hundred people, was about half full that evening. I quietly sat down in a pew towards the rear and watched attentively as the service got underway.

A young priest was officiating. He had physical features you rarely see in Franconia. He was probably in his mid-thirties, slim, erect, and with jet-black hair. He looked Latin American. I can remember it as if it were yesterday—the way he blessed the young couple in German—speaking like a native; the way he gave the sermon—short, but to the point.

About half an hour later, as I was leaving the chapel, I struck up a conversation with some of the wedding guests. No one knew who this priest was or where he came from, but they were extremely curious about him.

Someone said he was a local boy but had become a missionary. Someone else had heard that he had been adopted by German parents. They said his brother became an engineer and that this man became a priest.

Lost in thought, I walked back to the parking lot, got into my car, and drove on to Würzburg.

So lost in thought was I that I didn't even notice I was already on the *Autobahn*. For some reason—even without really wanting to—I had wound up on memory lane. I was back in Bogotá, on a foggy and misty autumn day in 1970—sitting next to my young wife at the airport. We had just gotten married and were on our way to Germany. I was looking forward to showing her my Franconian *Heimat*. There we were, sitting at *El Dorado*—Colombia's largest airport.

Waiting to board our plane, we were sitting around with a few dozen other travelers. A young couple with two small children settled near us, immediately piquing my interest. My ears picked up German words from the adults, yet the two boys—probably five and six years old, respectively—were whispering in Spanish.

For a while, I involuntarily eavesdropped on their conversation. The longer I listened, the more I realized the delicate situation going on. These two boys were on their way to Germany—apparently for the first time. It seemed they were looking forward to the rich country across the ocean, which they knew from hearsay only; but they were wondering what Germans eat and drink, what kind of clothes they wear, and whether they play soccer, too. But what these little guys were looking forward to most was all the fine German cars they knew they would be seeing.

The elder of the two—the six year old—was consoling his little brother, holding his hand and trying to distract him from the fact that they were about to leave their South American homeland forever. I noticed a long pale scar on the older boy's right thumb, which gave this harmonious scene a surreal touch.

While this was going on, the man and woman were fumbling around with a German-Spanish dictionary, trying to communicate at least a few words to the two boys. Unfortunately, the grown-ups' mangled pronunciation kept them from scaling the huge language barrier: the boys hardly understood a word the adults were saying.

I was impressed by the fact that the two boys were speaking about their new—*parents!*—in an exceedingly loving and kind way. Yes, these boys had, in fact, been adopted, as I was to soon find out.

After about fifteen minutes, I addressed the parents in German and offered to interpret for them—a gesture they greatly appreciated. In this way, I was able to make closer contact with my fellow countrymen who knew neither the language of Columbia nor its people.

Interestingly, both parents were from the Spessart region. They had just adopted the two boys in Bogotá. The new parents were probably about thirty years old and were dressed well, but modestly. In the few minutes that remained until boarding, they told me their story.

They had been married for some years, but it turned out she was unable to have children—a great disappointment for them. They had made friends with a pastor from Aschaffenburg who was a missionary in Columbia and, over time, the couple had entrusted to him their wish to adopt a child. The missionary had shared with them that it was relatively simple to adopt children from Columbia.

This was an option the couple had also read about in their church bulletin, so they accepted the missionary's help in establishing contact with the appropriate agencies in Colombia.

Only a few weeks later, the Colombian agencies were able to make an actual offer. Apparently, there were two young boys in Bogotá who had lost both parents and were now desperately seeking to be adopted. It took the German couple only a few days to decide to take both children. And here they were, returning to their *Heimat* with the two little boys they had just adopted. The German couple looked exhausted, but happy.

Lovingly, the young German couple took the boys by the hand. And willingly, the boys let their new parents lead them to the plane. Unfortunately, our seating assignments were not close to this charming family, so my wife and I could only wave to them from afar when we changed planes in Miami. They boarded a different plane, and that was the last I ever saw of them.

By now I had reached Würzburg. I took my bag, locked the car, and walked up the stairs to my mother's apartment. Just before I opened her door, something in my memory went "click"— connecting 1997 to 1970; Mariabuchen to Bogotá.

Could one of those adopted brothers possibly be the priest who

218

had just conducted the service, the priest with the jet black hair and dark skin? What were the odds? One in a million?

I closed my eyes, swayed back and forth, and suddenly had a flashback of the priest making the sign of the cross at the close of the wedding, "In the name of the Father and of the Son, and the Holy Spirit."

And he had a deep scar on his right thumb.

Arthur Pahl was born in Gladbeck, Germany and grew up in Würzburg, Germany. After an apprenticeship as a waiter, he completed his training for Hotel and Restaurant management in the Swiss Noble Restaurant trade, worked as a steward on an ocean liner, lived in Canada, Colombia, the USA and Brazil, was alternately a rice farmer, emerald dealer, taxi-driver, gravestone seller and stockbroker before he succeeded to steer back to his homeland of Germany, where he has since been working as a tour manager for international pilgrimage groups. On his journeys with pilgrims from all over the world, people told him of their lives, their fortunes and misfortunes, their worries and their destinies. Some were so unusual, they had to be told. That's how his first book Heavenly Paths came about. It was published under the German title: Verschlungene Wege in Germany, 2009. Six months later Himmlische Pfade was published. In April 2012 Gefühle brauchen Gefühle, Pahl's 3rd book was released and immediately translated into Portuguese, under the title:Sentimentos precisam de Sentimentos. Arthur Pahl has published 32 true stories in 3 books. His first book in English, Winding Paths of Life, was published in 2013. It entails 7 of his best stories translated from German to English. At the moment the author has dedicated himself to writing his first Novel. He lives between Frankfurt, Germany and Sao Paulo, Brazil.